THE SEVENTH ELEMENT

AN ELEMENTAL GUARDIANS NOVEL

ROSALIE LARIO

THE SEVENTH ELEMENT
Copyright © 2017 by Rosalie Lario

*****

All rights reserved. Without limiting the rights under copyright reserved above, no part of this publication may be reproduced, stored in or introduced into a retrieval system, or transmitted, in any form, or by any means (electronic, mechanical, photocopying, recording, or otherwise) without the prior permission of the copyright owner.

This is a work of fiction. Names, characters, places, brands, media, and incidents are either the product of the author's imagination or are used fictitiously.

Cover design by Sweet 'N Spicy Designs
Editorial Services provided by Red Ribbon Editing

*****

First Moon Goddess Press Edition: July 2017

Chapter 1

"**COME ON**, Jewel. We're gonna be late. Again."

Those words, spoken by my best friend Demetrio Rodriguez—or Deme, as I knew him—jolted me out of my sleepy haze. I ran a brush through my hair and threw my coat on, then grabbed my backpack before following him out the door of my cramped little dorm room.

"You're *so* lucky you don't have a roommate," he muttered under his breath.

"Only because she dropped out the third week of school. Next semester I'll probably be saddled with some sort of freak."

But I definitely got where he was coming from. I hadn't had to deal with her for long, but sharing a room with a stranger had been no picnic. Between her rampant panic attacks and her not-so-endearing tendency to lose something and then accuse me of stealing it, the whole experience had been right up there with my one-time root canal in terms of fun.

Still, I would have taken Lizzie any day over Deme's roommate, a grungy rock star wannabe whose idea of showering was trudging in the rain from one building to the next. For a clean freak like Deme, it had to stink. Literally.

"You should just sleep in the spare bed in my room," I suggested for the third time as we headed down the corridor for the rickety old elevator. I mean, we'd known each other practically our whole lives and were more like brother and sister than best friends. Plus, although he'd yet to admit it to me—or maybe even to himself—there was no way he'd ever look at any woman as anything more than a friend.

"Don't tempt me," he grumbled.

But I knew he wouldn't. Deme might be a rule-breaker when it came to how he dressed and styled himself, but that was it. The campus had a strict non-coed policy when it came to dormitories. Even visits from the opposite sex were limited to daytime hours.

"Remind me again why I let you talk me into an eight-thirty class?" I complained as we came to a stop in front of the elevator. "You know I'm *so* not a morning person."

"That's the understatement of the century," Deme murmured, pressing the down button. "I already told you, the best classes are early in the morning."

Whatever that meant.

Deme frowned as he glanced at me. "You wearing your bracelet?"

Rolling my eyes, I tugged up the sleeve of my coat to show him the bracelet he'd given me that morning. It was a raw red gemstone through which he'd drilled a hole and stuck a black leather cord. Deme had been into making jewelry ever since I'd known him, and he always insisted on us wearing matching pieces. It was a quirk I'd grown to love, especially since I knew what it meant.

We were family, no matter what.

I had precious little of that, so I appreciated the gesture, more than I could ever express to him. Given the similarities in our hair color and olive skin tone, I'd often thought we could pass for relatives, if not for my eyes. Their startling turquoise hue was a constant reminder that Deme wasn't my actual brother, no matter how much I might wish otherwise.

After eying the bracelet, I glanced up at Deme's head where his normally black, thick hair had been liberally streaked with red dye spray. He'd also styled it straight up, making him look kinda like he'd stuck his finger in a socket. "It matches your hair today."

He grinned at me, and the black liner ringing his eyes like a raccoon all but made his eyes disappear into his face. "Cause I'm cool like that."

"More like lame," I joked, but he was right. Something about Deme *was* effortlessly cool, like he would do whatever he wanted and didn't care what anyone else thought of him. I knew the truth, though. There were a few people whose opinions he cared about. They could crush him with one carelessly spoken word.

But that would never be me.

The elevator at last came to a stop on my floor, the doors opening with a menacing clang.

"This thing is a death trap," Deme muttered as we stepped onto the elevator and the cables seemed to give a little.

"At least we only have four stories to fall," I said with faux cheeriness.

He gave me a dirty look.

I had to admit, it amused me Deme was so afraid of heights. Of all the things to be afraid of, that seemed like such a weird one. Especially since we'd grown up with all the splendor of the New York City skylines. But he'd taken one look over the side of the Empire State Building observation deck during our fifth-grade field trip and was never the same again.

As the doors shuddered to a close and the elevator began its descent, I couldn't resist bouncing up and down a bit, lending an extra shake to the cab.

Deme blanched and instinctively grabbed onto the side. "Stop it."

"Ohmigod, we're going to fall!" I shrieked, pretending to be panicked.

His teeth gritted. "I. Said. Stop!"

Heh. I obeyed with a grin. "That's payback for talking me into waking up so early on a consistent basis."

The elevator screeched to a stop and before the doors could fully slide open, Deme went charging out of them.

My laugh followed him down the hallway leading to the front entrance. He was too easy.

We slipped outside the double doors of the dormitory and into the frigid morning weather. The cold did nothing to detract from the beauty of the Magevilt University campus. Thick ivy caressed the exterior of the eclectic mix of Gothic and Victorian buildings, and the stone fountain in the center of the green lawn permanently cascaded a rainbow-colored stream of water. To top it off, the grounds seemed to be encased in some sort of soft, ethereal light that made it feel a few degrees warmer than it really was.

Thank god for that. Even though we were only a few hours upstate from New York City, the fall weather was considerably colder than I was accustomed to.

Suddenly, I remembered.

"Crap." I ground to a halt. "My biology text. I forgot to grab it."

Deme scowled at me. "Woman, how many times have I told you to keep that thing in your backpack where it belongs?"

Resisting the urge to stick my tongue out at him, I said, "Not all of us have photographic memories."

Seriously, Deme could read something once or twice and remember most of it, whereas I came by my good grades the hard way. I had to really study for them.

Some things were *so* not fair.

He dug his phone out of his pocket and glanced at the screen. "Dammit Jewel, we have less than five minutes to get to class."

Professor Montgomery was a stickler about tardiness, almost as much as he was about bringing your textbook. Since he was one of the few teachers who assigned seating to his students, that meant I'd be getting an earful from him when I slunk in late.

At least we both didn't have to suffer.

"Go," I told Deme. "I'll be right behind you."

"You sure?" He glanced across the expansive lawn toward the building housing the biology class.

"I think I can manage to find my way on my own," I said dryly. "Go. Try to make it look like my seat is occupied. Maybe I can sneak in without him seeing me."

Deme scoffed. "I'll do my best. Good luck."

His tone said it all. Nothing got past Professor Montgomery's eagle eyes.

Damn.

With a defeated sigh, I turned back to the doors leading into my dormitory, Darkhen Hall.

By the time I made it to my room and back downstairs with the book, class had already started. Part of me wanted to just skip it altogether, but I knew that would be a big mistake. When Deme said the "best" classes were in the early morning, he meant the most difficult. I should have thought about that before I agreed to take biology with him. He might be able to get away with skipping a class here or there, but I needed every bit of learning I could get. So as much as it sucked, getting chewed out over coming in late was the least painful option.

I stalked back outside my dorm building to find the temperature had already warmed up by five degrees or so. Still, a blast of air made me wrap my coat more securely around me as I made my way across the lawn, past trees amid the autumn transition.

Preoccupied with the round of questions I knew Professor Montgomery would aim my way as payback for coming in late, I didn't see the two figures engaged in combat midway across the lawn—not until they went hurtling past me no more than twenty feet away. The men were trading kicks and punches, and I realized I knew one of them. It was the cute guy from art history, the class I'd chosen for the one elective I was allowed during my first semester.

And when I say cute, I mean quite possibly the most attractive guy I'd ever laid eyes on. He was tall, at least four or five inches taller than me, which would put him at over six feet. He had a lean, muscled physique and sandy brown hair cut into a tousled style. Though I tried not to stare in class, it was almost impossible. His face was striking, all angles and sharp lines, with full lips that could make any girl daydream. The guy looked like he could just as easily be modeling inside the pages of GQ Magazine as lounging in a classroom seat. Something about him made my mouth go dry while my knees simultaneously weakened.

Since I had about as much game as a high school band nerd—and I would know, I'd briefly been one—I made it a point to stay far away from him whenever I entered the classroom. Knowing me, I'd smile at him and probably end up tripping and falling flat on my face.

Lucky for me, one of my hidden superpowers seemed to be staying completely invisible to cute guys. I don't think he'd noticed me once during the few weeks we'd shared the same class.

After watching him fight for just a millisecond, something told me my little baby crush was about to turn into a super mega crush. Because *damn*, the boy could move.

Even though his brown leather jacket and jeans should have made it impossible, he leapt into the air and executed one of those crazy martial arts movie kicks with such ease and swiftness that something in my loins clenched. Actually *clenched*.

The guy he kicked—a dark-skinned man with short hair, a black turtleneck, and black pants—went flying through the air to land on his back. But I guess he was a Bruce Lee fan too, because he did some weird sort of kick with his legs and somehow leapt right to his feet. It happened so quickly, it took a few disbelieving blinks to even process it.

The guy in black did something weird with his hands, then shook them toward Art History Guy like he was flicking water off his fingertips. Art History Guy ducked and made the same strange motion back.

What the hell are they doing?

Whatever it was, I'd seen it once or twice before, walking around campus. Some guy would be shaking his hands, or a girl would be waving her arms spastically. I just figured they were drama students acting out scenes. But to see it here, in the middle of a fight. Now that was beyond odd.

Even weirder, although I didn't see anything, the man in black convulsed like he'd been tasered, then fell to his knees. But he visibly shook it off and shot back to his feet, almost quicker than I could follow.

What were these guys eating for breakfast? How could they even *move* that quickly? And what on earth was happening?

That was when I saw the guy in black slide something out of his pocket that glimmered like silver in the morning light.

Now, normally I'm the biggest wimp in the world, so I don't know what possessed me to yell out to Art History Guy rather than turn tail and run. But instead of screaming and fleeing, I shouted, "Look out! He's got a knife!"

What I didn't realize was it would immediately redirect both of their attention.

Right. Onto. Me.

When something like recognition dawned on both their faces, a disturbed knot settled in the pit of my stomach.

Umm ... Why were they suddenly staring at me like *I* was their target?

Discomfort morphed into flat-out fear when the man in black yelled something I didn't understand and immediately changed direction, heading straight for me at a dead run.

What the—?

Like the proverbial deer caught in headlights, I stood there, frozen in shock. The man in black fished something out of his pocket with the hand not holding the knife.

"No!" Art History Guy yelled. He broke into a sprint after the man in black. "Run!"

But nope. Wise as his words were, I didn't do that. By the time I convinced my feet to start moving again, the man in black was already upon me. I saw him drop the knife, and then the heavy weight of his body smashed into me.

"*Oomph.*"

I hit the ground with a hard thump, stunned by the impact from both the ground and the man who landed right on top of me. He must have been used to giving and taking hits, though, because he sprang into immediate action, yanking my hair to the side and pinching my neck.

"*Ow!*"

The man in black shifted off me and onto his knees, examining my face intently.

The shock of his impact had knocked the fear right out of me. I scowled and stared right back at him. "What the hell?"

That was when I saw the thing in his hand, the thing he'd taken out of his pocket while he was racing toward me. The thing, I realized, that he'd pricked me with.

It was a syringe. A freaking *needle*, for god's sake.

My mouth dropped open. "You stuck me!"

The fear came back, slamming into me just as forcefully as the man had moments earlier.

What was in that syringe? And why was my vision suddenly swimming, the image of his face swirling around in my head?

Before I could stutter out the question, Art History Guy reached us. I guess his idea of helping me was slamming his body right into the man squatting beside me. I let out a groan as they both tumbled over my legs, then kept rolling.

I didn't feel any pain, thanks to whatever the man in black had stuck me with. But then, I couldn't move either.

Helplessly rooted to my spot on the ground, I managed to turn my head to see the two men trading blows. Rolling over and over in their individual attempts to gain dominance.

The man in black tumbled Art History Guy onto his back. When he lifted his hand and silver glinted, I realized he'd managed to pick up the knife during their struggle.

My mouth opened to call out another warning, but nothing came out.

The man in black jabbed the knife toward Art History Guy's eye, and for one frightened moment I thought he was a goner. But at the last second, he managed to grasp the other man's wrist.

With a quick shift of his hips, he unseated the man in black. Swift as lightning—and when I say that, it actually *looked* like lightning had sparked off him—he rolled the man in black over and slammed the knife right into his chest.

My breath escaped in a startled puff as the man in black went up in smoke. Literally. One moment he was there, the next he was a stream of darkness dissipating into the air.

What. The. Hell?

Apparently, whatever the man in black had poked me with had some pretty serious hallucinogenic powers.

I blinked several times, but his body didn't reappear. Instead, Art History Guy turned and began to crawl toward me, concern marring the gorgeous lines of his face. But even as he approached, I felt consciousness slipping from my body.

Great. I finally get him to notice me, and it's because I'm dying.

How very typical of my life.

That was my last thought before I surrendered to the haze coating my vision.

Chapter 2

"**YEAH, SHE'S** here with me."

The quietly uttered words broke through my consciousness, echoing in my head like a drum.

Ouch. I winced, trying to lift my hand to my temple, but my limbs wouldn't cooperate with me.

"She saw him, all right," the voice continued.

It was gruff and somewhat gravelly, and, even though I'd never heard him speak before, I knew it belonged to Art History Guy. It was too sexy a voice to belong to anyone else.

"Yup, she had eyes on me when I killed him. Saw him go poof like a freaking smoke bomb."

With those words, the memories came flooding back to me ... being injected with something by some wacko. Having what I thought were hallucinations borne from whatever he'd stuck me with.

Could it have been something else entirely?

But what? How would it be possible for someone to disappear into a stream of smoke like that?

"I don't know," the voice said. "She strikes me as pretty clever."

When I realized no one was responding, I wondered if he was on the phone. Was this even happening, or was it another hallucination?

If only I could open my damn eyes. But like the rest of me, they appeared to be stuck in the OFF position.

"I'll try, but we may have a tough time convincing her otherwise. You'll have to prepare yourself for the possibility that she may start to figure it all out." More silence, then he added, "Uh huh, she's on her way now. Hopefully she can counter the effects of whatever they put into her … Yeah, okay. I'll keep you posted."

Footsteps sounded, growing farther and farther away, until they were gone completely.

In my dreamy haze of half-consciousness, I lost track of how much time passed. I must have conked out again, because next thing I knew, I heard that sexy voice once more. It started out low, the words unrecognizable, then grew louder as the footsteps advanced.

"She's been out since. What do you think they stuck her with?"

"I have no clue." It was a woman's voice that responded.

"Lord only knows what those assholes are up to," he murmured. "Can you draw it out of her?"

Warm hands pressed on my abdomen, and a brilliant light broke through my dark vision. The warmth on my stomach grew hotter and hotter, until it felt like it might scorch my flesh. I whimpered as a bright flash exploded, hitting me with a wave of power that sucked me right back into unconsciousness.

The slightly off-key words of a song I was sure I knew woke me from my slumber. I blinked slowly as the phrase 'No Woman, No Cry' floated over to me. Frowning, I continued blinking until my vision began to clear.

Why was I staring up at a strange coffered ceiling, and who the hell was drawling out Bob Marley's lyrics —and getting half of them wrong?

If I didn't know better, I'd say I was waking up after a Saturday night rager. But I was pretty sure it was the middle of the week, and since the most I ever drank was two or three wine coolers, that couldn't possibly be the case.

My gaze took in the details of the room. Light oak panels lined the wall, a set of double doors was closed, and tall windows let in a filtered stream of light. I was lying on a tattered brown couch, and a coffee table and another slightly smaller couch were right across from me.

Nope. Not familiar in the slightest.

I heard the clack of a billiard ball striking another to my right, and the same voice continued another phrase of the song.

Wrong words, I wanted to say, but it seemed inappropriate without looking at the face belonging to the voice. Or at least sitting up.

That was when I began to remember what had happened. The images and memories came floating back to me as they had earlier, but they were just as hazy as before. Even more so. It all seemed like a weird dream, like puzzle pieces that didn't fit together all the way. Like the last thing that had happened …

I had been lying here, half unconscious, when I'd felt the sensation of being burned by light. The memory was so intense I glanced down at my stomach, but I didn't feel any pain now.

Hey, where's my coat?

It was gone, as was my backpack. I had on my jeans, boots, and blue sweater instead.

At least my stomach was okay. When I set my hands there, I didn't feel anything unusual. Certainly no burning sensation, like I'd feared.

Taking a breath, I hoisted myself into a seated position on the couch. The world spun for a few moments before settling into its usual place. I glanced over to my right, blinking furiously at the sight of Art History Guy shooting pool at an ornate table across the room. His back was to me, giving me a nice uninterrupted view of the dark sweater he wore and those jeans I'd noticed on him earlier. It somehow felt wrong to keep staring, but *man*, did those jeans fit him in all the right places.

There was something completely surreal about sitting here, alone in a strange room with the hot guy from class, while he leaned over the pool table to line up a shot and sang like he didn't have a care in the world.

The disorientation was so intense I couldn't help but murmur, "Am I still dreaming?"

He froze in place, cutting off mid-chord, then rose and turned to face me. An easy grin transformed his face as he drawled, "Only if I'm in your dreams, sweetheart."

When I just sat there, staring at him dumbstruck, his smile slipped into a smirk. "Joking."

"Oh." I blinked at him owlishly.

What was even happening right now?

He gave me an understanding look. "Head's still funny, huh?"

"What?"

"You hit your head." He motioned toward me. "When that asshat who started a fight with me accidentally smashed into you."

"Fight?" The visions of the man in black came back to me. "He had a knife."

The guy gave me a blank look. "Knife? You must have hit your head harder than I thought. It was a good old-fashioned fistfight."

No, that wasn't right.

I frowned at him. "No, he had a knife. A syringe. He injected me with something."

When he continued to look at me like he didn't have a clue what I was talking about, I swung my feet over the side of the couch and tried to stand up. The world spun rapidly, and I immediately sank back down.

"Whoa, there." The shuffling of his boots sounded on the carpeted floor, and a moment later he was in front of me, kneeling to look me in the eyes. "You must still be confused from the hit."

Clearly, but something was off about this encounter.

I let myself meet his gaze, fighting the urge to blush at the glint of warmth in his eyes. "So there was no knife? No syringe?"

He shook his head. "Nope."

In a small voice, I asked, "So, he didn't turn into black smoke?"

Amusement lit up his face, and he let out a hearty laugh. "Now I know your head is still funny. We both know that's not possible, right?"

When he said it that way, it did make the whole thing seem implausible. I mean, things like that don't happen in the real world.

But man, it had seemed so real in the moment …

I let my fingers trail up my neck, to where I remembered the syringe piercing my skin. There was no tenderness, no indication whatsoever that anything was wrong.

The guy's face sobered. "I debated whether I should take you to the school infirmary. I hope I didn't make the wrong choice."

"No, I …" I lifted my hands to my head, smoothing my hair back. The matted chunks I felt told me I really didn't want to know how I looked right now. "I'm okay. Just a bit out of sorts."

He lifted a hand to my temple, and the tingling warmth of his touch melted away any resistance I felt. "You don't think you have a concussion, do you?"

"No, I don't think so." My head didn't hurt. I just felt … confused.

The guy rose to sit beside me. "I think we might have science together or something. You look familiar. I don't think we've met, though. My name is Lucas Zain." He flashed me a brilliant smile. "My friends call me Luc."

"Art history," I murmured. When he merely cocked a brow, I found my cheeks heating. "I think we're in art history together, I mean."

"Oh."

When he continued to stare at me expectantly, I realized I hadn't introduced myself. "Sorry, my name is Jewel. Jewel Harris."

Awkwardly, I stuck my hand out. He took it in his much larger one, and a bolt of static electricity shot up my arm, accompanied by the tiniest flash of light.

I gasped, snatching my hand back. "Did you see that?"

He frowned and shrugged. "What do you mean?"

Seriously. How could he have missed it?

When the thought hit me that maybe I'd imagined it, like some sort of residual side effect from the knock on my head, I squirmed uncomfortably on the couch. "Never mind."

This was all so weird; I couldn't make sense of it.

"Sorry you got caught up in the middle of my fight." He looked appropriately contrite. "That guy's been looking for trouble with me ever since the school year started. He's a douche."

"But ... he's not dead?"

"Dead?" Luc gave me a shocked look, then chuckled. "A bit bruised maybe, but no. Not dead. He ran off after he realized he'd pummeled an innocent girl to the ground."

Well, his explanation certainly seemed like a logical one. A lot more probable than the scenario I'd somehow conjured up in my head.

Then why did it still feel like something was off?

Rubbing my chilled hands along the arms of my

sweater, I asked, "How long was I out?"

His lips twisted. "Forty minutes. I was starting to get a bit worried there, but you looked so peaceful I didn't want to drag you halfway across campus to the infirmary in this weather."

"I'm okay," I repeated softly.

My gaze wandered the room, taking in some of the details I'd missed during my initial inspection. One of the walls housed floor to ceiling oak-paneled bookshelves filled with books that looked like they hadn't been opened in decades. A flat screen television hung high on the wall beside the large windows and, on the far side of the room, behind the pool table, was an ancient-looking piano with the most decorative case I'd ever seen.

"Where am I?"

Luc scratched his chin, his stubble doing nothing to detract from the square, masculine set of his jaw. "The common room in the MU Fellowship Hall. I usually hang out here between classes."

"Ah."

I'd seen the Fellowship Hall as I walked through the campus. The building was hard to miss. As I'd learned during my college orientation, it had once served as a chapel but was converted to college use when the university bought the land several decades ago. Now it was the site of the religious studies department. The exterior was made of red brick and had green wooden doors, along with decorative stained glass lining some of the upper windows.

"Are you a religious studies major?" I asked him.

He certainly didn't look like one. Not that I knew what they looked like, since I'd never actually met anyone who majored in the subject. But to me, the thought conveyed the image of a thin, wiry intellectual with round glasses and a collared shirt with a bowtie. Not a hunk with a leather jacket and worn jeans that hugged all the right places.

Then again, what did I know?

"Maybe. Not sure yet. I've got a few months yet to figure it out," Luc said.

Well, at least I wasn't the only one who didn't know what I wanted to do with my life. Though in my defense, I was only a freshman.

"Are you a sophomore?" I asked him.

"Junior," he drawled, shooting me a grin. "I'm Professor Raymond's teaching assistant. He's the head of the religious studies department."

Now that one shocked me. He didn't give off a scholarly vibe, and he sure as hell didn't look like any of the teaching assistants in my classes.

He must have read the surprise on my face, because his grin widened. "Not quite as dumb as I look."

"Oh, no, I—I didn't mean that," I stammered. "I just meant—"

Taking pity on my flustered state, he let me off the hook. "Just teasing, Princess."

His nonchalant nickname sparked a prickly rush of heat through my body. I didn't know if it was supposed to be a good or bad thing that he likened me to royalty, but either way it made me uncomfortable for some reason.

"It's Jewel," I murmured.

Luc motioned toward my face. "Because of the eyes?"

"So I've been told."

While my name didn't always seem to fit, like maybe it should belong to someone bolder than me, there was no denying the brilliant tone of my eyes.

Without warning, Luc rose to his feet. "Well, I have a class in twenty minutes. You sure you're okay?"

My stomach fell at the subtle dismissal and, feeling even more self-conscious now, I rose to my feet. When the world didn't spin on its axis, I nodded. "Yeah, I'm okay. Um …" I bit my lip as I looked around the room. "You don't happen to know where my coat and backpack are, do you?"

"Oh, right." He walked around to the back of the couch we'd just vacated and bent down. When he rose, he had both items in his hand. "I took them off you after I carried you in."

The thought of him removing my coat from my unconscious body sparked a wave of tightness. What was it I felt? Excitement over the fact that his hands had been on my body, however innocent it might have been? Or embarrassment at the circumstances under which it happened?

Honestly, I didn't know, and I didn't care to examine it any further.

"Um, thanks." I accepted the coat and shrugged it on, then took the backpack from him. "Well, uh, see you around."

I turned and headed for the double doors. It was only when I'd swung them open and stepped over the threshold that Luc spoke again.

"Jewel."

My breath caught. I stopped and turned back to

face him. "Yeah?"

He flashed me an easy grin. "See you in art history."

"Oh. Okay."

Wincing at how pathetic I sounded, I turned and headed down the long hall. There were closed doors on either side, as well as an intersection with another hallway, but a set of double doors at the end with an exit sign over them told me where to go. Thankfully my vision had cleared, and I didn't seem to be suffering any ill effects from the recent loss of consciousness.

Well, I thought sardonically as I walked out into the cool air, *at least now he knows I exist.*

Chapter 3

MY MORNING class had already ended, and since I was sure Deme would be wondering why I never turned up, I trudged through campus to track him down. The lawn was packed with students now, people milling in and out of the surrounding brick and stone buildings. Every now and again I'd see someone move their hands like Luc and the guy in black had earlier. It made me wonder what was going on, but whenever I looked closer, there was nothing to see. It was weird, but that bit of strangeness was the least of my concerns right now. I couldn't stop thinking about the hallucinations I'd had.

They seemed so real. Even now my brain replayed them over and over again, the image of the man in black dissipating into smoke so vivid in my mind. I remembered the feeling of the white, hot light shooting inside my abdomen.

Why did it seem like it had really happened?

Even though the sun was shining down onto the green lawn that served as the center of campus, highlighting the varying shades of orange and red in the surrounding trees, the biting breeze made me snuggle deeper into my coat. I tried not to think about Luc's hands being on it just a short time ago.

Luc. Even the name sounded sexy ... and so out of my league.

Oh, I was no slouch in the looks department; any old mirror could tell me that. Dark tan skin and turquoise eyes made for a striking combination, as many people I'd met throughout my life had told me. And my hair, which was generally stick-straight—though not so much now thanks to the unfortunate incident this morning—was one of my best features.

My appearance came from my mother. She died in a house fire when I was just a baby. Dad was a doctor, and it had been one of those rare days when he was actually off. He'd taken me to the park to give my mom a rest, and by the time we'd gotten back, it was already too late. All the pictures of her had gone up in flames, along with everything else that day. I had nothing tangible to remember her by and no family either, since she'd been orphaned when she came over to the States. All I knew was she was Hawaiian, hence the tan skin and dark hair. The eyes must come from my father's side, although his are a more washed-out shade of blue.

So no, it wasn't the way I looked that put Luc out of my league. It was the fact that I was so damned awkward when it came to guys. Always had been. And he seemed like the type who appreciated a confident woman.

That wasn't me, not even on my best day.

About twenty feet from the building housing the science department, I heard my name being called.

"Jewel. Yo!"

I stopped mid-stride and turned toward the sound of Deme's voice. He was speed walking toward me, his face a mixture of concern and annoyance.

"What the hell," he said the moment he was close enough to speak without shouting. "How could you blow off class? You know now Professor Montgomery's gonna have it in for you next time he sees you. That man is way too crazy about biology for his own good." He shuddered. "For anyone's good, really—"

"Deme." I grabbed his arm, cutting him off in midsentence because *man*, could he go on when he was in a mood. "Something happened."

He knew me better than anyone, and he could tell by my tone that this was serious. "What? What happened?"

"Um …" I glanced around. "You remember the guy from art history? The cute one?"

We were also in that class together, and there were no secrets between us … at least not on my side. Not when Deme could read me like a book.

A strange expression crossed Deme's face. "I told you, I heard that kid gets around. He's no good for you."

"No, it's not anything like that." When Deme raised one thick eyebrow in question, I continued in a hushed tone. "I kind of got in the middle of a fight he was having, and I got knocked out."

Deme's eyes grew wide. "What?"

He snatched my hand and dragged me over to a nearby stone bench. Given the frosty temperature, there was no one else around as he pulled me down on the seat.

"Argh!" I shivered as the icy cold of the stone froze my ass through my jeans. "It's cold."

He shook me. "Focus. Now tell me, what happened?"

As I relayed the morning's events to him, his expression went from amazed to dismayed. But when I told him about the hallucinations, about how I'd imagined being injected with a mysterious substance, his concern for me was palpable. And when I mentioned imagining a white light heating my belly, his face took on an impassive expression.

God, I hated that poker face. It felt like I saw it all too often lately. Considering I wore all my emotions openly, it was really starting to piss me off.

"That's crazy, chica," he said bluntly.

"I know." I pressed the heels of my hands into my eyelids, trying to alleviate the sudden pressure building there. "I know, but ... Deme, it seemed so real."

"It wasn't." He pulled my hands off my face. "You sure you don't have a concussion?"

"You sound just like him," I said with a giggle. "I mean Luc, the Art History Guy."

His expression told me he wasn't at all amused by the comparison.

Sobering, I lifted my hands to my head and felt around. "To be honest, it doesn't hurt *anywhere*. If I hadn't been knocked out, I would have a hard time believing I'd been hit at all."

"You must be Superwoman," he said dryly.

I shot him a dirty look. "Smartass."

"Seriously Jewel, just be thankful you didn't get

hurt. And next time keep an eye out for things going on around you. I've never met someone so lost in their own world."

When I merely stuck my tongue out at him, Deme rose and held out his hand. "Come on, woman. Let's get out of the cold. My ass is freezing."

Night had fallen by the time I made it back to my dormitory. After hitting my other two classes, I'd met with Deme again so he could catch me up on what I missed in biology. As I'd feared, it took hours to feel like I got a grasp of what Professor Montgomery had gone over that morning. Inwardly I cursed Deme for talking me into taking that class with him. Surely there had to be easier professors.

After a quick shower in the shared bathroom on my floor, I threw on a towel and brushed my teeth, then headed back to my room to change into my pajamas. For some reason I was exhausted, like I'd run a marathon or something. More than that, throughout the day, I felt like I caught the occasional flash of something strange in the corner of my vision. But every time I turned to look, it was gone.

"Maybe I *should* have gone to the infirmary," I murmured as I stepped into my flannel bottoms. I grabbed my t-shirt and slid it over my head. When the fabric grazed my neck, I recalled the feel of being pinched with something.

God, it had felt so real.

On impulse, I headed to the mirror above my short, wide dresser. As I pulled back my hair to look at the spot on my neck, I almost half expected to see a needle prick. But there was nothing. The skin there was smooth as ever.

"Just a hallucination, Jewel."

Even if it did seem like it truly happened.

There was no mistaking how real the dark circles under my eyes were, though. I stifled a yawn. Jeez, I hadn't felt this tired since Senior Grad Night, when everyone in my class had gone to a late-night theme park and stayed up until after sunrise.

I stumbled over to turn off the light switch, then barely made it to my bed before deep exhaustion claimed me.

The sky was dark, and I floated on a cloud. Lightning flashed all around me, illuminating my figure in the darkness. I moved my fingers, and a trippy ribbon of light trailed after them.

I'm dreaming.

The realization came swiftly. What was more, I'd had this dream before. Countless times. Only I'd forgotten until now.

I opened my hand, and a small glowing ball of light appeared in the center of my palm. It didn't surprise me. Somehow, I knew it would happen. Before my eyes, the ball grew bigger, until it was about the size of a basketball, lighting up the sky around me. Dark shadows danced just outside the perimeter of my light. I could see them, though logic dictated they should be invisible. The fingers of my other hand wiggled, and the shadows danced in time with them. I laughed at the sight, feeling pure joy over what I could do.

But then the shadows began to distort, growing wider, bigger. More frightening. I waved my fingers, trying to get them to leave, but it only made their movements more frenzied. The shadows formed into monstrous figures with jagged teeth, snarling and writhing in the air.

"No," I whispered.

At once the shadows lunged through the air, heading straight for me. I screamed and raised my hands to shield my face. Then I stumbled backward, directly off the cloud. Air buffeted my body as I fell. The ground raced up to meet me …

I gasped and shot up in the bed, the remnants of my dream swirling around my head. *What the hell?*

The images were vivid in my mind, along with something deeper. Some niggling remembrance of things forgotten. It hovered just beneath the surface, out of my current realm of comprehension. My hands trembled as I lifted them toward my face. I stopped in mid-motion.

"What. The. Hell?"

There it was. Faint, but unmistakable.

My skin was *glowing*!

Panic clawed at me as I wrangled out of my twisted bed covers and staggered over to the mirror. My own face looked back at me. Black hair hanging straight over my shoulders, turquoise eyes shining with anxiety. The dark circles beneath them had faded to a light purple. Everything was the same as it ever was.

Everything save one ...

Just beneath the surface of my skin, an unnatural radiance highlighted the sparkly shimmer in my eyes.

"What is happening?" My whisper cut through the air, reverberating throughout the quiet room.

I pressed my fingertips to my temples, willing my heart to stop its frantic racing. To my utter shock, as my heartbeat calmed, the glow began to fade until it was completely gone.

Minutes passed as I stared at my image in the mirror. Once again, I looked utterly normal. But I couldn't blame the glow on hallucinations this time. Not when the tightness in my gut told me something was off.

Between yesterday and today, something had changed. Something inside me. I knew it as surely as I knew anything. The glow was only the outer manifestation of what had already been done.

On shaky legs, I wobbled over to the window and opened the blinds. The green lawn in the center of campus lay before me. It looked almost the same, but I was seeing it through new eyes, as if a veil had been removed from my vision.

Familiar faces strode here and there, headed to class or to other parts of campus, but even though I'd seen them before, passed by them countless times, they were different now. One guy absently juggled a tiny ball of flame between his ungloved hands as he ambled toward the social studies building. Another was trailed by a child-sized tornado that seemed to follow him like a pet chasing after its owner. A girl I was pretty sure sat next to me in my woman's studies class partially reclined on the circular stone casing of the water fountain, and as she absently wriggled her fingers toward the water, it magnetized toward her and absorbed into her skin.

I rubbed my eyes, as if that would cure me of what I was seeing, but the vision remained.

"Holy fuck balls." There was no denying it, no chalking it up to some non-existent concussion. There was magic here.

I didn't know exactly *what* was happening or why, but I knew what I saw was real. I knew it deep in my heart. Just as I instinctively knew there was one person who could give me the answers I sought.

After frantically digging out a pair of jeans and a sweater, I grabbed my coat and backpack and left my room. I did have some vanity left, because I stopped in the bathroom long enough to brush my teeth before hightailing it out of the dormitory.

Normally this was where I would go find Deme in his dorm room, if he hadn't first come to collect me. But my feet didn't turn in that direction. Instead, I headed straight for the Fellowship Hall, my determined gaze set on where I was going.

It was hard not to get distracted when I now saw the world through new eyes. Every person on the lawn seemed to have some sort of supernatural quirk. A girl walking in front of me disappeared into thin air before reappearing again a moment later. When a stiff breeze shot through the lawn, some guy opened his mouth wide and swallowed the thing whole before emitting a loud burp.

O-kaaay.

I wasn't even going to touch that one right now.

A loud thump settled in my heart as I climbed the two steps to the Fellowship Hall. I burst through the door, racing down the hallway to the common room. He would be there. I didn't know how I knew, but I did.

The double doors into the common room were closed, but I could hear the racking of balls behind them, along with some laughter. Without thinking about it, I quietly opened one of the doors and peeked inside.

Just as I'd intuitively known, Luc was standing there at the pool table with a pool cue in his hand. Across from him stood another guy I didn't recognize. He had bronze skin that hinted at some sort of Middle Eastern heritage and deep brown eyes. His dark brown hair was cut into a short, sleek do, and he was clean shaven, emphasizing the angular lines of his jaw. He wore a black sweater and black jeans, which only served to highlight the deep tan of his skin.

Neither of them noticed me enter and, despite my panic, I found myself pausing at the threshold. I couldn't help it. The two of them together were striking. One darker, the other lighter, and both breathtakingly gorgeous. Latent hormones went zigzagging through my body.

Where do they make these guys?

Living in the modeling hub of the world, I'd grown accustomed to seeing good-looking people on the streets, but these guys took it to another level entirely.

For one crazy, lust-induced moment, I forgot all about the things I'd just seen. But then the darker skinned guy said something I couldn't hear, and Luc laughed. He absently lifted one hand off the pool cue and a streak of lightning shot from his fingers, zapping the second guy in the stomach.

"Ow." The other guy laughed as he reeled a few inches backward. He rubbed his abdomen, and then all seemed to be forgotten as he lifted his pool cue and lined up for a shot.

"Seriously?" I screeched, unable to help myself.

Both men jumped at the sound of my voice, hurling their shocked gazes in my direction.

"Ow?" I waved my hand toward the second guy. "He zaps you with lightning and that's all you have to say?"

The guy's brows shot up toward his forehead, and he turned to give Luc a confused look.

Luc, for his part, stared at me with something akin to growing horror. But then, as if just noticing what he was doing, he cleared his throat and schooled his expression into one of bemusement. "What are you talking about?"

This was all too much. A knot of anger coalesced in the pit of my stomach. "I'm talking about what you can do. What a lot of people on this campus can do, apparently!"

Luc traded a loaded glance with the second guy. "Sweetheart, you hit your head harder than I thought."

Yesterday his words alone would have made me question my sanity. But not today. Because I could suddenly sense, deep within me, he wasn't telling the truth.

I shook my head and crossed my arms. "You're lying."

Startled by my blunt accusation, Luc shifted uneasily. "You and I both know it's not possible to do what you're saying I did."

"Another lie." What the hell? I could tell easily now, like overnight I'd become some sort of human lie detector. "I *saw* it. I saw other things, too."

Carefully, as if he was stalling for time, Luc set his pool cue onto the table. "What sorts of other things?"

"Oh, let's see." I ticked the items off with my fingers. "How about a man eating the air. A girl absorbing water. A guy being followed by a tornado. And that's just to start."

When Luc gave a heavy sigh and exchanged yet another worried look with the guy across from him, it hit me. As I was racing over here, I'd secretly been hoping Luc could convince me everything I'd seen was a hallucination. But he wasn't going to be able to, because it wasn't.

It was real.

"Oh my god." My arms lowered as I processed what I'd just discovered.

Everything I'd seen was real. Not just today, but yesterday.

"What *really* happened to me yesterday?" I glanced down at his hand and, recalling the way lightning had shot from it, took a small step backward. "What *are* you?"

Luc bit his lip. The expression on his face made it obvious he was internally at war with himself.

Debating what to tell me next, no doubt.

"Dude," the dark-haired hottie by Luc said. His voice held a note of warning, and he and Luc exchanged some sort of silent communication. I didn't know what the hell they were doing, but it seemed like they were arguing over something without even using any words.

Finally, Luc took a deep breath and said to the other guy, "Aeron, can you go get the Professor?"

Aeron let out a long sigh, then nodded and headed in my direction.

My stomach gave a few anxious flops as he approached, but not because he was so attractive. For all I knew, he was one of *them* ... whatever they were. It took all I had to resist the urge to cower or run.

In the end, all he did was throw me a look of curiosity and a quick grin before stepping past me and heading out the double doors of the common room.

My gaze stayed on the door until his footsteps receded down the hallway. That was when I turned back to Luc. "Tell me the truth. What's happening here?"

Luc crossed the distance between us, stopping no more than two feet away from me. He gave me a deep, considering look. Then his lips twisted into a half-smile. "You sure you really want to know?"

Wasn't that the question of a lifetime.

Part of me wanted to say no and run back to my dorm room to crawl under the covers, pretending all of this was one long, bad dream. But I couldn't. The memory of the subtle glow beneath my skin prevented it.

"Yes." I took a deep breath. "I *have* to know."

When he swallowed, a trickle of what looked like lightning zipped from his Adam's apple up into his square jaw. It only served to highlight the perfect angles and lines of his face.

Almost too perfect.

My heart started to beat frantically in my chest as I recalled yesterday, when we shook hands. The trace of electricity I thought I'd saw, that I had felt zap my skin.

Lightning shooting from his fingertips. More than once.

The truth hovered there on the surface. On my lips. It couldn't be, not based on the reality I knew. But there it was, staring me right in the face.

"Ar-are you magical?"

Luc chuckled, as if he hadn't been expecting that question. "I guess that depends on your definition."

He was right. I'd asked the wrong question, and for some crazy reason I'd known it even before I'd asked.

My voice wavered as I uttered the question I'd been too afraid to ask first. "Are you human?"

He barely reacted, but from the way he stilled and his eyes widened the slightest fraction, I could tell I'd surprised him. The silence stretched out between us as he regarded me, taking my measure. At last, he gave a slow shake of his head. "Nope."

My breath hitched at his stark admission. Even though everything in my logical mind said it couldn't be possible, there was another, deeper part of me that had already known.

"So …" Somehow, I resisted the urge to shrink into myself. I managed to look directly into those too-perfect eyes. "What are you then?"

A sudden, inhuman stillness settled over him. His lightning-quick gaze bored into mine, as if he was deciding what I should know. His nostrils flared slightly as he drew in a breath. When he finally answered me, his voice was silky smooth. "I'm an elemental."

"Elemental?" The word sounded both foreign and familiar on my tongue. Had I heard it before? If so, I didn't know what it meant.

As if he guessed the direction of my thoughts, he nodded. "Simply put … I'm from another dimension."

Chapter 4

"ANOTHER DIMENSION?"

My voice echoed too loudly in the common room. Even as I knew he spoke the truth, my rational brain tried to deny it. "You want me to believe you're from another *dimension*?"

Before Luc could respond, a deep, thick voice with an English accent rumbled from behind me. "But you do believe it, don't you, Miss Harris?"

My breath catching, I whirled around. A tall man with a trim figure and salt-and-pepper hair curling below the collar of his light-yellow, Oxford dress shirt had entered the room. He wore wire-framed glasses, and he sort of had a George Clooney, sexy older guy vibe going.

The man gave me a tight smile as I stared at him in shock. "Good morning, Miss Harris. My name is Theobald Raymond."

My mouth dropped open. "Th-the head of the religious studies department?"

"The one and only."

Now I understood why so many of the freshman girls had giggled when they talked about wanting to register for a religion class. With looks like that, it would be a miracle if all his classes weren't filled to capacity.

Professor Raymond stepped farther into the room, and that was when I noticed the guy who'd recently left right behind him. Aeron, Luc had called him. He entered the room behind the Professor, giving me wide berth. Under the circumstances, I appreciated the gesture.

"So you … you know about *him*?" I pointed at Luc, well aware I'd made him sound like some sort of monster.

But well, hadn't he just admitted to basically being an alien?

"I know about a lot concerning the other dimensions, Miss Harris."

"He's an expert," Luc added nonchalantly.

Well, isn't that just awesome?

I wanted to freak out, but Professor Raymond looked so assured, so dignified, that it helped me stay calm.

"I suppose you must have many questions," he said.

"Yeah." Understatement of the century. Except, given what I'd just learned, I didn't know where to start.

My blank stare must have clued him in on that fact, because after a moment of loaded silence, Professor Raymond turned back to Aeron. "Mr. Dunn, would you be so kind as to place a note outside my office door stating the office hours have been cancelled for today?"

Aeron nodded and left the room, clicking the door shut behind him.

"Come." Professor Raymond flashed me a friendly smile as he motioned toward the couches. "Let's sit and we can discuss it. I do believe this may take a while."

It didn't take a genius to figure that out, because if there were other dimensions that could somehow interact with our own, then I sure as hell was about to have a lot of questions.

Something about the Professor put me at ease. I couldn't begin to explain why, considering what I'd just discovered. But given he was the head of an entire department at the university, I figured he had to be pretty trustworthy.

Right?

The steady thump of my heart against my ribcage had me sucking in deep breaths as I did what the Professor suggested and followed him over to the seating area. When he took a seat on the small couch across from the larger one I'd woken up on yesterday, I sat in the same spot I was in when Luc first introduced himself to me. I shrugged out of my coat before sitting.

Luc followed us over and sprawled carelessly beside me, so close he could reach out and touch me if he were so inclined. My body automatically poised for flight, the tiny hairs on the back of my neck standing on end.

"Relax, Princess." Luc's lips twisted into an amused grin. "I don't eat human flesh."

Professor Raymond gave Luc a wry look. "Mr. Zain, your attempt at reassurance is somewhat lacking."

Luc sat up straighter and mumbled, "Sorry."

The Professor's expectant gaze returned to me, and after a few moments of tense silence, I realized he was waiting for me to speak first.

"Oh ... uh ..." Where to start? Taking a breath, I began with the most recent question in my mind. "What's an elemental?"

"Hmm ..." He cleared his throat. "That's a difficult one to explain without first explaining about the existence of the other worlds."

Other *worlds*?

Okaaaay ...

"Where exactly are these other worlds? Are they in another galaxy?"

Based on Luc's hearty chuckle, I'd gotten my guess wrong.

Jerk. It wasn't as if I dealt with something like this every day. I threw him a dirty glance, but all I got in response was a saucy wink that made my cheeks grow hot.

"No," was Professor Raymond's calm response. "They are on other planes of existence."

That earned him a vacant stare. "Huh?"

"Like I told you"—Luc absently crossed one ankle over the opposite thigh, bringing him even closer to my personal space—"other dimensions."

Wait.

I wasn't a huge science buff, but I did remember some of this from my high school science classes. "Are you talking about parallel universes?"

The Professor's lips twisted. "Yes, in a way. Are you familiar with the concept of the multiverse?"

"A little." Luc's proximity temporarily forgotten, I leaned forward in my seat. "But I thought it meant a parallel universe is created whenever you make a choice about something. So, for example, somewhere out there might be a world where I decided not to go to college."

Professor Raymond nodded. "That's one theory, but not exactly the one I'm discussing."

"Oh." His words deflated my excitement. "Okay, then. You lost me."

"I'm speaking of mutations in space creating alternate universes with differing physical constants."

When I gave him a blank stare, he pitched forward, motioning with his hands. "Imagine, if you will, a world where the inhabitants get their sustenance not from food, but from darkness. Or air."

"Or light," Luc added cheerily.

My gaze fell back to Luc, who absently rolled his ankle as he regarded me.

"Are you serious right now?"

Professor Raymond nodded at Luc. "Mr. Zain, perhaps it would be helpful if you would show Miss Harris the book."

"Yeah, 'cause who doesn't believe everything they read," Luc muttered under his breath. When the Professor continued to stare steadily at him, he sighed and rose to his feet. "Fine."

A low whistle sounded from Luc's mouth as he ambled over to the bookcases and poked around, finally withdrawing a hardcover book that had a nice layer of dust on it. He blew on the cover, and some of the dust wafted off.

When he brought the book to me, I couldn't help

but stare at it. The cover was ancient, made of what appeared to be ornate leather. Areas of it were tattered, revealing semi-rotted wood beneath. Several metal clasps served as a lock of sorts.

"This looks like it belongs in a museum or something."

"Or something," Luc drawled, placing it into my hands before sitting back down beside me.

I examined the book. Part of me felt guilty for even touching it. It looked like one good fall was all it would take for the thing to disintegrate.

When I glanced at the Professor, he nodded in reassurance. So I placed the book on my lap and gently pulled back on the metal clasps, opening it. The pages were worn vellum, confirming what I'd already surmised. This book was damn old.

My fingers traced over the ink on the first page, and I repeated the words I saw there. "The Book of Elements."

"Please continue," Professor Raymond urged.

I turned the page again, to the first passage. "In the beginning, there were but six elements: earth, air, water, fire, aether, and nether."

"Aether, in a sense, means light," the Professor explained. "Nether is darkness, or the absence of light."

Nodding, I continued on. "Out of these elements sprang gods, immortal beings with a multitude of abilities. But in time the gods grew lonely, and each created a world complete with mortals in their own image."

My gaze flew to the Professor. "What does this have to do with anything?"

He arched a thick brow at me. "Keep reading."

Shrugging, I continued. "The worlds lived in relative balance and harmony until the nether god, in his greed, desired to rule over all the worlds. To accomplish this he created elementals ..."

I gasped at the word, my gaze landing on Luc.

He gave me a reassuring nod. "Go on, Princess."

Suddenly, I wasn't so sure I wanted to. Something told me that once I read the next words, my world would never be the same again.

But then, wasn't that already true? Even if I didn't read this, I could never go back to where I was the day before yesterday. Not after what I'd seen.

I would always wonder.

So, after a deep, stabilizing breath, I went back to the text. "To accomplish this he created elementals, warriors infused with some of his supernatural abilities who traveled to the other worlds to establish dominance. In response, the remaining gods created their own elementals, guardians tasked with watching over their world. And so, the elemental guardians were born ..."

As my voice trailed off, I looked up at Professor Raymond. His steady gaze told me everything I needed to know.

But I didn't believe it. I couldn't.

It was crazy.

With an incredulous laugh, I glanced over at Luc. "You expect me to believe that these *elementals* actually exist and you are one? I mean ... the powers of a god? Come on!"

Luc's composed expression didn't waver.

Faced with his all too perfect features again, I couldn't help but recall what he'd done earlier to Aeron. The way he'd moved during the altercation with the man in black—if it wasn't a hallucination. I was rapidly beginning to think none of it had been.

Holy crap.

My face sobered as I regarded him with growing understanding.

This was real. *He* was real.

"What are you?" I asked flatly, for the second time in less than fifteen minutes.

"I'm a light elemental," he said evenly. "From a parallel world known as Aethera."

"And you … you have powers."

It wasn't an inquiry this time. Not when I knew the answer. But he acted as if it was anyway.

"I can create lightning. Manipulate it."

A wooden nod was all I could manage. I'd already seen what he could do, so there was no point in disbelieving it. My mind raced with questions. I didn't know where to start. "How did you get here?"

Luc glanced at the Professor before answering. "There are holes between the dimensions. We call them portals. They allow for travel between the worlds, if you know where to find one."

A soft laugh escaped me. I didn't know how to feel about that revelation. "Is everyone from your world an elemental?"

"Nope." Luc uncrossed his legs, leaning forward to rest his elbows on his knees while he looked at me. "Most of the other worlds are populated with mortals, just like Earth has humans. But in every world, there's a portion of the population that is elemental."

Professor Raymond chimed in. "The best way to describe elementals is they are like your royalty on here on Earth. In fact, a good portion of the royals on this world *are* elementals."

My mouth dropped open. "You're telling me Earth has elementals, too?"

"Of course."

The earlier glow of my skin burned in my memory, and a sudden thought occurred to me. "Oh my god, am *I* an Earth elemental?"

Professor Raymond gave a startled laugh. "Certainly not. Whatever would make you think that?"

I couldn't sense any lies in his words, not like I had before with Luc.

"This morning." I glanced down at my hands, but they looked the same as always. "When I woke up, there was, like, a *glow* beneath my skin. Just under the surface."

"A glow?" The Professor exchanged a glance with Luc. "Hmm …"

"What?" Nervous energy raced through my body, making me shift in my spot. "What does that mean? Is something wrong with me?"

Neither of them responded at first.

Almost to the breaking point, I hovered on the edge of my seat, fighting with everything I had not to jump up and shout, "What is it?"

"It must be an effect of the substance you were injected with," Professor Raymond finally murmured.

His words felt flat, but again, I could discern no lie there.

Then it hit me.

Anger coursed through my veins as I shot out of my seat and glared accusingly at Luc. "You told me I imagined that!"

Shrugging, he averted his gaze. "I didn't want to worry you."

My finger jabbed in his direction. "You mean you didn't want to tell me the truth."

He winced slightly, then mumbled, "I didn't see any point when there seemed to be nothing wrong with you."

"You …" I clenched my teeth to bite back the litany of curse words that longed to escape my mouth. "You let me walk away with some unknown drug inside me! Don't you think you should have told me, so I could at least get checked out or something?"

"I'm afraid the fault lies with me, Miss Harris." When I turned my furious gaze to Professor Raymond, he offered a placating smile. "I wasn't sure what you had been injected with, but I knew no doctor would be able to detect it. Besides, based on what we know of the assailant, it seemed most likely that whatever was in the syringe would have a temporary effect at most."

His words didn't make much sense, but at least I was getting somewhere now.

"What do you mean? What do you know of the assailant?" I started to sit back down, when I came to another realization that propelled me back to my feet. My trembling hand covered my mouth as I stared at Luc. "Wait … you killed him!"

Luc's shoulders tensed. "Believe me, sweetheart, it was in self-defense. It was either me or him, and given that he attacked you, lord only knows what he might've done to you if I hadn't got him first."

Most of that felt like the truth, but a niggling sensation in my stomach told me he wasn't giving me the whole story.

The jellylike sensation in my legs told me it would probably be wise to sit, so I slumped back onto the sofa. "Okay, tell me who he was. Why did he turn into black smoke when you stabbed him? Or did I imagine that, too?"

It was the Professor who answered, ignoring the snarkiness of my last question. "Much of what you read in the Book of Elements is true. Though of course the existence of the gods is in question, we do know each of the six worlds has beings who are born with powerful abilities."

"Elementals," I murmured.

"Exactly. And it is true that, for as long as there have been records of time, the elementals from the dark world—Netheren, as it's known—have attempted to take over the remaining five dimensions."

I shot a quick glance at Luc. "The man Luc killed?"

"He was a dark elemental," the Professor confirmed. "When an elemental is killed, he or she returns to that which they are made of. Their primary element. In this man's case, it was darkness."

"Hence the dark smoke," I murmured.

"Exactly. Aether and nether are opposing forces, light and dark. Based on their lineage, Luc and the man you saw were mortal enemies."

I resisted the urge to snort at his use of the term 'mortal.' It didn't seem to apply here.

"So, where do I come in on all of this? Why did he go after me?"

The Professor shifted in his seat. He was quiet for so long that my imagination took over, making me fear all sorts of improbable reasons. Just when I was about to burst with anxiety, he said, "As you might have guessed by now, this university is no ordinary one. It's one of the few schools on Earth that shelters elementals from this and other dimensions. A safe zone, if you will."

"Is everyone on this campus from another world?" It certainly seemed that way from what I witnessed when I was rushing over here.

"Many, but not all," was his even reply. "And there are a fair number of regular humans on campus as well. Don't forget, you are here, too."

There was no sense of falsehood in his voice.

My mind raced as I attempted to process the Professor's words. "Why would elementals need shelter?"

Luc chimed in on that one. "Various reasons. Infighting with elementals of their own kind, in some cases. Others of us are here as guardians under the Interworld Treaty."

"The *what* now?"

A half-smile formed on his lips at my puzzled expression. "It's an agreement of protection between the heads of all the worlds, other than

Netheren. The theory is that each world is better protected against dark elementals when it has various other types of elementals guarding it."

A strangled laugh escaped me. I pressed the heels of my hand to my eyelids. "You're giving me a headache."

"Sorry." Luc's voice was sympathetic. "I know it's a lot to take in all at once."

He was right. Too much, in fact. I would have to think this all over later. But for now, there was one thing I *needed* to know. "So, again, why did he stick me with a needle?"

"The Netheren elementals aim to create imbalance here on Earth as well as in the other dimensions. It is their first step to taking over each world." The Professor crossed one ankle over the other. "My guess is he injected you with something so you would be able to see the abilities of those here on campus. It was an attempt to create confusion."

I blinked. Could it really be that simple?

"You mean, I was just in the wrong place at the wrong time?"

Professor Raymond nodded. "Had the man slipped past Luc, no doubt he would have injected as many people as he could. His ultimate goal was chaos."

Chaos. The word sat there on the tip of my tongue, begging me to repeat it. It seemed all too appropriate, in fact, given what I'd just heard.

"And the glow?"

"I'm sure it's a side effect." Professor Raymond gave a decisive nod. "It may return, but like the other effects of the injection, it should soon fade permanently."

His tone was so assured that I wanted to believe him. I didn't have any reason not to. But still, something lurked beneath the surface of my comprehension, making me more than a little uneasy at the Professor's words.

Racked with confusion, I let my gaze wander back to Luc. I didn't trust him as far as I could throw him, but for some reason I'd been able to tell earlier when he wasn't being truthful with me. "Do you agree with Professor Raymond that the effects I'm seeing are temporary?"

"He's the smartest guy I know." Luc met my gaze directly. "Especially when it comes to elementals. He knows everything."

There was no doubt he spoke the truth, so I took him at his word. It wasn't until much later I would realize he'd never actually answered my question.

Chapter 5

"YOU SURE you're okay?"

Luc's deep voice broke through my fog. I peeked over at him as we walked side by side through the campus lawn. Luren Hall was to our right, the Gothic-style four-story building that was probably my favorite on campus. Round turrets rose off each corner, making it look sort of like a medieval castle. When I first visited here, it brought back all my childhood fantasies of pretending to be a princess. The effect was slightly ruined by the busy first-floor bistro where students had lined up outside, waiting to get their Starbucks fix.

Professor Raymond left us minutes ago because he had to go teach a class. He'd told me I was welcome to come back and see him if I had any more questions, which I appreciated. I was sure that once the shock wore off, there would be *plenty* I realized I hadn't asked.

The moment the Professor left, I realized I was alone in the common room with Luc. I told myself the uncomfortable shiver that racked my body was due to him being non-human, but if I was being honest with myself, that was only part of the problem. Now that I knew he was an elemental, he was even more intriguing than before. Yeah, so he was a being from another dimension who apparently had supernatural powers – but he was also an incredibly attractive guy.

And he has powers!

I mean, who wouldn't secretly think that was the biggest turn-on ever? There was only so much a girl could take.

I'd mumbled something about needing to get to my next class, which was an excuse but also accurate. To my shock, Luc insisted on walking me to the building which housed my English literature class.

When Luc arched a brow in my direction, I realized I hadn't answered his earlier question.

"Am I okay?" I let my gaze wander to the far side of the lawn where three students were taking turns waving their fingers at nearby shrubs, causing them to writhe and twist into different shapes. "No, I don't think I am."

Luc let out a soft grunt. "I'm sure it's a lot to take in. Anyone would feel that way."

"I guess." Biting my lip, I forced my gaze away from the group. "How did I not notice any of this before?"

"Enchantment." Luc slid his hands into the pockets of his leather jacket. "The president of the university is a light mage, gifted with the ability to create illusions."

"So I was right. You *are* magical."

"I guess you could say so." His brow quirked. "Our abilities are what you would call elemental magic. The president casts illusionary spells so the human students don't notice anything outside of their realm of the ordinary. The substance you were injected with must counter the effects."

A disbelieving laugh crept from my throat. "I can't believe all this."

"There's a lot you don't know about yet," he murmured.

Apparently.

Curious, I let myself take in the lines and angles of Luc's face. If there was any moment I could stare at him and get away with it, it would be now. "Aethera, that's where you're from too, right?"

"Yup." He threw me a half-grin. "I can't create illusions, though. I only have the ability to manipulate lightning."

"So there's a range of abilities on each world?" I asked him.

"Exactly."

A stray breeze wafted in the air, and I burrowed further in my jacket to counter the chill. "What's it like there?"

"A lot like here. Only on my world, the elementals aren't hidden. The mortals on Aethera are aware of them, so illusion, light manipulation, you name it, all of it is practiced openly."

I couldn't imagine it.

"And you're here as a guardian?"

Luc nodded. "My family signed on to protect Earth several generations ago. Starting with my great-grandfather. Once I turned eighteen, it was my turn."

My brows furrowed as we continued walking. "So, you didn't have a choice as to whether or not you came to Earth?"

"I swore an oath to protect this world." He threw me a sidelong glance. "It's an honor to serve here."

Based on his sharp tone, I'd unintentionally insulted him.

"Sorry," I said with a wince.

"Don't worry about it." Luc flashed me a quick grin. "I know this is all new to you."

A sudden thought hit me, and I stopped in my tracks. Luc slowed to a halt beside me, an inquisitive expression on his face.

My fingers crept up to my neck, to the spot where I remembered being pricked. "I checked that night. I didn't have any needle marks."

He grimaced, and I caught a flicker of shame in his eyes. "While you were passed out on the couch, I had a friend come in and heal you. She's originally from my world, too."

My mouth dropped open. "People on your world can *heal*?"

He shrugged. "We were hopeful she might also cure you of the effects of what you were injected with, but I guess that didn't happen."

"Guess not," I said softly.

His blue eyes gazed into mine, alive with sympathy. I might have imagined it, but it almost seemed like a bolt of energy flashed through his irises.

"I'm sorry you had to go through this." Slowly he stepped closer, as if giving me time to back away. When his hand slid from his pocket, my pulse leapt. But I didn't move, not even as his fingers smoothed a stray strand of hair from my forehead.

His fingertips brushed against my temple, and a

spark of energy warmed my skin where he made contact. This time I almost expected it, though. I didn't even flinch.

"I'm glad I know," I murmured truthfully.

It was crazy, yes. My world was a whole lot scarier than it had been a few days ago. But I wasn't sorry.

Now I knew anything was possible.

Luc's gaze momentarily drifted down my body. Confused, I followed his eyes, but there was nothing unusual there, just my coat wrapped snugly around me. When he brought his eyes back up, something dark and wild flashed in them. But it was gone so fast I might have imagined it.

Huh.

He dropped his hand and stepped back, giving me a tight smile. "Looks like we're at your building."

I glanced over to the left.

Wow, he's right.

We'd walked all the way across campus. I'd been so caught up in our conversation, I hadn't even noticed it.

"Um ..." Reality intruded. My cheeks heated at the thought that I'd probably been gawking at him like some sort of moony-eyed stalker or something. "Thanks for walking with me and explaining everything."

"Anytime, sweetheart." That rakish drawl was back in his voice. "See ya in class."

Secretly, I was overjoyed I wouldn't have to wait that long to see him. But it was confusing because ... well, he wasn't human.

A cacophony of emotions flitted through me as I watched Luc turn and head back in the direction we'd come from. I'd just found out about the existence of other dimensions and beings from other worlds. That should be enough to keep my mind occupied for months, but apparently there was enough space left to also think about one very intriguing non-human.

Realizing I'd been staring for far too long, I turned back toward the building just in time to see Deme heading straight for me. He didn't look happy to see me, either.

Oh crap, what am I going to tell Deme?

How could I begin to talk about what I'd just learned without sounding completely off my rocker?

"Why were you hanging out with that guy?" Deme asked the moment I was in earshot. "I told you he's bad news."

I recoiled at the grumpiness in his tone, my own news momentarily forgotten.

"Now we're late to class, too." He snatched my hand and headed for the doors to the building. "I swear, Jewel, sometimes you have no sense."

"Chill," I snapped. "We were just talking."

Seriously, I loved Deme, but sometimes he acted *too* much like a brother.

The bell rang just as we entered the classroom, leaving Deme muttering under his breath as we slipped into our seats. The annoyed expression on his face deterred me from even attempting a conversation with him.

Honestly, I was sort of glad I hadn't brought it

up now. For some reason, the thought of telling Deme about everything I'd learned, about supernatural beings, made my stomach tight.

He was the person who was closest to me in the world, but clearly he couldn't see the things I did. His gaze didn't even stray to the guy in the front row who kept morphing from human form into a condensed mass of air. Or the girl next to him who stacked up a pile of paperclips on her desk ... without using her hands. The clips just danced across her desk, stacking on top of one another as if they had a life of their own.

What if he doesn't believe me? What if he thinks I'm certifiable?

With a sinking heart, I realized I wasn't ready to share what I'd learned with Deme. Not yet.

Somehow the entire day passed by without me confiding in Deme. At first he was too grumpy, but later, once he'd gotten the monkey off his back and returned to the lovable Deme I knew, I found I didn't want to ruin his mood.

When I said goodbye to him after dinner without broaching the subject, I promised myself I would tell him the following morning. Get him to believe me ... somehow.

But then, as I drifted off to sleep that night, the dreams came back.

I was floating on the dark cloud again, nothing but darkness surrounding me. Then the lightning began to flash all around me, and I realized with a burst of delight that it wasn't any old lightning. It was Luc …

Somehow he had *become* the lightning.

The dark shadows that lived at the edge of the clouds began moving, as if they had a life of their own. On impulse, my fingers lifted. Wiggled.

The dark shadows snaked closer.

I'm controlling them, I realized with a start. They writhed and twisted in a seductive rhythm, edging closer to me on the cloud. A feeling of power, ripe with sweetness, rippled through me.

Mine.

I woke with a gasp, clutching the twisted bedsheets to my body.

Though the remnants of my dream danced along the surface of my memory, the filtered light streaming in from the break in the window blinds told me it was morning already.

"Damn," I sighed. It felt like I'd just gone to bed. My dreams were messing with me, robbing me of the restful slumber I so desperately needed after the events of the past few days.

I lifted my shaky hands toward my face, intent on rubbing the sleep from my eyes, when the soft glow penetrated my mind.

"Oh no. Not again."

Radiant white light shimmered just beneath the surface of my skin, almost as if a light bulb had been implanted inside me. After wrestling the covers off, I raced over to the mirror.

"Crap." The glow was still there, just like yesterday morning, only today it was stronger, more obvious. My turquoise eyes practically gleamed against my shimmering skin. "I look like a freaking alien."

While the greater part of me was internally freaking out, I kind of had to admit I looked pretty cool. I mean, in the grand scheme of things, there was a lot worse that could have gone wrong than glowing skin.

But on the other hand ... *Eek!*

A weird, itchy sensation flitted across the palm of my right hand. It felt almost like energy crackling across my skin. Puzzled, I lifted my hand, palm up. A glowing orb formed there.

"What the hell?" I whispered. The ball grew bigger and bigger, until it was roughly the size of a beach ball. It floated off my hand and I inched backward, keeping my eyes locked on it. The ball began to zoom around the room, pinging off the walls in a haphazard ricochet until it suddenly zipped back toward me, hitting me square in the chest.

I gasped as my body absorbed the ball of light, bringing with it a heady sense of power. Static electricity bent the air, raising my hair on end. I turned back to the mirror in disbelief as my hair thickened before my very eyes, growing shinier and curling at the ends. It settled around my shoulders in a sensuous mass. The glow beneath the surface of my skin faded, leaving behind perfectly flushed cheeks.

"You have *got* to be kidding me!" Whatever *that* had been, it left me looking like I'd just spent hours at the salon. Better, in fact. No amount of hair product could create waves this bouncy or locks this shiny. Not to mention the blemish-free complexion requiring not a stitch of makeup.

For a long moment I just stared in the mirror, unable to help it. I still looked the same, just like a more perfect version of myself. At the same time, a heady sensuality coursed through my veins. It almost felt like some part of me had been asleep all my life, only now to awaken.

Hell, I even felt stronger. My body was amped up, like I'd just downed a couple of Monster energy drinks.

Some hidden urge propelled me to wrap my fingers around the edge of the dresser right in front of me. I lifted it, expecting nothing to happen, but to my shock the bulky piece of furniture tilted as if it weighed no more than a feather.

"No fucking way!" This couldn't be happening. Not only did I now look like some sort of super vixen, but I had superhuman powers as well? "What the hell was in that syringe?"

The shaky timbre of my voice floated around the room as fear melded with shock and excitement, dilating my pupils until they practically overtook the turquoise of my irises.

For all I knew, this was a normal byproduct of being stuck with whatever was in that needle, but I couldn't walk around campus all day pretending like it was nothing.

"The Professor," I gasped. Maybe he would know what was happening and how long I could expect this to last.

Of course, that train of thought led to another. How did the Professor know so much, anyway? As

I dressed, I made a mental note to ask him.

I made it halfway down the hall before bumping into one of my floor mates, a girl who was friendly but I didn't know well. She had a towel in her hand as she trudged toward the bathroom. When she saw me, she gave me a yawning smile and glanced away, only to shoot her gaze back a mere moment later. Her eyes widened. "Wow, you look great today. Are you going somewhere special?"

Without breaking my stride, I called an answer out as I headed to the elevator. "No, um … just class."

This time I didn't even pause to take a detailed look around as I made my way back to the Fellowship Hall. The images of shooting flames and a tiny waterspout blurred by my vision as I single-mindedly stalked across the lawn.

Only, once I stepped into the Fellowship Hall, I realized I didn't know where Professor Raymond's office was. There was no placard indicating which way to go. Before it hit me where I was heading, I found myself walking back to the common room. I don't know how I knew Luc would be there, but the sudden racing of my heart prepared me for the sight of him. Thankfully the newfound sensual power racing through my veins made the thought of facing him that much easier.

Taking a deep breath, I placed my hand on the doorknob and turned it, then stepped inside.

Yup. There he was, leaning against the back of the couch we'd both sat on yesterday.

Today he wore a thick, cable knit sweater in a shade of blue that would no doubt look fantastic with his eyes, a pair of worn jeans, and those same biker boots he'd worn the last two times I saw him. He had one ankle crossed over the other as he perused a book in his hands, and since he didn't look up as I entered, I figured it must be engrossing enough that he hadn't heard me come in.

Based on the worn leather cover, it was the same book I saw yesterday – the Book of Elements. I didn't know what to say about that, so I leaned against the doorframe. "Doing some light reading?"

Luc straightened with a start, carelessly tossing the book behind him onto the couch seat. I stifled a gasp and fought the urge to rush forward and check whether it had been damaged. Seriously … did he not *care* how old it was?

"No, I—" He took one good look at me and the words died on his lips. From the look on his face, it wasn't hard to read his thoughts. "Whoa. You look … nice."

Part of me wanted to blush, but the rest of me was too focused on the reason why he thought I looked so nice now. "Funny story." I pushed away from the door and sauntered into the room. "So, I woke up glowing again this morning, and when it faded, I turned into this." I pointed almost accusingly at my own face.

"Huh." Based on his clueless expression, he didn't seem to understand why this would be an issue.

"That's not all." I held up my palm. Again a tingle of electricity raced through me, and a glowing orb formed.

His brows crept up on his forehead. "Wow."

Seriously? I clenched my fist, and the ball of light disappeared. Why was he not getting the gravity of this situation?

"Think that's cool? How about this?" I glared at him as I stalked over to the pool table and set both hands on one edge, then easily hoisted the heavy oak table into the air.

His eyes bulged and he grinned wildly. "*Awesome.*"

Sudden anger built within me. Even though it was because of this crazy situation and not anything he'd done, my displeasure was directed at him. Setting the pool table down, I turned to face him and set my hands on my hips. "Really? I'm turning into a comic book character, and all you have to say is it's awesome?"

As if he sensed how close I was to losing it, Luc sobered. "Look, there's no big reason to be concerned. I'm sure it's just a side effect of the syringe."

Even as he said it, something in the tenor of his voice had me spitting out, "I don't believe you."

Wait, why had I said that? I didn't know, but just as before, I sensed he was … well, maybe not lying exactly, but holding something back.

Luc's eyes widened, and I was sure he looked as shocked as I felt.

My anger coalesced into a thick knot in the pit of my stomach. Even as it threatened to overwhelm me, I realized Luc wasn't at fault. He was just the one who happened to be here, and I was responding by taking out my frustration on him. I took a deep breath in effort to calm myself. "I want to speak to the Professor. Do you know where he is?"

Luc nodded. "He's teaching a class right now. He should be done in about fifteen minutes, if you want to wait."

Glancing at my watch, I sighed. I had a class starting at that time, and even though part of me wanted to blow school off completely given what was happening, I also knew I would pay for it in the end if I did. "No. I have algebra. I'll come look for him afterward."

"Okay."

Luc's voice sounded closer, and I looked up to see he'd taken several steps toward me. The heady power beneath my skin slithered at his proximity, and I had to hold my breath at the instinctive urge to close the distance between us.

What the hell is going on with me?

As if he sensed my confusion, Luc's face softened. "I can't imagine what you're going through right now. You're doing an amazing job of handling it."

It didn't feel that way, but I appreciated the sentiment. A tiny streak of lightning appeared to flash in his iris, and it reminded me of my dream. For some reason, I found myself confiding in him. "I-I've had weird dreams the last two nights."

His brow arched. "What kind of weird?"

"I was standing on a cloud. Dark shadows danced just outside of it, but I could see them."

Luc's expression remained impassive. "Anything else?"

"I-I could do that weird glowing ball thing, like I showed you. And …" I took a breath. "And there was lightning. It seemed alive, almost."

Another streak of light flashed in Luc's eyes, but his voice was even when he said, "I'm sure it's normal to have unusual dreams given what you've been through."

That's it?

My eyes narrowed. "Don't you think it's strange I can actually *do* one of the things I dreamt about?"

Luc gave me a nonchalant shrug. "It's possible you subconsciously knew you could already do it, and that's why it showed up in your dream."

That sounded like a non-answer if I'd ever heard one. Something told me that was all I was going to get from Luc at this point.

"Listen." He reached his arm out, closing the remaining distance between us, and set his hand on my cheek. "You're not going to have all the answers, but I can promise you're going to be okay. The world is still spinning on its axis. You're gonna be fine."

Even while I appreciated his effort to calm me—and honestly—it was working, I couldn't help but snicker at his words. "Yeah, there just happen to be a few more worlds than I knew about yesterday."

"True." His lips twitched. "But it's not like the end of the *world* or anything."

A reluctant snicker escaped me. "Haha."

The click of heels on the floor sounded a moment before a feminine voice spoke, her tone cold as ice. "Sorry. Am I interrupting?"

Luc's hand jerked away.

Jumping at the note of barely disguised rancor, I turned my head to see a tall, pretty girl about my age with long, wavy blonde hair standing at the threshold into the common room. Even though she wore the same thing I did, jeans and a sweater, something about the way she wore them gave her an otherworldly feel. To top that off, the bitchy glare she lobbed my way could freeze a raging fire.

I froze as the thought hit me that she could be Luc's girlfriend. From the way she was looking at me, she certainly acted like she had some sort of vested interest in him.

Luc scratched the back of his neck, looking the slightest bit uncomfortable. "Jewel, this is Thea. She's another one of Professor Raymond's teaching assistants."

When Thea gave an uneasy shift in her spot and lowered her gaze, a sense of discomfort drifted off her. I immediately understood what is was. Even though she was acting like a catty girlfriend, she didn't have reason to be. Otherwise he'd have introduced her that way, right?

Thea lifted her eyes back to Luc. "I wanted to run by some notes with you before the Professor's next class."

Lie. The word rang in my head like a bell. But I wasn't about to bust her balls over it. When it came to a guy like Luc, I could understand jealousy. So even though I didn't care for the way she was looking at me, I would drop it. For now, at least.

"Yeah well, I'd better head to my next class anyway." Schooling my face into a bland smile, I said to Luc, "Thanks for the help. See you around."

He grinned at me. "See ya in art history."

My mind spun as I walked past Thea and out into

the hallway. What was happening to me? Could I really sense whether people were telling lies? Was this stuff happening all due to whatever had been in the syringe? And if so, how long until I was back to normal?

Though a secret part of me had to admit this wasn't all bad. Super strength topped off by not having to wear makeup? There were worse things ...

I had almost made it to the building exit when the soft sound of voices coming from behind a partially closed door stopped me. The voices sounded familiar. Familiar enough to make me turn around and search out the sound.

When the noise floated toward me again, I turned at the intersection into the adjoining hallway. I continued forward, slowing my steps without even knowing why. After a moment, actual words began to filter out.

"... Worried ... doesn't know ... what should I do?"

Why did that voice sound so familiar?

At last I came to a stop before a partially closed door. It had taken a good minute or so to make my way here from the entrance.

How on earth did I hear this from all the way in the front of the building?

I had no more than a moment to ponder the thought before the voices started again.

Suddenly I knew why I'd been drawn here.

The first voice made total sense. It was Professor Raymond. But the second ... that one had my breath stuck in my throat.

Deme?

Why would he be *here* of all places, talking to the Professor? He wasn't taking any religious courses this semester, so he had absolutely no reason to be in this building at all.

"Until we've heard otherwise," Professor Raymond said, "you should continue on as before."

There was a brief pause, then Deme said, "I don't like it. She hasn't confided in me, and she tells me *everything*."

My heart began to hammer against my ribcage, the sound so loud in my ears I almost wondered if *they* could hear it. I'd known Deme all my life. Even now I easily recognized the worry in his tone. I knew everything about Deme.

Didn't I?

"Perhaps she is simply processing everything and will confide in you soon."

Another moment of silence passed before Deme said, "I don't know, Professor. She's smart. I think she's going to start figuring things out, and then she's going to ask me."

The tone of dejection in his voice wrenched me, even while his words threatened to shred my heart in two.

What was he saying?

"You know what you have to say," was the Professor's even reply.

"Yeah, but …" Almost in a whisper, Deme added, "I don't want to lie to her. Omitting the truth is one thing, but an outright lie?"

A shaky gasp tore from me as pieces of the puzzle began to fall into place, one by one.

All this time I'd believed it was my father who suggested I check out Magevilt University, but now that I really thought about it, wasn't it *Deme* who'd brought it up first?

Oh my god, how could I forget?

I remembered it clearly now, sitting with Deme at the eat-in counter in my kitchen while he pored through the stack of college brochures he'd requested. My dad shuffled in and peered over our shoulders. He thumbed through a few of the brochures before tossing the Magevilt one in front of us and pronouncing it seemed like a good school.

Now that I recalled it, I could clearly see Deme's eagerness when my dad had spoken. The way he'd convinced me to go check it out with him. How he'd said it was *special.* Unique.

No, it's not possible.

It couldn't be.

But then the Professor said the words that would instantly change my life forever.

"She will never know. As an Earth elemental, you can block her newfound ability to see through a lie."

Just like that, my world came crashing down around me. Stars exploded in my vision and I stumbled back, afraid for a moment I'd fall.

Deme ... *my* Deme ... was an elemental?

No. No.

It wasn't possible. We'd been friends our whole lives. I would have *noticed* something like that. Wouldn't I?

But then I remembered what Luc had said yesterday. Some elementals could practice magic so humans couldn't sense otherworldly abilities. Top it off with what I'd just overhead the Professor saying …

The very real possibility that this could have happened with Deme slayed me.

"No," I gasped, clutching my stomach to dispel the wrench of pain in my gut. No, I knew Deme. He was practically family. He couldn't have kept this secret from me all our lives, could he?

From the sudden silence on the other side of the door, my whispered denial had been louder than I'd thought. Either that, or they could both hear as well as I suddenly could. A moment later the door flew open, and the gazes of the Professor and Deme were right on me.

The look of absolute shock on Deme's face was surely a match to my own. As we locked eyes, a cacophony of emotions flitted through his face and I *knew*. Things were never going to be the same again.

"Jewel," he began. "I—"

"No," I cried out, backing away. I clapped my hands over my ears when he moved to take a step forward. "Save it. I don't need to hear your lies!"

His face crumpled just as I turned and began to race through the corridor, heading for the front door.

"Jewel, wait."

From the sound of his footsteps, he was chasing after me, but I wasn't in a listening mood. Not when I knew I couldn't trust a word coming out of his mouth. And thanks to whatever temporary juice that syringe had given me, I now seemed to be faster than he was because I outpaced him easily.

The door to the common room flew open just as I came to a screeching halt at the intersection in the corridor. Thea and Luc tumbled out, and I had a fleeting moment to note the concern on Luc's face before I veered toward the building exit.

"Jewel!" Deme yelled out again.

"Let her go."

The sound of Luc's voice floated toward me as I tore through the exit and sped out into the cold. I was beyond grateful for his words, because right now the last thing I needed was to speak to someone who was probably going to lie to me again.

Chapter 6

A STIFF breeze blew past the thick comfort of my coat as I stood at the edge of Freemont Falls. They were located just a short bus ride from campus, and they were a popular spot for MU students to visit during the weekends. Deme and I had been here a few times since school had started. The majestic beauty of the cascading water had captivated me from the first moment I saw it. Set in between two mountains, several rocky, sloping walls fed into a gorge below. At some point a footbridge had been constructed at the top of the falls, and even though it was old and dilapidated, the bridge's proximity to natural formation made for an incredible sight. Droplets of water sprinkled onto the bridge, making for a delightful walk during the summertime. Right now though, with the stiff breeze whipping through the gorge, it was cold as hell. Which meant it was also deserted by everyone but me.

I've never been out here by myself before.

That sad thought only fed into my dejection. Funny how stark and desolate it seemed now that I was alone. Oh, it was still beautiful out here. The normally green trees lining the top of the mountains had taken on a myriad of fall colors, and leaves fluttered off the branches and down into the water by the handful. But it felt different to be here by myself.

That was the worst part of this whole thing. With Deme, it had been like we were partners in crime. No matter what we went through growing up, we'd always been together. The fact my mother had died when I was a baby and his father had taken off when he was three only bonded us deeper.

Now all I could do was wonder how much had been a lie. All this time I'd thought we were like family. But no, we weren't even the same race.

Or were we? The Professor had said Deme was an *Earth* elemental.

I guess I didn't know enough about elementals to know the answer. According to the Book of Elements, they were these sort of cosmic warriors created by gods. And they didn't die like normal people did. The man in black had burst into a dark shadow.

So yeah, seemed like a different race in my book.

My cell phone beeped several times. I knew without looking it was Deme, texting me to find out where I was. Upset as I felt, I knew he was worried about me. But conversation was the last thing on my mind right now. I wouldn't even know what to say.

Shivering, I dropped onto the wooden slats of the bridge and hugged my knees into my chest. I was cold as ice out here, but at the same time I didn't want to leave. I didn't want to go back to campus and face Deme again. Not before I'd processed what was happening.

How could he keep a secret like this from me his whole life?

That's what bothered me most. Elementals were

born, not made, so he must have always known. Yet he'd told me nothing. Not even a hint of this whole other world going on beneath my very eyes.

A sense of betrayal cut through me, so deep and so excruciatingly painful that I could barely catch my breath. My best friend had been living a lie all these years. He'd learned everything about me, pretended I, in turn, knew everything about him, when in reality that couldn't be further from the truth.

Bitter thoughts consumed me, keeping me paralyzed on the footbridge until my incessant shaking and chattering teeth made me realize I hovered on the edge of hypothermia.

I scrambled to my feet, wincing at the stiffness of my frigid joints, and stumbled across the bridge and through the woods until I was back to civilization. The waning sun told me I'd been out for hours, far longer than I'd been aware.

Oh Deme.

How could he have lived with this for so long without telling me? I didn't understand.

A short bus ride later, I was back at the perimeter of campus. Nothing but woods surrounded the ten or so acres around it. It looked different now that I saw it through fresh eyes. So different.

My jaw dropped when I suddenly realized there was some sort of invisible barrier around the campus. Although I couldn't see it, I could *feel* it, like a slight atmospheric shift in the air. I must have been so distraught that I missed it completely on my way out. But now, with my syringe-enhanced body, it was unmistakable. Taking a shaky breath, I stepped past the barrier. There was a slight *pop* as it allowed me in.

Weird.

Blinking at the strangeness of it all, I continued walking until I hovered at the edge of the lawn. There was my dormitory, just over to the left. I didn't know how, but somehow I knew Deme was waiting for me there. I knew I wasn't ready to face him yet, but before I consciously made the decision, I found myself heading back to the Fellowship Hall. Crazy how that seemed to be rapidly becoming a habit.

Before I even reached the front entrance, one of the doors began to open. A second later, Luc appeared on the other side.

My stomach did a funny little flop as I came to a halt.

Luc said nothing, just stood there expectantly until I realized he was holding the door open for me, waiting for me to come inside.

Belated nerves built up in my stomach as I stepped over the threshold and turned back to greet him shyly. "Hi."

Though his face looked more serious than I'd ever seen before, Luc flashed me a brief smile. "Hey. I had a feeling you'd end up back here at some point."

There was no covering the surprise in my voice. "You waited for me?"

"Of course." Luc led me farther into the building. "You know, you probably shouldn't go off campus right now. Certainly not on your own."

"Why not?" I came to a sudden stop as it hit me.

"Wait, how did you know?"

Luc hesitated, discomfort wafting from him. He absently rubbed the back of his neck. "I'll explain. Come on."

Rather than lead me to the common room as I'd expected, he made a left turn at the same hallway I'd raced down earlier.

I hovered at the intersection of the corridors. "We're not going to the common room?"

He shook his head. "Not right now. There's something I want to show you."

Although I couldn't imagine what, anything was better than focusing on Deme's betrayal. I caught up with Luc and let him lead the way down the hall.

"I'm sorry about your friend," he murmured softly.

Unexpected tears began to swim in my vision, and I blinked them away. "Thanks," I murmured, because really, what more was there to say?

The building was eerily quiet, and I realized for the first time it felt like this the other times I'd been here, too. "Where are all the other students?"

He gave me a half-grin. "The classrooms are accessed through the other side of the building. This section houses mostly the administrative offices. Not too many students come through here."

Something about that struck me as odd. "Then why have a common room on this side?"

Luc's grin widened. "You caught that, huh? This side is used by Professor Raymond's assistants."

He made one more turn at an intersection of corridors, then came to an abrupt halt before a set of ornate double doors. Before I could make another inquiry, he pushed one of the doors open. I gasped at what was revealed before me.

The space on the other side of the door was enormous. Based on the asymmetrical, high-beamed ceiling, this was the room that had once served as the worship area of the chapel. Long, decorative chandeliers hung from several different spots on the ceiling, casting an orange glow reminiscent of candlelight.

Although the room no longer housed pews, the parts of the floor I could see had tiny anchor holes from where the pews had at one time been bolted down. Now several large rectangular wooden tables took up most of the floor space. Stained glass windows lined the upper part of the room, and the ceilings had been painted to match them while the wooden beams were gilded. It was, in a word, breathtaking.

"This is amazing," I breathed, my eyes glued on the elaborately painted ceilings.

"It is indeed." It was Professor Raymond who spoke, shocking me from my thoughts.

When I lowered my eyes, I realized there were several people inside the room. In my excitement over how gorgeous the space was, I'd completely missed that. My gaze flicked from the Professor, to Thea, to Aeron, the dark-haired hottie Luc had been playing pool with in the common room. They stood behind one of the large tables, which had books strewn all over the surface. Scraps of loose paper also littered the table here and there. Based on the chairs skewed behind them, they'd all been sitting before Luc and I entered.

What are they doing here?

I turned my questioning gaze back to Luc, and he answered my unspoken query. "Thea and Aeron are also part of Professor Raymond's team."

My brow furrowed. "You mean they're teaching assistants, too?"

"No." Professor Raymond leaned forward, setting his hands on the table. He'd partially rolled up the sleeves of his white dress shirt, yet somehow it made him look even more scholarly and authoritative. "He's speaking of the Guard."

My eyes flitted from his face to Aeron and Thea's impassive ones, then back again. "The *what*?"

The Professor's lips gave a little twist. "Step inside, Miss Harris. You're about to learn the truth about Magevilt University."

There was a gravity to his tone that made anticipation build in my chest as I entered the room. Professor Raymond's words echoed in my head.

You're about to learn the truth.

More than anything, it was what I wanted. Yet, at the same time, I didn't really know if I was ready. Or if I would ever be. Because somehow, I knew things would change forever.

But then … given what I'd learned about Deme, they already had.

The echo of Luc's booted feet on the wooden floor let me know he was right behind me as I stepped over to Professor Raymond's table. I barely had a moment to glance at the opened books, some of which contained illustrations and others plain text, before the Professor spoke again.

"What I told you before about the other dimensions was true. There are six different worlds, as I explained, each with its own physical constant. And, as Mr. Zain was kind enough to explain,"—he nodded at Luc—"elementals from five of the six worlds are recruited as guardians under the Interworld Treaty."

"Okay." I nodded in understanding. "That much I remember."

Professor Raymond gave me a calculating look before continuing. "What I didn't tell you before was that I am a commander of the Gaian Elemental Guard."

I blinked at him. "Huh?"

The Professor straightened to his full height, the orange lights from the chandelier above him giving his salt and pepper hair reddish highlights. "Each world has one or more groups of guardians – elementals from the five worlds battling Netheren – who are bound to serve that world."

Luc had told me his family had signed on generations ago to protect Earth. That must be what he'd meant; he was one of these Gaian guardians.

As I looked from the Professor, to Aeron, and then to Thea, I began to understand. I motioned to Aeron and Thea. "You two are also elementals."

Though it wasn't a question, Aeron nodded anyway.

I pointed to the Professor. "And you're the leader?"

He gave me a sharp nod. "Of the Northeastern American quadrant. There are three others on this continent, and a total of eight Guard units here on

Earth."

Clearly, I was missing something. "What makes you qualified to be their leader?"

"I'm also an elemental," he said evenly. "From Gaia—or Earth, as you know it."

Luc casually leaned against the edge of the table, looking at me as he added, "On top of that, he's an esteemed scholar of elemental lore."

Okay, well … I was beginning to think that maybe I *was* the only normal one on this campus.

Somewhere amid all this discussion, I'd begun sweating in my heavy overcoat. Unzipping it, I tugged my arms out of the sleeves. "So you're an elemental, too. Along with apparently everybody else on this campus but me."

Stark silence greeted me in response, and I jerked my gaze back up to study the Professor's face. My heart began to thump rapidly when I read his expression. Though it was stoic, something about the way he'd stilled frightened me. Add to that the flicker of sympathy I read in Aeron's gaze, and I was genuinely scared now.

When I turned to Luc, he gave me the most serious look I'd ever seen him make. "That's where you're wrong, Princess."

My chest tightened in response to his compassionate tone. I licked my suddenly dry lips. "Wh-what do you mean?"

An all-too familiar voice sounded out from behind me. "I'll tell her."

Gasping loudly, I whirled around to face the figure who stood in the doorway. The washed-out blue eyes of the man I'd known my whole life stared back at me.

I drank in the sight of his familiar tall frame. His sandy brown hair partially fell into his eyes, same as it always did. This was a man I knew like the back of my own hand.

My father.

"D-dad? What are you doing here?"

He said nothing, only gave me a sad smile, and that was when his words registered.

"Wait, tell me what?"

"What Luc means, Jewel ..." My normally self-assured father took an audible breath, looking uncertain for quite possibly the first time I'd ever seen. "Is that you're an elemental, too."

Chapter 7

I STARED at my father as his words coursed through me, spreading a chill throughout my body. My first instinct was to dismiss what he'd said as some sort of joke. It was too crazy, the thought laughable. But then the haunting dreams of the past two nights flashed in my memory, paralyzing me. My suddenly wooden legs were rooted to the ground.

The things that had been happening to me … the different sensations I even now felt coursing through my veins …

"But … the injection," I whispered.

That was the reason for all the changes in my body. Wasn't it?

Something pained flitted across my father's face. He took another deep breath. "We had your powers bound when you were a baby. I honestly thought it would be the best thing for you, to grow up normal. We believe the injection was designed to release your latent powers."

We believe …

He had glanced at the Professor when he said that. Somehow that look, more than anything, devastated me. Because it meant he'd been conversing with the Professor without my knowledge.

"No," I whispered, clutching my stomach to ward off the sharp jab of pain there. Nausea built within me, and I swallowed compulsively until it went away.

My father took a step toward me, then paused. "I'm sorry, Jewel. I truly thought I was doing what was best for you."

"No." I gave a vehement shake of my head, denial still rooting its way through my veins. This couldn't be true. I couldn't be one of *them.* I was just me, the same person I'd been my whole life.

Yet even as I processed the thought, I could feel the heady, sensual power slithering beneath the surface. This thing hidden within me, this power, had been awakened. And from the way it practically vibrated against my flesh, there was no need for anyone else to tell me what I already knew.

Now that it was out, there was no shoving it back.

I stared at my father, still frozen in shock. The implications of what he'd just told me made my mind reel. From the wheezing of my breath and the splintering of my vision, I was seconds away from a full-blown panic attack.

This can't be happening. It can't.

I thought Deme's betrayal was bad. *This* … this was a million times worse.

My father must have read my emotions, because now he did move. He stepped toward me, lifting his hand in supplication. For one of very few times in my life, I saw uncertainty on his face. Weakness. "Jewel, I'm sorry. You have to believe I only wanted the best for you. I did all this to protect you."

"No." I backed away before he could reach me. Right now, the last thing I needed was him to touch me. "I-I … don't."

Wrapping my hands around my shoulders, I willed my body to calm itself. To my surprise, the heady power lurking inside me spread itself out, surrounding me like a blanket and lending me strength.

It was only when I could trust myself to speak again without breaking down that I asked him, "If I'm a-an elemental … are you?"

He knew what I was secretly asking, there was no mistaking it. Because his eyes welled and he shook his head. "No, Jewel. Though I love you as much as I would any birth daughter, you didn't come to me in that way."

My breath expelled in one long shudder as the veracity of his softly spoken words rang through me.

Just when I'd thought my heart couldn't break anymore …

Every inch of my body shook as I hovered there, stuck between the urge to run screaming out of the building so I wouldn't have to hear any more of his painful admissions, and the desire to know the truth about myself.

The latter finally prevailed.

I *had* to know.

"Why? Why did you lie to me? Why would you hide who I am? And why, for god's sake, did *they* know all of this before me?" My arm swept out as I asked the last question, motioning to everyone else in the room. I knew it surely as I knew my father was telling me the truth now. The only person surprised by what had just been revealed about me was *me*.

My father's sigh echoed throughout the cavernous room. "Sit down, Jewel. I'm going to give you all the answers you seek. I promise."

Truth, my inner compass sang out.

When Luc grabbed the nearest chair and slid it over to me, murmuring a soft "Here," I didn't hesitate to sit down. Not when my jellylike legs felt like they'd give out at any moment.

My father exchanged a glance with Professor Raymond, then steeled his shoulders. "Theobald tells me he explained to you what elementals are."

Who? After a moment, I remembered that was the Professor's first name. "H-he, um … he said they're, like, people from each of the six worlds who have powers."

"Yes. And he explained that elementals are considered royalty?"

"Something like that," I muttered.

My father clasped his hands behind him and began to pace throughout the room. I knew from a lifetime of experience he was entering full-on lecture mode. How ironic this was one of the few times I was eager to hear what he had to say.

"What I don't believe he told you is that elementals operate on a sort of caste system. They are called houses. Those in the first house would be considered the ultimate in royalty. They are the official rulers of each of the worlds."

I blinked at him. "Okay."

Pausing, my father gave me a deep look. "You, Jewel, are a daughter of the Aetheran first house."

My breath caught in my throat as I processed the double whammy he'd just lobbed at me. I choked on air, then let it back out in a noisy exhale. Not only was he telling me I was some sort of royal, but …

With a disbelieving laugh, I shot out of my seat. "Are you telling me I'm not even from this freaking planet?!"

"Jewel," my father murmured.

His stern voice and familiar tone of reproach had me sitting back down before I even processed my reaction to it. My brain might now know he wasn't my actual father, but my body sure as hell didn't.

"Tell her the whole story, Timothy," Professor Raymond prodded.

The familiar way in which he addressed my father by his first name clued me in that the two of them might be even more chummy than I'd thought. My hunch was confirmed when Dad spoke again.

"Jewel, Theobald and I have known each other for decades, ever since we met when I was in medical school."

Jesus … decades. The depth of my father's dishonesty floored me, but I couldn't focus on that right now. If I did, I would fall apart.

"Go on," I prodded.

"I displayed an aptitude for medicine and a levelheadedness that proved to be an asset for one of my professors. One day he pulled me aside and explained that Earth is just one of six worlds, and each of the worlds is served by elemental guardians."

"That must have been a shock," I said, infusing a layer sarcasm into my tone.

"Yes, but," he shrugged, "it also made sense. And when he asked for my assistance in treating an injured elemental, I knew he was telling the truth. The differences were right there, in the blood."

I couldn't imagine what sort of differences there might be, but then I wasn't a doctor. At least I knew now why my father had insisted on treating my scrapes and booboos as a child. He didn't want anyone else to find out what I was.

"The elemental I treated was Theobald." Dad nodded to Professor Raymond. "At the time, he was a member of the Aetheran Elemental Guard. We formed a friendship and kept in touch over the years whenever he'd return to Earth as part of his duties."

When I glanced at the Professor, he gave a sharp nod confirming my father's words.

"Several years passed during which I continued to grow as a doctor. The professor had recruited me to treat any injured elementals who came through the area, though it was top secret, of course. One day Theobald came to me and explained that Aethera and Netheren were currently battling."

I remembered my prior conversation with Professor Raymond. "They were fighting because Netheren wants to take over the other dimensions?"

"Yes ... and no."

I arched my brow at my father, but it was the Professor who spoke. "I served the Aetheran ruler at the time, Lady Elena, as a member of her Guard. Though she was very young when she took the throne, in her early twenties, she was a skilled fighter and a good ruler over the light elementals."

My head whirled toward him as he continued.

"Lady Elena was also very beautiful. She had the most striking turquoise eyes." He smiled at me. "Your eyes."

My blood chilled at his mention of the woman who'd apparently birthed me. I took a shuddering breath and willed my heart to slow its marathon race in my chest.

"You were six months old then, and your father had died before your birth."

My real father, he meant. I licked my lips. "H-how?"

"I'm afraid we don't know," the Professor said. "What we do know is the ruler of the Netheren first house, Lord Adrian, had gotten word through his spies of your Lady Elena's beauty, and he decided he wanted her for his own."

Luc chimed in. "What you don't know, Princess, is that procreation between the dimensional races is strictly forbidden."

Now Luc's moniker for me made a little more sense. While I wasn't exactly a princess, I was royalty as far as Aetherans were concerned and of the highest caste. He really *had* known about me before I did. Argh, that so pissed me off!

Scowling at Luc, I asked, "Why is that?"

Professor Raymond slid a weathered scrap of paper across the table toward me.

Blinking, I grabbed it and read the words, which looked like they'd been hastily scribbled in red ink. "Should two elements ever be joined, any progeny resulting from such a union will become the seventh element: chaos. Chaos shall reign supreme."

I threw a questioning glance at the Professor. "What is this about?"

"These words were copied eons ago from an ancient book, the Book of Fates, before it was lost in battle with Netheren."

"Another old book?" I scoffed. "That seems to be a thing with you elementals."

Professor Raymond frowned at my derogatory tone. "Someone bled to pen these words on paper. That is how much they meant to him or her."

His not-so-subtle rebuke sparked an echo of shame through my body. It also made me want to barf. That was *blood* on the paper?

Apparently sensing my chagrin, the Professor continued. "According to lore, the Fates are three immortal seers. Some say they sprang into existence at the same time as the elemental gods. Others say they were created by the gods. Whichever one it is, they prophesied what would occur in the event there was ever crossbreeding between the races."

"Chaos," I murmured.

He gave me a deep look. "As you can imagine, this is exactly what Netheren would like."

I bit my lower lip as I considered his words. "The Netheren ruler wanted to mate with the ruler of Aethera."

My mother, I thought with a deep pang. Funny how finding out she was different than I'd thought made the hurt that much deeper. It wasn't as if I'd ever known her. But still, she'd been royalty for god's sake, not a doctor's wife. *And she was killed for it.*

"Exactly." Professor Raymond took the slip of paper back, carefully tucking it inside another book. "As you can imagine, this didn't sit well with Aethera. So, when the Netherens invaded, there was a mighty battle."

"What happened?" I whispered.

"Your mother was killed in the battle," Professor Raymond murmured.

Though I'd expected as much, it still hurt to hear it. What I didn't expect was the way Luc's shoulders tensed, his eyes brimming with some sort of undefinable emotion, as if maybe he knew what I was feeling right now.

I took a deep breath before asking the Professor, "What then?"

"In his fury over your mother's accidental death, Lord Adrian decided he would steal you away instead." A flicker of something that might have been sympathy sparked in the Professor's eyes. "The rumor was he intended to raise you to the age of majority and then breed you himself."

My gut took on a sudden, nauseating churn at the thought of what he'd just said. Swallowing hard, I forced myself to say, "Go on."

"To avoid this, the Aetherans tasked me with taking you away. Keeping you safe."

Even as he spoke, the sensual power that had awoken within me flowed through my veins like molten lava. It made me realize how different I truly was.

How fooled I'd been all along.

"So you brought me to …" My gaze flicked back

to the man I'd known as my father my whole life. "To Dad."

My father nodded, his face softening. "I promised to keep you safe. We decided you would be better protected if you appeared human, so we bound your abilities."

My brow scrunched as I considered that. "But how? How were you able to do that?"

I mean, I could *feel* them, and they were strong.

My father sighed and stalked closer. When he knelt on one knee, looking me in the eyes, I knew I wasn't going to like what he had to say. I dug my fingernails into my jeans.

"Theobald put me in touch with a powerful Earth elemental."

He hesitated, and I nodded for him to go on.

"Many Earth elementals have the power to ground the abilities of other elementals. Usually it's just temporary, as it's very difficult to do. But occasionally there's an elemental whose powers are so potent they can make the effects last longer." My father lowered his gaze, then visibly steeled his shoulders before glancing back at me. "Deme's grandmother is an extremely gifted Earth elemental. She uses minerals to absorb powers. That's what she did with you."

My heart dropped to my stomach. Deme's grandma was the one who'd bound my powers?

Great.

"What about Deme?" I whispered. "Did he know all along?"

My father gave an audible sigh. "Not until he was old enough to understand, of course. The problem was the binding needed to be continually reinforced."

"What do you mean?"

Professor Raymond chimed in. "Magic like that, it doesn't last forever. But if bolstered by something like a grounding mineral, it will hold."

Dad's lips gave a sad twist as he glanced toward my wrist. "The bracelets. The necklaces."

My shocked gasp tore through the room. I lifted my arm to display the rough red stone on the black leather cord. "*This* is the reason for all the matching jewelry?"

"Deme's lesser grounding ability is reinforced through the matching stones you both wear. The stones run out of magic after a few days. They have to be regularly replaced. When you were both small, we simply placed them on you, but after you got older, you needed a different explanation …"

"So, Deme cleverly figured out he needed to lie to me about his passion for jewelry-making," I said sarcastically.

"Don't be mad at him." My father gave me a sad smile. "If you must be mad at anyone, choose me. Deme loves you, and he only tried to protect you. Besides, he's wanted to tell you ever since he found out. His grandmother is the one who forbade it."

"Because we *all* agreed it was too dangerous for you to know," Professor Raymond added evenly.

They were right. Some part of me recognized that. Deme had only been a baby when all of this happened. He was just as much a victim to circumstance as I was. But I still had a right to be mad at *them.*

"Look what good all these secrets did." I snorted and yanked the bracelet from my wrist, barely even feeling the pain when the leather cord dug deeply into my skin before snapping under my newfound strength. "Guess I don't need this anymore."

"Jewel," my father murmured, but this time the quiet admonition in his voice gave me no pause whatsoever.

Shooting out of my seat, I gave my father wide berth as I began to pace the room. God, it hurt. Part of me wanted to rage at all of them. The other parted wanted my daddy to take me into his arms and make all the pain go away. But I wasn't a little girl anymore. Hell, I wasn't even *his*. Never had been.

"Okay, so now I know." I faced the group, steeling my heart against the pain I read on my father's face as he rose and sat in the chair I'd just vacated. "Tell me what really happened to me the other day."

My gaze flicked over to Luc, and he answered. "You were injected by the Netheren, Jewel. And no, we don't know exactly what it was, but best we can figure, it was something designed to break the grounding magic Deme's grandmother did on you."

I gazed down at my fingers, where the lazy power had settled beneath my skin. When I held up my palm and concentrated, the glowing orb of energy reappeared. "Then this ... this is actually something I can do? Not some temporary effcct of whatever was in that syringe?"

"It's a fairly common ability on Aethera," Professor Raymond said. "Eventually, you'll learn to manipulate the light."

"It's useful when fighting the bad guys," Luc chimed in. "Counters some of their shadow abilities."

Everything they'd said rang of truth, which led me to my next question. "The feeling I get in the pit of my stomach, like someone is lying to me?"

Luc nodded. "Another Aetheran ability."

"One many Earth elementals can block," the Professor said.

I thought back to how the Professor had been able to convince me I was human even after I'd begun to glow and nodded. It made sense now, how he'd been able to fool me.

"So why?" I clenched my fist, and the glowing orb disappeared, the residual energy slinking back under my skin. "Why did this happen to me? Was I really just at the wrong place at the wrong time?"

Because given all I'd heard, that was beginning to seem like a fantasy.

"No, Jewel," Professor Raymond said. He glanced at my father, then back at me. "Lord Adrian is still out there, and our sources tell us he's still looking for *you* all after all these years."

My father took a deep breath and stood. "We think you were injected because he suspected you might be Elena's daughter, and he hoped to reveal your true powers to confirm the fact. Just as has been done."

The dread on his face made my skin tighten. Sucking in a shaky breath, I whispered, "So what does that mean?"

"That means, Jewel, you are in trouble."

Chapter 8

SEVERAL PAIRS of eyes stared at me with varying grades of concern. Thea looked like she'd just as soon hand me over to the other side than sit here, while Aeron regarded me as if I was an interesting new species he'd just discovered. And Luc, he had the same unreadable look on his face. As for the Professor and my father, their worry spread over me like a thick, smothering blanket.

It made sense, I guess. Out of all the people in this room, Professor Raymond was the one who'd been present during the battle between the two worlds. He knew more than anyone what was at stake. And my father ... well, despite the fact he actually *wasn't* my father, there was no denying his love for me.

"So an evil elemental from another dimension wants to capture me and impregnate me with his demon spawn." Just saying the words made me feel like I wanted to simultaneously run out of the room screaming and break out in hysterical laughter. Instead, I settled for a "Huh" and resumed pacing the large room.

Before I could get more than two paces in, my

father closed the distance between us and enveloped me in the warm hug I knew so well after practically a lifetime with him. The unyielding tears building beneath my eyelids threatened to spill over, and I blinked heavily to dispel them.

I wanted so much to surrender myself to the comfort of his arms and pretend he was still really my father. But I couldn't. And right now I didn't want to focus on that. It would break me down; I knew it as surely as I was breathing. I could break down later. Now, I needed to find out what I had to do.

"So what?" I pulled away from him to lob the question at the Professor. "What do I do now? Keep pretending to be a human and continue on with school, like none of this ever happened?"

Because there was no way I'd be able to do that. Not a chance.

"No, Jewel." The Professor stood with a deep sigh. "We tried to keep you safe, to keep you oblivious to the dangers surrounding you. You may disagree with our methods, and if so, I'm sorry for it. But we did it out of love for you and your world, and for *that* I could never apologize."

Angry words burned my throat, begging to be freed, but I couldn't deny the truth of what he spoke.

No—*hell* no—I didn't agree with the lies about what I was. But that was a conversation for another time. Especially when it came to my father.

So rather than argue, I asked, "What then?"

Professor Raymond glanced from Luc, to Thea, and then Aeron. "You were in danger when you left campus alone today, Miss Harris. We had guardians keeping an eye on you from a distance, but given you've been injected and your powers are manifesting, you're prime for discovery by Lord Adrian. We must teach you about your world, so you can protect yourself in case we cannot. We must help you learn how to use your emerging powers."

"And teach you to fight," Luc said bluntly. "You already know powers can be magically blocked."

"Yes," my father echoed sadly, "you should also learn to fight, just in case."

My heart wrenched at the tone of despair in his voice, even as I processed their words.

"Yeah." I nodded my head. "Okay."

They were right. It was time for me to learn more about who I really was ...

And what I could do.

"You didn't have to walk me back to my dorm." I gazed over at Luc through the relative darkness of the campus. Even though the nearest street lamp was dozens of yards away, I could see him as clearly as if he stood beneath it. Apparently better night vision was one of the perks of being an elemental.

Yay for that, I guess.

Funny how it didn't even register as shocking to me anymore. Not after the day I'd had.

"I wanted to," Luc said simply, digging his hands into the pockets of his leather jacket.

"Besides, if I hadn't, your father would have insisted on doing it, and you looked about two seconds from clocking him with the nearest chair. Given your new strength, that might've ended badly."

The image of me belting my dad with a random piece of furniture made me laugh out loud. It was ridiculous. Or at least it would have been a few days ago. Now, well, I suppose nothing was a given.

The thought was enough to sober me up. "I guess I don't really know him at all."

"Nah, Princess," he said, stopping abruptly. "Don't do that."

Grinding to a halt beside him, I said, "What?"

"Don't act like you don't know the guy." A spark of temper flashed in his eyes, along with a jagged streak of lightning. "Yes, he lied to you, and that totally sucks. I get it. But the man raised you from a baby. He was there for every step, every fall, every tear."

My eyes widened at the heat in his tone, but he continued, oblivious.

"He fed you, he clothed you, and he gave you every bit of love he had to give. So don't tell me you don't know him. Because whether you agree with his methods or not, that man was more of a father to you than you could ever comprehend. And I don't know him well, but from what I do know, he sure as hell loves you like one."

Realizing my jaw had dropped somewhere to the vicinity of my chest, I snapped it shut. "Wow … that was sort of a hot button for you, wasn't it?"

As if he just realized he'd gone off on me, the

tension melted off Luc's shoulders. He gave a low, embarrassed chuckle. "Sorry, uh ... dad issues, I guess. They make me much more aware of when there's a good one around."

After considering that for a moment, I gave him a sharp nod. "Fair enough."

He might be right about my father, but that didn't mean I was going to forgive him instantaneously. A lifetime of lies was too deep a betrayal to simply brush off like a speck of dust. But there was no denying he'd done everything he could to protect me, and that did bear consideration.

Only I'd do that later, when I was alone in my dorm room and could bury my tears in a pint of Chocolate Chocolate Chip Haagen Dazs. Or two.

As we resumed walking, the events of the past hour raced through my mind. After the Professor and my father insisted I learn how to use my powers, how to fight, I'd discovered why Thea, Aeron, and Luc were present at the meeting. They were the ones who were going to teach me.

Thea was also Aetheran, and she'd been the one who healed me when I'd been unconscious. Healing was a pretty rare ability, so, as she'd bluntly told me, she didn't hold out any hope I would develop the power. But she agreed to teach me what she knew of Aethera, as well as how to use leverage while fighting a larger opponent.

I didn't hold any illusions there. She was going to make my life hell.

Aeron was also going to spar with me, as he put it. From the way he grinned when he said it, I had a feeling I was going to learn a lot from him. Some of it would probably be painful.

As for Luc, he was going to teach me how to wield my light and how to manipulate it. Given that I now sensed the hidden energy flowing through every inch of my body, I was most excited for this. It had nothing to do with the fact I'd be spending time with him.

Right.

My father had wanted to take me somewhere for a late dinner, to talk to me in private, but I wasn't ready. I told him I needed some time to process what he'd shared with me and that I wasn't hungry anyhow, which couldn't be more true. From what I just learned, while I might feel like regular food eased my hunger, it was a self-imposed illusion brought about by years of believing food was what I needed to survive. Though I didn't think I could ever give up my pizza, as an Aetheran I gained sustenance from light, not food.

The thought made me snicker. What the hell kind of freak show was my life right now? I ate freaking *light* for god's sake, and I'd been so programmed to believe I was human I'd never even realized it!

My dormitory came into view, and I screeched to a halt. Though I couldn't see him from this distance, I could sense Deme was there, right outside the main entranceway. Waiting for me.

A tremor shivered down my spine. I just couldn't. I couldn't deal with him now. Not after everything that happened today. Not after my dad.

Luc took one look at me and said, "He's your best friend. You're gonna have to face him sometime, you know."

"I know," I whispered. But not tonight.

He glanced toward the direction of my dormitory, where I could sense but not see Deme waiting, then turned back to me with a twist of his lips. "Want to practice using your powers?"

"Now?"

When he nodded, I said, "Hell yeah!"

Luc laughed and snatched my hand into his much larger one. "Come on. I'll show you where I like to go when I want to practice alone."

"Okay." His hand easily warmed mine, little shocks of electric current passing back and forth between us. To my surprise, the energy exchange felt kind of nice.

No, that was a lie. It felt *very* nice.

I allowed myself a moment to enjoy it, but when I glanced back to where I knew Deme waited, something stopped me. "Hold on a second."

He let go of my hand, and I dug my cell phone out of my pocket. I found Deme's number and shot him a text.

Just need some time to process all this.

A few seconds later his response came through.

Are we okay?

Chewing on my lip, I hesitated before typing.

We will be.

His response was instantaneous.

Love you.

Despite everything, despite all the conflict raging within me, I found myself smiling.

Me too.

When I slid my phone back into my pocket and glanced at Luc, he gave me a questioning smile.

"All good?"

"Yeah."

He reached for my hand again, then turned and walked across the grass. I almost broke into a jog to match Luc's long-legged pace as we headed toward the edge of campus, where the streetlights didn't reach. The only illumination out here was from the moon. Surprise, surprise, it was more than enough for me to see clearly. A flutter tickled my stomach.

Maybe being an elemental isn't so bad.

Unless you counted the insane dark elemental trying to capture me.

Just like that, my excitement faded.

Luc came to a stop in front of a small, rectangular building that had a circular dome in the center of the roof. I recalled seeing the strange white building once or twice, but I was hardly ever on this side of the campus, so I'd never paid it much mind.

"What is this place?"

He let go of my hand, and almost immediately the frost in the air chilled my flesh. I slid my hand into my pocket, silently lamenting the loss of his warmth.

"It's the campus observatory." He shot me a wicked grin. "I like to break in here at night."

Throwing him an incredulous glance, I murmured, "You're serious."

"As a dead man," he pronounced, leading me around to the backside of the building. That's when I noticed how close to we were the edge of campus. I never would have realized if not for the same invisible barrier I'd noted earlier when I got off the bus.

"What is that?" I motioned toward the barrier, which appeared to be emitting some sort of low-frequency pulse.

Luc arched a brow. "You can sense that now, huh?"

I nodded.

"It's meant to be protection, to prevent those who aren't invited onto campus from finding it." He let out a snicker. "Clearly it's not foolproof."

No, I guess not. Otherwise I would never have been injected by the man in black and would still be obliviously living my old life.

And I never would have met you, I thought, looking a Luc.

Well, maybe this wasn't *all* bad.

He came to a stop in front of a door, his gaze raking the ground. "Aha." Kneeling on one knee, he lifted a rock about twice the size of my fist and snatched up an object from beneath it.

When he held it up to me with a grin, I couldn't help but shake my head. "You have a key?"

Luc winked at me. "Stole the original off the custodian's keyring when he wasn't looking and returned it after I made a copy."

A laugh escaped me at the thought of all the work he'd gone through to get a spare key. "This must be some place."

"You'll see." He turned to unlock the door, then left the key in the lock when he opened it.

A lifetime of following the rules had my heart hammering in my chest as I followed him inside. It seemed silly to fear getting caught trespassing given all I'd discovered in the past few days, but I guess years of being the doctor's well-behaved daughter couldn't be unlearned just like that.

We were standing inside a dark room with several rectangular tables lined up against the wall. Based on the objects and stacks of paper strewn about, this was some sort of research area for the astronomy students. Luc headed to the right, leading us to a closed door. He turned the knob and opened it, motioning for me to enter.

When I stepped into the small, pitch-black room, it only took a moment for my new and improved eyesight to adjust. Once it did, I saw a thick rectangular column made of white-washed brick right in the center of the circular room. Atop it rested a large telescope. My gaze immediately drew up to the top, to where it practically brushed the domed ceiling. "This is the main part of the observatory, right?"

The door clicked behind me, and Luc said, "Yup. Check this out."

I turned to see him head over to a panel on one side of the room. He pressed a button, and there was a mechanical grinding sound. Muted moonlight began to spill into the room, drawing my gaze back upward. I gasped at the sight of a panel in the domed roof opening, revealing the night sky. Stepping farther into the center of the room, I stood right next to the large telescope.

"Part of the roof opens up so you can see through the telescope," Luc explained. "The dome is detached from the remainder of the building too, so you can move it around 360 degrees to see different things in the sky. Here."

He pressed another button and the whole roof began to rotate, so the open panel migrated from the right side of the room to the left.

"Holy shit!" I swallowed hard to dispel the hint of nausea rising within me. Looking up at the dome while it rotated sort of made me feel like I was in a circus funhouse with one of those spinning wheels causing everything to tilt off its axis. I gave Luc a curious look. "Are you into astronomy?"

Luc shrugged as he came to join me in the center of the room. "Not particularly. From my experience, most of the interesting stuff is down here on the ground." At my quizzical look, he elaborated. "The dimensional doorways."

"Oh." I hadn't known that. "I guess I didn't give much thought to *how* you get from one world to the next."

"Don't blame you. It's been a rough few days."

That was an understatement.

Luc took one look at the expression on my face and chuckled. "Honestly, given all that's been thrown at you, I don't know how you're still standing."

I smiled. He was right. Maybe I was stronger than I was giving myself credit for.

"So how exactly *do* the dimension doorways work?"

"Sort of like the barrier around the school. It doesn't look different. Everything looks the same on the other side, but you can sense something is there. When you step through, it's sort of like popping a bubble. Except you end up in a diffcrent world."

My stomach gave an uneasy flop at the thought of travelling to another dimension so easily. What if you went into one of the doorways without even realizing it? "Where's the nearest one? What happens if you go through? Can you come back out?"

He let out a low laugh. "We'll go over all that stuff, but I wouldn't worry about it too much right now. The doorways are in obscure spots. No chance of stumbling upon one; you'd really have to be looking for it. And yeah, you can come back through, no problem. Usually."

That last bit made the hairs on the back of my neck stand up. Did I even want to know what he meant?

But then I had another thought. "Wait, if you're not into astronomy, why even come in here?"

Luc gave me a rakish grin. "Haven't figured it out yet?"

He motioned throughout the room, and I studied the space in confusion for one long moment before it hit me. "The moonlight."

"Yup." He lifted his hand, his arm brushing the side of mine as energy crackled between his fingertips. "Your ability is similar to mine. You wield light. But mine requires more of an energy exchange, so it needs a light source to work."

He aimed his fingers upward, and a stream of lightning shot through the open dome up into the sky. "Now try yours."

Biting my lip, I lifted my hand and a glowing orb formed there.

"See if you can aim your light up through the top," he said.

Concentrating, I willed the orb upward. It floated off my hand, hovering close to my face for a long moment before zipping back down to my palm and reabsorbing into my skin.

"Oh." Disappointment deflated my tone.

"It's okay. No one gets it right away. Here."

Luc unzipped his leather jacket and slipped it off his shoulders, tossing it carelessly to the side. He was right. It was warm in here.

I followed suit, unbuttoning my coat and removing it before carefully setting it down beside Luc's.

"All right," he said, "try it again."

I lifted my hand and the glowing ball formed, sitting right there on the top of my palm with an electric tingle.

"Here." Luc slid behind me, setting his hand beneath mine to hold it steady. "Whenever I aim my energy somewhere, I think of where I want it to go. Then I order it there. Try that."

His request was easier said than done when he was standing close enough for me to inhale the heady scent floating off him. It was part masculine spice, part lightning storm, and one-hundred percent arousing. And with his chest pressing against my shoulder, his hip at my back, I could hardly think, much less concentrate.

"It's part of you," he murmured. "It may take some time, but eventually it'll do exactly what you want."

Taking a deep breath, I concentrated on the top

of the dome, willing the light to go there. But once again it merely lifted a few inches before bouncing right back into me.

"Damn." My hopes fell, along with my hand. "At this rate, I'll be an old lady before it does what I want it to do."

If only I'd started practicing when I was younger, I'd no doubt be a pro by now. But that choice was taken from me, along with all knowledge of who and what I really was.

Yeah, guess I was a little bitter about it.

"Nah, it's fine." He lifted my hand, steadied it. "You just started. Try again."

Patience was never really my strong suit, but Luc's insistence lent me strength. We continued trying for what might have been minutes or even close to an hour, until I was finally able to block out the distraction of having Luc stand right behind me. I willed the orb to form and focused on directing it where I wanted to go. This time, instead of just dropping back down, it began to grow.

"That's it." Luc's grip tightened on the back of my hand. "Now aim it up."

Steadily it continued to grow, rising a few inches off my palm. I clenched my teeth and directed it upward, and to my surprise it began to rise. Higher and higher, until it hovered near the top of the telescope.

"That's great," Luc said excitedly. "Now zap it all the way out."

With a burst of concentration, I fixated on the opening in the top of the dome. The ball shot up, and for a second I thought it was gone. But then it froze, growing even bigger, and zoomed back down. I gasped as it burst right above us and the light showered down, absorbing into my body in an exhilarating deluge of power.

When Luc inhaled deeply behind me, his body giving an involuntary shudder, I realized the orb had hit him right along with me.

"Whoa." He let out a euphoric chuckle. "That was *awesome*."

A giggle rose within me at the thought that he'd just gotten inadvertently whammied by my light. Well, at least it hadn't hurt him. In fact, he seemed to have enjoyed the power surge.

I whirled around to face him. "Now you know what the past few days have felt like for me —"

The rest of my words died in my throat when I realized how close we were standing to each other. The front of our bodies practically touched. The electric discharge from his natural ability combined with the power boost I'd just given him sparked a ripple of electricity along my skin. And man, did I *like* it.

When Luc's exhilarated grin faded into something more serious, as his hooded eyes gazed down at me, I got the impression he felt the exact same way.

My palms settled on his chest just as his hands closed over my arms. The wave of energy started again from where our bodies touched, bleeding through our clothing until my skin practically crackled with power. I could almost feel the heat rising off our bodies, warming the air around us. The scent of summer storms and spice washed over me.

I was leaning into him before I even processed my movement. His head moved toward mine at the same slow rate. The sweet minty scent of his breath flooded my nostrils an instant before his soft lips brushed mine, the touch so fleeting it was like the delicate caress of butterfly wings.

My heart began to pitter patter inside my chest, desire and energy and excitement flooding every square inch of my body. But before I could do more than take a shaky breath and lean in to deepen the kiss, he shot backward with a muttered curse, leaving nothing but space where his body had just been.

Staggering at the sudden loss of his presence, I opened my eyes and blinked in confusion.

Luc had placed a good couple of feet between us. He closed his eyes and lifted his face toward the ceiling, running his hands through his hair before clasping them behind his head in clear exasperation. "Sorry, Jewel. That was my fault and a really bad idea."

Hurt slammed through me as I stared at him in silence. I didn't know why he thought it was a bad idea, when to me it had seemed like a very good one. His rejection stung more than I could've imagined.

Was it that my power had temporarily intoxicated him?

Oh my god, could that be it?

Because if so, then me trying to kiss him was tantamount to trying to jump his bones while he was half passed out drunk. And suddenly I felt very,

very stupid.

Luc opened his eyes and must have read some of the emotions on my face, because his expression softened. "It's not you. I mean, obviously. It's just … there's a lot you don't know."

"Yeah, I guess there is," I muttered, knowing my cheeks must be flaming red. I'd basically just gotten the "It's not you, it's me" speech, and right now I wanted to crawl under a rock and die. It took everything I had not to turn and race out of there. Instead, I tried to save face by manufacturing a yawn. "Well, it's getting late and it's been a long day."

Even though he must've known what was up, he didn't mention it. Instead he said, "Yeah, you're right," and moved to retrieve our coats from the floor. As he handed me mine, he murmured, "You should get some rest tonight. Professor Raymond wants you to start learning about Aethera."

The thought of facing Luc again tomorrow made me want to stay huddled under my blanket for the rest of the semester. But I forced a smile on my face and said, "Can't wait."

I could fall apart once I got back to my dorm room. This mortifying incident was just one more thing to add to my long list of reasons why.

Chapter 9

THE FOLLOWING day I managed to sleep in until well after two o'clock. Finding out my father and best friend had lied to me all my life, on top of trying to control what I now knew were permanent powers, seemed to have done a real number on my body. I'd been so exhausted when the alarm clock went off in the morning that I didn't even consider dragging myself out of bed.

When I finally pried my eyes open, all my classes were over and my energy was back up to normal – if this new feeling of sensual power flooding through me was what you'd call normal.

A soft glimmer drew my gaze down to my arms.

"Crap. I'm glowing again."

It was subtler now, like a flashlight had been turned on beneath my skin, but there was no mistaking it.

Leaping out of bed, I headed straight for the mirror. It felt a bit narcissistic to be examining myself so closely, but heck, it wasn't everyday one began to glow. I had to admit, it did wonders for my complexion. And for my hair! It was still as bouncy and shiny as it had been yesterday, nothing like my normally lifeless dark locks.

Things could definitely be worse in the looks

department. But since I didn't exactly want to walk around lit up like a glowworm, I closed my eyes and concentrated on pulling back the electric tingle I felt dancing on the surface of my skin. It settled into me, and when I opened my eyes the glow was gone, yet the perfect hair and skin remained.

A reluctant grin twisted my lips. "A girl could get used to this."

After our embarrassing little *not-a-kiss* encounter night, Luc had mentioned meeting back at the old worship room to learn more about Aethera. I washed up and dressed, saying another silent thanks for the fact makeup no longer seemed to be a requirement, then headed to the little café on the ground level of my dormitory before setting out for the Fellowship Hall. It hit me again when I was grabbing a muffin that I technically didn't need to eat any of this stuff. Absorbing light gave me all the sustenance I needed. But, well ... old habits die hard. Besides, I loved the way food tasted. I didn't see myself giving it up anytime soon.

The campus looked different today. Not somewhat scary, like it'd been when I first started noticing things. Just different. A whole new world had been opened up to me, and now that I saw it, I couldn't believe it had been here before, right out in the open yet invisible to my magic-bound eyes.

After an hours-long cryfest last night, along with some much-needed ice cream, I'd begun to process some of what I'd learned.

As much as it hurt to know everyone I loved had lied to me all my life, I could sort of understand why. My father might not be my biological dad, but

I never questioned his love for me. It was there in every conversation, every time he tucked me into bed at night. Of course he would do anything in his power to protect me. I might understand it, but that didn't mean I agreed with it. Or that I was so easily ready to forgive him.

He should have told me. Given me the option to explore what I was, to master my powers.

Even if it meant you'd grow up in fear your whole life?

Yeah, that was the rub. If the tables were turned and I was the worried parent, I couldn't say I would have done anything differently. I hated I could so easily see his side of things, but I could.

Either way, it still hurt. A lot.

The pain was the very thing that made me avoid the part of campus where I knew Deme was most likely to be. I wasn't ready to talk it out with him just yet.

The Fellowship Hall was as quiet as usual when I entered it. I headed down the halls toward the room Luc had shown me yesterday. One of the doors was partially open, and when I pushed through it, Thea and Aeron were waiting for me instead of Luc. They were both sitting at one of the tables, with open books in front of them. They glanced up when they heard the clack of my booted feet on the wooden floor.

My gaze scoured the room before returning to the two of them. As casually as I could manage, I asked, "Where's Luc?"

Aeron gave me an easy grin, his chocolate brown eyes twinkling under the orange-tinted lights of the many chandeliers. "He had some business he needed to deal with. You'll be working with us today."

"Oh." Fighting to hide my disappointment, I approached the table while slipping off my coat. "What are we doing?"

Thea motioned toward the seat set directly across from them, her mouth set into a grim line. "Sit. You're going to learn more about some of the other worlds."

Well don't look so excited about it.

But hell, I couldn't blame Thea. I wasn't exactly jumping for joy at the thought of working with her, either.

Clenching my teeth to fight off a scowl, I took the proffered chair and glanced at them expectantly. "So?"

Thea picked up the book in front of her and turned it around before plunking it down closer to me. "This is Aethera."

A picture of Aethera? I couldn't deny I was curious to know what my homeland looked like.

My heart thumped as I brought the book closer to me and scanned the vividly painted images laid out on the pages. They depicted a mountainous landscape, but my excitement died down when I saw it didn't really look different from here. The sky was a little bit bluer, but other than that I didn't see much.

"That's it?"

When I brought my gaze back to Thea, she gave a nonchalant shrug. "It never gets dark there. Other than that, it is pretty similar to Earth."

My lips curled in distaste as I mulled over her words. I'm sure I'd feel differently if I'd grown up there, but having grown up on Earth, in a world of day and night, the thought of never having a nighttime seemed sort of sucky to me.

I riffled through a few more pages of the book, which seemed to be some sort of Aetheran version of a grade school science textbook. After making a mental note to borrow the book for a more thorough read-through, I glanced up at Thea. "Yeah, seems pretty much the same."

One of her thick, blonde brows arched. "The difference is light is the primary food source. It's not consumed in the way food is here on Earth, though. You mainly absorb it through your pores."

That much I'd already gathered.

"You can swallow light too," she added in a bored tone, "but just as a way to up your energy."

"The Aetheran version of a caffeine kick, if you will," Aeron chimed in.

"Weird." I blinked as I looked back and forth between them. "What about the normal people on Aethera? Non-elementals. What are they like?"

Thea shrugged. "Just like mortals on this world, apart from what they consume. Life spans are like here on Earth, and they can die just as easily."

Aeron leaned forward, setting his forearms on the table. "Other than the primary physical constant and a few other minor things, all six of the worlds are pretty similar to one another. You'll find there aren't too many differences between the mortals on each of the worlds. It's only among elementals that you'll start to notice real variations."

I tried to wrap my brain around the idea. "Why is that, I wonder?"

"Who knows?" Thea retorted, her tone implying it was silly for me to care.

Aeron shot her an amused look before turning back to me. "According to myth, when the elemental gods created their worlds, they did it to alleviate boredom. The mortals were made to be weak copies of them. They looked similar in appearance to the gods, but had none of their powers. When the nether god decided to take over the remaining worlds by creating beings with special abilities, he forced the other five gods to do the same or risk having their worlds dominated."

"Right." I motioned for him to go on.

"Each of the gods have abilities based on their element. When the gods created their elementals, they infused each of them with some, though not all, of their own abilities. In this way, the gods remained superior to elementals. That's how there is such variation between them."

It made sense. "What can Aetheran elementals do, besides heal or manipulate light?"

Thea let out an exaggerated yawn, lifting her hands over her head. "Some can travel at the speed of light. Others can wield lightning. Then you have your mages, who can use light to spell others. And your truth-seers —"

"Wait. You said truth-seers?" The word sounded unfamiliar on my tongue, but I could guess what it meant.

Aeron nodded. "Yes, that feeling you get in your gut when someone is lying to you. That's your own personal truth compass. Good ability to have, if you ask me."

Thea snorted at his words.

"What?" Aeron retorted hotly. "You think if it's not the ability to heal, it's worthless? Newsflash, other abilities can be useful, too."

She rolled her eyes. "Sure they can, Viper." He scowled at her, and she lifted her cell phone from the table to glance at the screen. "Well, this has been fun, but I have class. See you guys later."

Without waiting for a response, she grabbed her backpack off the table and rose, heading for the door.

I watched in confusion as she left. Clearly a lot of that was over my head, but it was sort of a relief to know I wasn't the only one Thea didn't seem to like.

"Sorry about that," Aeron said as Thea stalked out the door. "I think she *only* sleeps on the wrong side of the bed."

My forehead scrunched as I regarded him. "What did she mean by viper?"

He made a face. "Long story."

Which meant he didn't want to talk about it. Well, too bad. I did. I was tired of things I didn't understand.

"I have the time," I retorted, gazing at him evenly.

His fingers drummed on the tabletop, and he took a breath. "Tell you what. Let's go over some fighting techniques and then I'll tell you."

Aeron pushed back from the table before I could respond, heading farther into the room. The space was wide and open there, devoid of anything we could bump into and ruin.

My palms tingled with anxiety as I stood and followed him. For the first time, I noticed he was wearing black on black again. I had to admit it was a good look for him. It highlighted the stark angles of his face and the bronze glimmer of his skin.

When he grinned at me, I noticed I'd been staring and fought back a blush. "Why do I need to learn to fight anyway? Do you think more of the Dark Lord's men will be able to sneak onto campus?"

He lifted a black brow. "Dark Lord?"

"I have to call him something, don't I?" I shrugged. "Somehow that seems more appropriate than Lord Adrian."

"Guess so," he said before pushing up his sleeves. "You need to learn to fight so you don't get your ass taken if he does manage to find you and you don't yet have command of your powers. Believe me, that would be in no one's best interest."

"But," I absently tugged my fingers through my hair, "what good is fighting when I'm up against someone with magical powers?"

"You never know what could happen. You might have powers that counteract each other. It's happened before. Then you'll need to rely on your fighting skills. Or they might be so caught up in using their own powers that you're able to get the jump on them when they least expect." Aeron took a spot in the center of the empty space and beckoned me to come forward. "Best to be prepared for every scenario."

I guess he was right. Nervous energy filled me as I approached him. "Um, this is probably a good time to mention I've never been in a fight in my life."

"You'll get used to it," he laughed. "Now hit me."

I blinked at him. "What?"

"Hit me." When I didn't move, he reached out and grabbed my wrist, gently closing my hand into a fist and positioning it. "Keep your wrist straight. Aim for my face."

He backed up expectantly and I stared at him, trying to muster up the courage to do as he asked.

"Don't worry," he prodded. "I can take whatever you throw at me."

Given that I'd never hit anyone ever, I had no doubt about that. Still, even though I knew it was in my best interest to learn how to fight—hell, I *wanted* to—something within me hesitated at the thought of hitting him. He had such a handsome face, all sharp lines and dark curves.

When a full minute passed and I hadn't moved, Aeron shot me an amused look and reached out, shoving me hard in the shoulder. I reeled backward, then scowled at him. "Hey."

He did it again, and this time I practically stumbled.

"Stop it!"

The third shove brought me down to my knees.

"Make me," he sneered.

Gritting my teeth, I rose and charged toward him, shooting my fist toward his face. Easily sidestepping me, Aeron grabbed my wrist, sending me fumbling around in a semicircle.

"I've seen preschoolers faster than you," he scoffed, laughter lighting up his dark brown eyes.

Now he was beginning to piss me off. Recovering, I aimed my other fist at him. It connected with the side of his jaw, making a loud sound as flesh met flesh. A hint of pain jarred my hand.

Aeron let go of my wrist, stumbling backward slightly. The side of his face I could see went slack with surprise, and when he turned toward me, his jaw was a fiery red where my fist had struck it.

It was then I remembered my sudden increase in strength. I clapped my hands over my mouth and started forward. "Oh no, I'm so sorry—"

His delighted laugh stopped me in my tracks. He rubbed his cheek as he gazed at me. "Nice. I actually felt that one."

Frowning at him, I lowered my hands. "So, you're okay?"

His hand shot out and caught me on the face, sending me whirling backward. A hint of burning pain spread along my cheek. Even as I grabbed it, I recognized he'd purposely hit me a lot softer than he could have. Still …

"You hit me!" I accused.

He gave a nonchalant shrug. "Half of learning how to fight is being able to take a hit."

I couldn't argue with his logic. At the same time, no one had ever hit me before. Sudden moisture obscured my vision, longing to break free of my eyes. Ashamed of my instinctive urge to cry, I blinked it back.

Aeron's face took on a knowing look. "It's normal," he murmured, his voice soft. "Happens to everyone at first. It's part of what you have to conquer."

God, he was right. I blinked furiously as his words penetrated, trying with all my might to hold in the tears. "*Shit.* I'm so in over my head right now."

I mean, it wasn't enough to deal with being lied to by everyone I loved. I also had to process that I was some sort of otherworldly royalty, not even freaking human. Oh, and I was also a pawn in an ages old power struggle, which meant I had to worry about getting snatched up by some sicko with a penchant for world domination.

What else could possibly go wrong?

Aeron's face softened. "You're doing great."

"Yeah. Fabulous," I muttered, swallowing past the lump in my throat. A few stray tears escaped down my cheeks, and I angrily wiped them away. "I can't even take a half-assed hit without crying. Don't tell me you didn't hold back, either, because I can tell when people are lying now, remember?"

He let out a soft laugh, and stepped toward me. His hand reached to my cheek, to where he'd struck me, and he stroked the skin lightly. "Don't be so hard on yourself, Jewel. I cried the first time someone hit me, too."

There was something sad in his tone, some untold story. At the same time, I knew his words were an attempt to make me feel better.

It was working.

"It's not every day you find out you're a non-human who's been in hiding since infancy from a powerful dark elemental," Aeron murmured.

Maybe he was right. Maybe I was being hard on myself.

His hand was warm where it still touched my face. My stomach did an anxious little flop as I locked eyes with him, his chocolate brown gaze pouring into me as if he could see my very insides. Something about him disarmed me on a primal level. It was more than his looks, which were quite classically dark and handsome. I remembered what Thea said to him earlier and suddenly it seemed important to know.

"Why did Thea call you a viper?"

He stilled, and his hand slowly dropped to his side. His voice was neutral when he responded. "Because of what I can do. I can poison someone with the touch of my lips. Weaken them almost to the brink of death."

My breath sucked in, and I instinctively took a step back. When Aeron let out an almost imperceptible flinch I forced myself to freeze. Shame buffeted me at my involuntary reaction. Aeron had been nothing but nice to me.

"I …" My voice shook and I paused, worrying my lower lip between my teeth. "I didn't realize that was an Aetheran ability."

But even as I said it, it hit me he had never claimed to be from Aethera. I had merely assumed because he'd been here with Thea to train me.

As if he read my mind, Aeron's lips gave a sardonic twist. "Not Aetheran. It's not entirely uncommon, however, in Netheren."

A gasp escaped me, and this time there was no stopping my backward stagger. "You—you're Netheren?"

His dark eyes imperceptible now, he gave me a slow nod, though he didn't make any move to close the distance between us.

Wait ... what did this mean? From everything I'd heard, Netheren was a dark, evil place, and its elementals had been created specifically to dominate the other dimensions.

"Ar-are you a spy?"

He let out a hollow laugh. "If so, I'd be a pretty horrible one given the Professor, and everyone else for that matter, knows exactly what I am."

"Then ..." Every instinct in my body told me to either flee or fight. The hidden energy flowing through my veins danced into my palms, furiously itching the skin. But I forced myself to stand there, to give him the benefit of the doubt. After all, he had every chance to overpower me and he hadn't. "Then why are you here? I don't understand. Aren't you the enemy?"

When he gave the tiniest of winces, I almost regretted my words. But given that it was his people who were hunting me, I needed to know.

"I'm from the third house of Netheren. Theoretically, yes, my kind should be battling yours and seeking to dominate you."

Sensing a but, I kept my mouth shut.

"My father, you could say, was a rebel. He believed the worlds should try to harmoniously coexist rather than battle each other." He took a breath and raked a hand through his hair, pain glinting in his eyes. "He, along with the rest of my family, everyone in the third house, were executed for treason. I managed to escape and found refuge here on Earth. I was eleven years old."

My mouth dropped open at his admission. Eleven years old? I couldn't imagine living through something like that at such a young age. "I-I'm sorry."

"Don't be." He gave me a small smile that faded just as quickly. "Wasn't your fault."

"So ..." I licked my dry lips. "You ended up joining the Professor's Guard?"

Aeron nodded. "It was the Professor who took me in when I arrived here on Earth. Some of the other elementals wanted me imprisoned. They thought I might, as you suspected, be a spy."

Though I could clearly understand their concern—I mean, it had crossed my mind—the thought of him going through all that at the age of eleven, right after losing his whole family, crushed me.

"Professor Raymond lobbied for me," Aeron continued. "He protected me those first few years, even gave me room and board."

"He's a good man," I whispered.

Aeron's brow lifted. "Just like your father."

The reminder of my father was like a stab to the heart. Even still, I understood what Aeron was not-so-subtly getting at. He thought I should forgive my father for lying to me.

"I know," I said simply. "I just need time."

Aeron nodded. "I get it."

I gave him an appreciative smile.

"All right, come on. Let's work on your elemental magic."

"I don't have much of it."

He gave me a wolfish grin. "Well, let's see it."

I formed my glowing orb, and he spent the next hour or so trying to help me figure out how to wield it. But every time I tried to make it do something, it would either fizzle out or just stay right there in my hand. Finally, after the third time I'd thrown my hands up in frustration, he glanced at the watch decorating his wrist.

"Listen, I think we should call it a day. I have class in twenty. You can always try to kick my ass tomorrow."

A laugh escaped me at his teasing words. "I have a feeling it's going to take a lot of training to be able to kick your ass."

His lips curved into a smile. "Damn right."

I tugged my coat back on as Aeron headed for his backpack, which he'd laid onto the table where he'd earlier sat. Just as I was about to say goodbye, his voice stopped me.

"Jewel." When I gazed at him inquisitively, he headed toward me, stopping just a foot away. His lips curved into a teasing grin. "Not always."

I stared at him blankly. "Not always *what*?"

"My kiss." His grin widened and he leaned in, his face inches from mine. "It's not always poisonous, only when I want it to be. Just thought you should know."

My mind reeled from the implication of those words, and I stood there frozen as he turned and went striding out the door.

Chapter 10

IT HAD been three days since my life had been totally upended by the stranger with the syringe. Three days since everything around me had changed at an explosive rate. That was pretty much all I could think about when I woke with a new ability. At least, that's what I chalked it up to when I opened my eyes and dark, dancing shadows loomed over my bed.

I almost screamed at the sight of them, but when I scrambled into a seated position, the shadows flew back to hit the wall, twisting and writhing as if they'd been magically pinned there. Curiosity got the better of me, and I examined the shadows, realizing they formed loose figures. They were miniature in size, but one kind of had the outline of an angel, complete with wings, while another had sharp pointed teeth reminiscent of a vampire. There was a strange sort of pressure in my chest that compelled me to breathe deeply.

The shapes swirled together and formed a dark, miniature tornado, like they were being sucked into a vacuum. They coalesced into thin lines which absorbed directly into my nostrils, sending a wave of energy flowing through my body.

"Great. Now I can make shadows."

Call me the queen of useless abilities.

With a beleaguered groan, I wrestled out of my covers and got ready for class. Today was the day. The day I would face Deme again after learning the truth about who he really was. Although I did appreciate him giving me my space these past few days, I still didn't know how I was going to face him, or what I would say when I saw him. I only knew I couldn't keep missing out on class. Not if I wanted to pass this semester.

Since I had art history, I made sure to examine myself in the mirror before I headed out. It never hurt to look one's best.

Yup, still Me 2.0.

To think all these years I'd bemoaned the lack of body in my hair, and all it took was a little elemental mojo to give me the look I'd always wanted.

When I got to art history, it was later than I'd anticipated. Class was just starting, so I was saved from having to chat with Deme as I slid into the empty seat beside him. He wore his hair in structured curls atop his head today. The dark locks were spray painted a bright sunshine yellow, and he had to be wearing a whole container full of hair mousse to keep the style frozen in place. It sort of made him look like a deranged cockatoo, which was probably the look he was going for. Deme liked to make a statement, even if that statement was, "What the fuck?"

He said nothing when he saw me, but there was no mistaking the relief on his face. I glanced over to where Luc usually sat, but he was nowhere to be found.

About five minutes in, the professor began to wander the room in full-blown lecture mode as he debated the mental sanity of Van Gogh. Taking advantage of his distraction, Deme leaned into me. "You okay?"

I nodded at him. I was as okay as I was going to be right now. My eyes trailed over the room one more time, then I whispered, "Do you know where Luc is?"

"No." Deme gave me a sharp glance, and for some stupid reason it made my skin flush. He noted it, and his expression grew suspicious. "I hope nothing happened between you two. I still think that guy is bad news."

Did our little butterfly kiss qualify as something? I didn't know, but since Deme didn't seem to like the thought of me hanging out with Luc, I said, "No, I—"

"Silence, please," the professor interrupted, his voice harsh as he shot me a glare. "Unless there's something you'd like to share with the rest of us?"

Half the class followed his gaze, looking over at me curiously.

I slunk lower in my seat, wishing the ground could swallow me up. My voice was a squeak when I said, "No."

He gave me one last dirty glance before turning and resuming his speech.

Deme and I didn't talk for the rest of the hour, though I had a hard time keeping my concentration anyway. Now that I could see magic, I wondered how I'd ever missed it. The stuff was everywhere.

Two rows in front of me, a girl was taking notes with a fancy metal pen that appeared to move of its own volition. Both her hands were busy taming her wild red hair into a thick braid. Another student had a notebook in front of him and no pen at all. Instead he slid the tip of his finger along the page, and the words burned into it. The scent of singed paper wafted over to me.

Not even the professor was immune from all the supernatural occurrences I was witnessing. Every now and again as he paced the room, he would disappear from one spot and then instantly reappear in another, like he'd moved so quickly my brain couldn't process it.

How the hell had I not noticed any of this stuff before? How blind I'd been. I lived in a completely different world now, one rife with magic and mystery.

After class was over, Deme grabbed my hand before I could escape like I'd thought about doing and led me out of the classroom. I followed quietly as he walked us over to a set of outdoor chairs and tables that were set up for studying right outside the building. During the summer and spring, the tables were never empty. But given the frigid temperature today, we had no problem snagging one of the tables.

Deme pulled out a chair for me, then snatched the one next to it and dragged it closer, turning it around so he could sling one leg over the seat and face me. His arms crossed over the back of the chair.

"Jewel." He let out a long sigh, his eyes

momentarily shutting. Then he opened them and raked over me with an earnest expression. "I'm so sorry for lying to you. For hiding stuff from you. You have to believe me, I never wanted to do that. I—"

"Stop." I reached out across the space separating us and set my hand atop one of his. "I get it, okay? I'm not happy about it. I wish you would've told me, but I understand you were trying to protect me."

His face lit up with relief and he let out a long sigh. "So ... we're good."

"I mean, I don't know if it's going to be like before," I told him honestly. "I understand the reasons why, but you really fucked with my trust."

"But I—"

I held up a hand, stopping his protest. "Like I said, I understand why. It's just, it's going to take some time, you know?"

Deme's shoulders rose and fell, and he looked mildly disappointed. "Yeah. I get it."

I allowed my gaze to sweep over him, trying to see him through new eyes. He didn't really look any different, not the way some of the elementals I'd seen on campus did. He looked like the same Deme I'd always known. It brought me more relief than I could have imagined.

"So ... you're an earth elemental."

His lips curved upward. "Yup."

"What can you do?"

"Well ..." His mouth twisted. "You already know I can temporarily ground the powers of other elementals."

I nodded. "What else?"

"This." He maneuvered his chair a few inches to the side, aiming his gaze down to the ground. He flicked his fingers in front of him, and a tiny spot of earth began to churn. Some of the dirt floated up, forming a small square brick that landed in his palm.

My brows furrowed. "Um … wow?"

Deme let out a low chuckle. "I can manipulate earth. Small scale stuff like this. Or even bigger stuff like earthquakes."

"Oh. Wow!"

"Yeah, it's pretty cool." He grinned at me, but then it faded. "Listen, I'm glad we got a chance to talk. I have to go do something for a few days … a-a mission."

"What?" Snuggling deeper into my coat, I leaned forward. "For who?"

Deme frowned, his voice soft. "I can't tell you. Not yet."

A sudden burst of anger flooded me, and I shot to my feet. "Deme, I thought we were done keeping secrets!"

Sighing, he swung his leg back over the chair and rose. "I don't have the authority to tell anyone anything yet, but I promise, as soon as I do, I'll let you know." When I continued to glare him, he set his hands on my shoulders and leaned in to kiss my forehead. "I'm sorry, Jewel. Please understand."

Groaning, I tried my hardest to give him the benefit of the doubt. "*Fine*. When will you be back?"

Deme pulled away. "A few days, a week at the

most."

"Okay," I said grudgingly. Against my will, my hands reached out and grabbed his coat. I pulled him in for an embrace. Mad or not, he was still family. "Take care of yourself."

He hugged me back. "You too."

When I got to the Fellowship Hall, the corridors were devoid of life, as were the common and worship rooms. I remembered Luc's absence in class, and a feeling of unease settled in the pit of my stomach. Heading back toward the exit, I was almost there when I heard the soft echo of a voice. This time I placed the voice immediately. Turning, I headed down the corridors toward the room where I'd discovered Deme and Professor Raymond talking before.

"They're out meeting with their respective contacts," I overheard Professor Raymond say. "We've canvassed the area, but we've seen no signs of anything unusual. Of course, you know as well as I do that means nothing."

There was more silence, then the Professor said, "Yes, we'll have to initiate that part of the plan. She may give us some difficulty, however."

I knew without being told I was the "she." Coming to a stop in front of the door, I didn't bother to knock before turning the knob and shoving it open. It slammed hard against the wall, the doorframe rattling and reminding me of my newfound strength.

Professor Raymond, to his credit, didn't react in surprise at the sight of me. He continued speaking into his cell phone. "Yes, well, we won't have to wait too much longer. As it happens, she is right here."

Glaring at him, I crossed my arms. "I don't appreciate you talking about me behind my back."

Even if the Professor's expression didn't tell me how juvenile I sounded, I would have recognized it myself. I fought back a hot blush, concentrating on my anger instead. "If something is going on that involves me, I deserve to know what it is."

One of the Professor's thick brows arched. "Perhaps you are correct, Miss Harris." He held out the phone, continuing to regard me evenly. "Would you like to speak with your father?"

Wincing, I took a step back. Dad tried to call me last night, and I'd ignored his call. I didn't know what to say to him other than, "Would've been nice to know I wasn't human!"

I didn't want to merely erupt in anger.

At the same time, I knew he only had my best interests at heart, and that made it difficult to stay angry.

Taking a breath, I answered the phone. "Hi, Dad."

"Hi, baby."

The sound of his voice collapsed the wall of anger I'd erected around my heart. I let out a sigh. "What's happening?"

"Some of the older members of Theobald's Guard were attacked just outside of town last night," my father replied, his voice matter of fact.

"One claims he saw Lord Adrian amongst the group of attackers before they managed to get away."

My breath sucked in at his mention of the Dark Lord. "He's ... he's here?"

Professor Raymond sighed and slipped his glasses off his face, wiping them with a cloth. It was the first time I'd ever seen him look weary.

"We don't know," Dad said to me. "As of now, it's an unconfirmed report. It would be very unusual for him to personally travel to another dimension. He is weaker here and at bigger risk of being overtaken by the Guard. If he *is* in fact here, we fear he may be closing in on your identity."

"But ... but how?" I staggered over to one of the seats opposite the Professor's desk. "Wait. Do you think he figured it out when his lackey didn't come back, the one who stuck me with the syringe?"

"Theobald suspects that man was one of many scouts he sent out, as he has done throughout the years. Grasping at straws in an effort to determine where you were."

Professor Raymond's hearing must be as good as mine, because he heard my father all the way across the room. Nodding, he spoke up. "Given the rate at which we end up confronting them, I imagine few of Adrian's scouts actually return. That in and of itself wouldn't be suspicious."

"Then how?" I whispered into the phone.

"We don't know," Dad said in the clinical tone I'd grown to know so well over the years. "We don't even know if our suspicions are correct as to whether he is on Earth."

From what he said, it didn't sound like they

knew much at all. "What was the next part of the plan, then? The part you didn't think I was going to like?"

I glanced over at the Professor as I said that, but his gaze remained focused on the desktop.

"Theobald and I agree it would be safest if you moved into the Fellowship Hall," my father answered.

It took a moment to realize he wasn't being facetious. "Seriously? Where am I going to sleep, on top of one of the tables in the worship room?"

Professor Raymond cleared his throat, speaking up before my father could respond. "Actually, there are bunkers located below ground level."

When I stared at him in disbelief, the Professor continued. "We believe the campus is fairly safe, of course. But, as you learned several days ago, the wards guarding this school are not foolproof. Given that the other on-campus members of the Guard reside in the bunkers, it seems the safest place for you to be for the time being. And since you've much to learn, your proximity accomplishes several purposes."

My mind reeled as I processed his words. They wanted me to move out of my cozy dorm room and into the Fellowship Hall. *Underground*, for god's sake.

Where the rest of the Guard lived.

This meant I'd be living under the same roof as the boys. That was a marked change from the rest of the campus's non-coed policy. But then, it wasn't like most people knew about the bunkers, was it?

You'll be living with Luc, a voice inside me

noted.

An army of butterflies instantly took flight in my stomach.

And Aeron ... and don't forget Thea.

That last thought was enough to draw me out of my mini freak-out. "Do I have to share a room with someone?"

Because if he expected me to suddenly become BFFs with Thea, then no effing way. I would take my chances with the Dark Lord, thank you very much.

My father chuckled into the phone, as if he sensed my reluctance to give up my privacy.

The Professor gave me a small smile. "No. There are enough rooms for you to have your own."

I fidgeted as I considered their words, and a tiny stream of power flowed unbidden from one hand to the next, lighting up my fingertips like a flashlight. I stared down at them, taking in the newness of what was happening to me.

If nothing more, the opportunity to master my abilities was worth moving into the bunker. Plus, I'd probably have access to all those ancient books I longed to get my hands on. More than anything, I wanted to understand who I was. Where I came from.

I spoke into the phone. "Looks like they have a new roommate, then."

"Good," my father said, clearly relieved. "I really think it's the best plac—"

He cut off abruptly, and I squeezed the received tighter. "Dad? Are you still there?"

"Oh ... yes."

His voice sounded somewhat uneasy.

"Is everything okay?"

"I just thought I saw something," he murmured. After a pause, he said, "Never mind, I was mistaken."

My forehead scrunched. "Where are you?"

"I'm at the hospital. I'm just about to go into a surgery, so I'll let you go. You'll move in there right away, right?"

The worry in his tone was a stark reminder that, while he might not be my flesh and blood father, he loved me every bit as much as one.

"Yes, Dad," I said softly.

"Good." He paused again. "I love you, pumpkin. I'll come see you as soon as I can get away."

"I'd like that," I murmured. Despite everything, he was still my dad.

Chapter 11

"**WHAT DO** you have in here, rocks?" Luc let out a fake groan as he hefted my rucksack onto his shoulder.

I gave him an exaggerated eye roll. "It's books and clothes, genius."

After my meeting with Professor Raymond, I dragged myself to the other two classes I had for the day. I made it back to my dormitory just before sunset, and Luc was standing by the main doors, leaning against the brick wall like he didn't have a care in the world.

"Hey roomie," he'd called upon seeing me. "Need some help packing?"

My body had drummed with nervous energy as I let him into the building, well aware the sun would be down soon and I'd be breaking the dorm rules by having a boy in my room. But since I wasn't going to be living here anymore anyway, who cared?

As Luc accompanied me upstairs, we passed a few of my dorm mates. Their appreciative glances weren't lost on me. One had even given me a thumbs up sign when he wasn't looking. Try as I might to hold it back, I was sure my blush had turned my skin the color of a ripe strawberry.

Once we were in my room, I'd grabbed my

rucksack and stuffed all my essentials into it, fighting back yet another blush when I got to my underwear drawer. But even though amusement had shone on his face, he hadn't said a word, other than to drawl out, "Nice room."

After loading my smaller backpack with the rest of my necessities, I'd slipped it over my shoulders while Luc grabbed the rucksack. Now, as we headed out of the building into the night, Luc gave me a hooded glance. "How ya doing, Princess?"

His nickname made me wince. "Don't call me that. It's obnoxious."

Luc snorted. "So am I."

I laughed at his words, but my next thought sobered me up. "Did you find anything? I mean, the Professor told me one of the guardians thought he saw the Dark Lord."

"Lord Adrian?" Luc scrubbed at the shadow of whiskers on his chin. "Nah, there's nothing to confirm that. The guy who called it in is one of the newer members of the Guard. It's very likely he just freaked out and thought he saw something he didn't." He gave me a sidelong glance. "Takes a while to build those nerves of steel, you know."

Thinking back on my earlier training session with Aeron, I could see exactly what he meant. One little hit, and I'd practically been reduced to a blubbering mess.

I took a deep breath. "You really think I'm safe on campus?"

His storm blue gaze shone through the darkness as he regarded me. "I do. The wards have been reinforced, and the patrols were doubled. Plus, you've got me."

Luc's easy grin belied the seriousness of his tone. I appreciated his attempts to put me at ease. The thought that some crazed elemental from another dimension might snatch me up and make me his baby mama was enough to keep me up all night.

Students milled here and there as we strode across the lawn. Soon enough we stood in front of the Fellowship Hall. However, rather than head toward the front entrance, which looked as if it was locked for the night, Luc went around to the side.

I followed him curiously, watching as he came to a stop beside a set of metal doors painted a burnt orange. Luc dug a key out of his pocket and slid it into the lock.

"I never noticed these doors here," I murmured.

He gave me a sideways grin. "No one ever does. They stay locked 24/7." Opening the door, he moved aside for me to enter. "You'll get your own key, too."

The door opened to a set of concrete stairs heading below ground level. They went down about twenty steps before ending at a wall, where another set of stairs were set in the opposite direction. Overhead chandeliers lit up the space, casting dark shadows in certain spots.

When I stepped inside, I saw this hallway was closed off to the rest of the Fellowship Hall. Other than the staircase, we were surrounded by four walls. No chance of an unaware student randomly stumbling upon the area.

The door slammed shut behind us, and I felt

Luc's presence at my back. His masculine storm and spice scent washed over me, making me stifle a shudder.

"Looks sort of creepy, doesn't it?" he drawled.

"My sentiments exactly."

I didn't protest when Luc stepped past me to lead the way down the stairs. My heart rate quickened as I followed him, each step feeling like I was going deeper into the earth. Which I guess I was.

As we headed down the second flight of stairs, a large, brightly lit room came into view. It was sort of a great room, with half a dozen chandeliers decorating the ceiling and two rectangular wooden tables taking up the center space. Surrounding the tables were several cozy armchairs laid out in various spots, along with wooden bookcases built into the walls that were the same tone of wood as the floor.

A random burst of excitement hit me as I wondered what information those books might contain, but the thought was eclipsed by the five pairs of eyes glancing up at me from the table.

I'd interrupted some sort of meeting.

My uneasy gaze raked across the faces of the people sitting at the table. Two were familiar: Thea and Aeron. The others belonged to a girl and two guys I'd never met before. They seemed close to me in age, though, and one of the guys looked vaguely familiar. I surmised they were the remaining student members of the Guard.

Pausing at the foot of the stairs, I realized they were all waiting for me to say something. I bit my lip anxiously. "Hi."

Aeron's lips curved into a smile and he rose. "Hey, Jewel. Come on in and meet everyone."

His friendliness served to combat some of my shyness. Throwing him a grateful smile, I stepped farther into the room.

Luc set my rucksack on the ground. "Jewel, you already know Thea and Aeron." He pointed over to the girl I hadn't met. She was tall and pale, and she had beautiful, long, dark red hair. "That's Sarah. She's from Auren, the air dimension."

"Hi," Sarah said, giving me a cordial wave.

Next he moved on to the guy I'd never seen before, who had a bright red mohawk decorating his head. "That jerk over there is Payton. He's from Pyrem, the fire world."

Payton made a lewd gesture to Luc with his tongue while flipping him the bird. But his smile grew sweet as honey when he turned to me. "Nice to meet you, Jewel."

Finally, Luc pointed at the guy who looked like he might be in one of my classes. He was tall with dark, spiky hair and eyes the color of the ocean. "That is Kai. He's a water elemental, from Aquea."

The power beneath my skin practically pulsed in the presence of everyone here, almost as if my elemental nature recognized its kin. With a quick prayer my fingers hadn't suddenly started glowing again, I lifted my hand to wave at them. "Hi, everyone. Nice to meet you."

"Glad to have you here with us," Sarah said.

"It's not every day we meet someone like you," Payton added. When my surprised gaze shot back to him, he elaborated, "You know, a member of the first house."

Yeah, I knew, but I hadn't expected any of them to acknowledge it. Or to even care, really. I mean, this was America. Land of the free, home of the brave … where no one gave a damn where you came from.

But then, none of them were exactly Americans, were they?

Man, I was so in over my head here.

"Call me Jewel," I said quickly. If they all started calling me "Princess" like Luc did, I was going to lose it.

"We're all members of the Gaian Elemental Guard," Aeron said. "We're here to keep you safe."

I gave him an appreciative smile just as Thea let out a loud yawn and picked up her cell phone to glance at the screen.

"Bored?" Aeron teased her, clearly amused.

"I didn't get much sleep last night with all the upheaval about the *alleged* Adrian sighting." Her accusing glance made it clear it was somehow my fault. "I'm going to bed."

She rose and stalked off in a huff, but when no one paid her any mind, I sort of figured it was a regular thing. I turned back to see Luc stifling a yawn himself. Suddenly, I did feel guilty.

"I'm sorry," I murmured to him. "I feel responsible for all of this."

He gave me a look that told me that was all shades of crazy.

"Yeah, definitely your fault for being born and all."

I broke into a reluctant laugh at his sarcastic

response.

"Come on." He winked at me as he lifted my rucksack onto his back once more. "I'll give you a quick tour and show you to your room."

After mumbling a quick goodbye to everybody, I followed Luc past the tables to the other side of the room, where a heavy set of double doors led to a corridor that went both left and right. The walls were a gray polished concrete and the floors a brown-veined marble. He turned right and pushed through a set of swinging doors. They led into an industrial-sized kitchen with more marble flooring and tiled walls. The space was so massive that another rectangular table with six chairs had been set right into the center of it.

"We usually eat breakfast in here." His face took on a hopeful expression. "Can you cook?"

My father never learned how, and so he didn't teach me. We had a housekeeper who cooked dinners for us twice a week, and we'd usually eaten out or ordered in every other meal.

When I gave him a dubious shrug, he looked crestfallen. "Damn. Neither can any of us."

Luc turned and walked out of the kitchen, leading me down the other side of the corridor. The long hallway had eight or ten closed doors set into it. He pointed to the first one on the left. "That's the bathroom. We all share it, so good luck. I've found the earlier you get up the better your odds are."

Great. Guess I was about to become an early bird if I wanted to remain freshly showered.

"That's my room." He gestured to the second door on the right without pausing. After continuing down two more doors, he stopped in front of another one set into the right side. "This'll be yours."

My chest tightened at the thought I'd be staying only three rooms down from Luc, but I said nothing as he turned the knob and opened the door, motioning for me to enter first.

Stepping into the small space, I looked around. There wasn't much to see. The walls were the same polished gray concrete, the floors the same marble. The room was just large enough to accommodate a full-sized bed, complete with wooden headboard, a nightstand with a lamp, and a small matching desk placed in the corner. The bed was covered with a brownish-beige bedspread that looked like it could have been stolen from the nearest cheap hotel. The room kind of smelled like one, too.

"Not as big as your dorm room," Luc drawled. "Not very pretty either, but it should do."

"This is fine."

It hit me that I was going to live here for the foreseeable future. A wave of anxiety wafted through me, and I shouldered off my backpack, dropping it onto the bed before turning and blindly taking a seat there myself.

"This is sort of a lot to deal with," I muttered, more to myself than anything.

Luc's face softened and he dropped my rucksack beside the bed before sitting next to me. His shoulder nudged mine. "You'll adjust. You're strong."

I let out a soft snicker, because I sure didn't feel strong right now. "Yeah, right."

"You don't think so?" he murmured. He wrapped his hands around my wrists, sparking a tingle of electricity where our skin touched. He turned my hands palm up. "Look. There's your power. Just simmering below the surface. Glowing. Waiting for you to take command of it."

Sure enough, my skin itched at the thought his words provoked. Twin orbs of light formed on my palms. I sucked in a breath of air at the sight of them. I'd never actually formed two before. "I wish I could control it. It seems so random."

"I think you're putting too much thought into it. It's more of a gut feeling. Instinct, if you will." When I gave him a doubtful glance, his lips twisted upward. "Look at the light. Can you make them merge?"

Focusing, I concentrated on willing them to do just that. But other than floating up a few inches before dropping back onto my palms, they didn't do anything. Then I thought about what Luc had just said. That it was more instinct than thought.

I let out a long, deep breath, relaxing my shoulders. When I got the urge to draw my hands closer together, I obeyed it. Instantly, the two globes merged into one bigger one, almost as big as my head.

"That's it," Luc murmured as I shifted my hands upward and the globe began to float in the air.

My eyes followed it as it rotated above our heads, casting a hazy glow throughout the space. Then, like a bubble, it gently floated down before bursting over our heads, sending a stream of energy cascading into me. The heady power slithered under my skin, adding an extra layer of bounce to my hair.

When Luc took a slight, shaky breath, I looked over to see his eyes lit up like a lightning storm, crackles of blue light streaking through his irises.

He smiled at me, his voice low when he said, "You probably don't realize it yet, but the power flowing through you is strong. Once you learn to control it, you're going to find there's a lot more to you than you think."

"Maybe you're right," I whispered as the power settled over me, adding a sliver of sensuality to my slightest movement.

I couldn't help but think about the other night, the shock of excitement his soft kiss had wrought. As my gaze fell to his full lips, I knew I wanted to do it again. But deeper this time. For real.

Static electricity charged the air between us. His gaze lowered, and I knew he was thinking the same thing.

For one long moment, I thought he was going to do it. He might have even moved his head a few centimeters closer. But then, as if he remembered something, he blinked and cleared his throat, then sat back.

His voice sounded gruff when he said, "I should probably go. We could both use a good night's sleep."

A protest lay on the tip of my tongue as I gazed into his still charged eyes. If he felt anything like me, the little burst of energy I'd showered us with would be able to keep him going for another hour at least. But clearly there was something going on that made him think this thing between us, whatever it might be, was not a good idea. And I didn't know how to combat that, not with my next-to-no experience when it came to the opposite sex. So rather than ask him to stay, which was what I really wanted to do, I merely nodded my head. "Okay. Thank you for showing me around."

"Anytime." A playful grin transformed Luc's face and he bumped my shoulder with his. "Welcome to the bunker."

He rose from the bed and strode out the still open door without closing it. I stared after him, my gaze remaining on the now-empty hallway as I thought about what he'd said. Maybe he was right, maybe I was overthinking the whole power thing.

"Crap." Sighing, I hopped off the bed and headed for the door. But before I could close it, the door directly opposite me opened with a soft click. The polite smile that crept to my lips died a quick death when I saw who was on the other side.

It was Thea, and she looked none too happy to see me, either. Given she wore a black tank top and matching sleep shorts, both emblazoned with hearts, I gathered it was her bedroom right across from mine.

Double crap. Because her face was *so* the first thing I wanted to see in the morning.

She leaned against the doorframe and crossed her arms, her blonde hair falling in long waves over one shoulder. "I'd be careful if I were you."

I glanced from left to right, looking for some imaginary menace, before realizing maybe *she* was the one I should watch out for. Mirroring her "I don't give a fuck" stance, I said, "Really? Why is that?"

"You shouldn't make the mistake of thinking he's into you. Because I can assure you, he's not. At least not in any but the most superficial of ways."

Even though her words sparked an anxious thump in my ribcage, I tried to play it off by letting out an amused scoff. "Were you spying on us through the slit under the door or something? Because if so, that's creepy."

She didn't answer. Instead she said, "Don't say I didn't warn you."

I lifted a brow. "What makes you so qualified to know whether I should be careful or not?"

To my surprise, her shoulders drooped for one brief moment, and some strange emotion flitted across her face.

"Because I've been there before. That's why."

With those soft words, she pushed off the doorframe and stepped back, closing her door with another click.

I blinked at the closed door, bewilderment warring with suspicion. What exactly had she meant by that? And did I really want to know?

Thinking the answer was probably no, I shut my door before turning to unpack my bags.

Chapter 12

IT TURNED out living in the bunker wasn't as bad as I'd feared it would be. After the first day, I figured out if I woke before nine in the morning, I was more likely to get bathroom access. Like typical college students, my new roommates preferred to sleep in whenever possible. I did too, but I liked showering more.

I also learned that, when my bunkmates weren't in class or out patrolling the campus and surrounding town, they were probably either upstairs hanging out in the common room, or in the worship room where they liked to practice their fighting and magical skills.

That wasn't so bad either. After I got over the initial shock of getting hit, I found myself picking things up fairly quickly. My newfound strength certainly didn't hurt. I practiced with anyone who was available, and the differences in their fighting styles were quite clear.

Luc was all about explaining technique, repeating the same move over and over until I had it down, while Aeron had a more straightforward "hit me and I'll hit you back" philosophy.

Sarah taught me how to use my smaller height and weight to my advantage, while Kai and Payton focused strictly on elemental combat. I learned that when I concentrated, I could use my light orb to deflect their water and fire, which made it a lot more useful than I'd originally thought. It sort of turned me into a bouncing ball of light that reflected their own weapons back onto them. It was pretty awesome when it worked. But I had a little burn mark on the inside of my arm to remind me I still needed to practice concentrating.

Too bad I didn't heal at super speed. Hours of daily practice left every muscle in my body sore and achy. Since Thea certainly hadn't volunteered her healing services, it meant I constantly walked around with a reminder of my last few practice sessions.

Thea was the worst when it came to sparring, too, mostly because she didn't seem to be practicing so much as trying to beat the crap out of me. Given her many years of experience over me, I'd say it was mission accomplished. Apparently, we'd *really* gotten off on the wrong foot, and I had the aches and pains from her to prove it. Even now as I stepped out of biology class, I could feel a twinge in my jaw. Thankfully the little glow of energy I'd managed to master settling under my skin daily served to mask most of the bruises.

Not so much the soreness, though.

I opened and closed my mouth to dispel the discomfort, then headed toward Professor Raymond's office. I found Luc just outside the doors of the Fellowship Hall. He was heading inside too, and when he saw me, he gave me a crooked grin as he held the door open for me. "What's up,

Princess?"

Rolling my eyes at his moniker, I stepped inside the building. "Nothing. Just looking for the Professor."

He nodded and followed me, the door slamming shut behind us. "He should be in his office this time of day."

"Thanks." I moved to brush past him, but he stopped me with a hand on my arm. Even through the layers of clothing and the coat I wore, I could swear I felt a trickle of electricity pass from him to me. Shivering, I asked, "Something wrong?"

His eyes warmed with concern as he placed a hand on my chin and gently lifted my face. I winced at the sharp stab of pain in my sore jaw, and his face grew hard.

"You're bruised. Thea didn't heal this?"

Shrugging, I averted my eyes. "I didn't ask."

Which was true. Thea wasn't the most approachable of people on a good day. Add to that her clear disdain for me, and I put my odds of getting healed by her slightly below winning the lottery.

Luc made a sound of disapproval low in his throat, and his fingers trailed down my neck. It sparked a line of energy down my throat and into my chest, instantly hardening my nipples. I shivered, feeling my cheeks grow warm.

His gaze trailed downward, almost as if he sensed my body's reaction, and I realized that sometime during our discussion he'd shifted closer to me. We were inches apart now, close enough for me to breathe in his masculine scent. I could see the way his pupils dilated, darkening his eyes.

My tongue reached out to wet my lips, and when his eyes followed, I realized he was thinking about kissing me. I certainly wanted him to. A real kiss, not that little butterfly kiss that had been more frustrating than quenching.

My whole body clenched at the thought of his lips on mine, moisture forming between my thighs. I knew he would be spectacular at it.

Hell, he was probably spectacular at a lot of things.

The slamming of a door deeper inside the Fellowship Hall made us both jump. I gasped and we stared at each other, whatever spell we'd momentarily been under broken.

Luc cleared his throat, running a hand through his hair. "Well, I guess I'll see you later."

"Okay," I murmured.

When he headed down the hall, the heels of his boots hitting the floor, I gave into the dreamy sigh that had formed in my throat. Damn, I wanted him to kiss me. Like, yesterday. With this newfound, sensual power flowing in my veins, I *almost* had the guts to make the first move.

Almost, but not quite. I guess no matter what, I was still the person I'd always been. I just had a few new upgrades.

I walked down the hall to the Professor's office. His door was open when I arrived, and he sat at his desk going over something on his computer. I knocked on the open door, and when he poked his head up, I asked, "Any word on Deme?"

He shook his head and adjusted his glasses.

"Nothing new."

Several days had gone by since Deme left. Wherever he was, he must not have reception, because he hadn't answered my texts.

After he left, the Professor informed me Deme had gone on some sort of secret mission for the Guard. He wouldn't tell me anything more than that, though, and I was worried about my best friend.

Absently rubbing at my burn mark, I asked, "If you hear from him before I do, can you ask him to contact me?"

The Professor nodded and his face took on a sympathetic expression that made him look even more like George Clooney than usual. "How are you doing, Miss Harris?"

"Good." I fidgeted with the straps of my backpack. "I'm learning a lot, figuring out my powers."

"Yes, but ... how are you?"

Oh. He wasn't talking about honing my skills. He was talking about my emotions. Given what I'd learned about myself in the past few days, he probably expected me to completely lose it. And honestly, I'd sort of felt like that was a possibility a few times.

"I'm adjusting," I finally said. And it was true. Slowly, for sure, but I was getting there.

"Good," he murmured. "Your father assured me you would be strong despite the gravity of what you discovered. I'm glad to see he was correct."

A lump formed in my throat, and I blinked hard. My father had always believed in me.

Luc's earlier words came back to me, his assurance that Dad was my father in every way that mattered. He was right.

Clearing my throat, I said, "Yeah, well … I'd better go."

I turned away and headed down the corridor toward the worship room. Energy hummed in my veins as I walked. I felt different than I had before my powers had been released.

Stronger. More energized. More alive.

Not human.

Yeah … most importantly that.

Somehow, it was beginning to feel normal now.

I was just about to turn the corner when a soft murmur of sound stopped me cold. It was Luc's voice, and the low tenor of it made me think he didn't want to be overhead.

"Not a good idea," he whispered.

"Why not?" a female voice responded, a hint of challenge in her tone. She sounded familiar, and when I held my breath and took a quick peek around the corner, I confirmed the voice belonged to Thea.

My gut twisted at the sight of them. She had Luc all but pinned against the wall right outside the open doors of the worship room. One of her fingers was wrapped around a loop in his jeans, flirtatiously tugging the lower part of his body closer to hers.

Retreating to my side of the corridor, my back hugged the wall as I processed what I'd just seen. There was a sense of familiarity to her touch that made me want to gag.

"Women have needs too, you know," she

continued teasingly. "We're both adults. So why not?"

"You know there are other factors," he said.

"You didn't care about her then," Thea snapped, the honey in her tone fading. "What changed?"

He took in an audible breath. "I—"

The echo of a footfall sounded out from farther down the hall. A second later, Kai's voice broke through the space. "Hey guys, what's up?"

He sounded deliberately cheery.

There was a shuffling of sound, and then Luc said, "Hey, bro."

The undertone of relief in his words was evident. It cut through me even in my confusion.

"Well." Thea let out a little cough. "I'd better go. I have class."

I froze, scared she was going to head my way and I'd be called out for inadvertently spying. But then her footsteps retreated, telling me she'd left by whatever way Kai had come in.

There was nothing but silence for a few long moments, then Kai said in a low, joking voice, "Someone's thirsty."

"Shut up," Luc shot back, clearly not amused.

"You should do us a favor. We'd all benefit from the better mood."

"Asshole." Luc let out a good-natured chuckle. "You know I'm pretty much celibate these days."

"You weren't that one night."

"Exactly," Luc agreed. "Last thing I need is to mess up again. I don't want to give her the wrong idea."

"Guessing it's too late," Kai joked, the sound of

his voice growing fainter. A door slammed and both their voices grew indistinguishable.

My mind reeled as I peeked around the corner, confirming the two of them had gone into the worship room and closed the door.

So Luc had hooked up with Thea.

I'd all but assumed that after her words to me a few days ago, but it still felt weird to hear it.

No, not weird. More like a knife to my stomach.

I was jealous, I realized. Some part of me had claimed Luc from the moment we'd almost kissed. Finding out he'd given himself to someone else even for a night made me want to throw up.

Which is probably exactly how Thea feels about you.

Nothing had happened between us, but clearly she'd sensed the attraction, at least on my part.

Oh, damn. Now I could see why she disliked me so much, and I kind of couldn't blame her.

I *hated* that.

But what had Thea meant when she said to Luc, "You didn't care about her then?"

Who had she been talking about? That was a puzzle I couldn't work out.

With one last glance toward the worship room, I turned and headed for the common room. I couldn't face Luc right now. I needed some time to mull over what I'd learned.

Later that night, I was back in my room at the bunker, poring over the Book of Elements. I'd been in the common room earlier, perusing the bookshelves, when I'd found it there. Since the Professor had never said I *couldn't* read it, I'd guiltily snuck it into my backpack, feeling like I was stealing. But since I had every intention of returning the book, I convinced myself I'd done nothing wrong.

The book contained a lot of mythology about the elemental worlds and information about how they interacted with one another. According to the book, the worlds were created as sort of mirror opposites. Aether and nether, i.e. light and dark, were opposites, as were earth and air, fire and water. When Thea told me Aethera had no nighttime, what she'd neglected to advise was that Netheren was *all* night. The people from that world lived off the energy of darkness as opposed to light. And on Auren, the air world, clouds were made of a substance so strong buildings could be built on them. Most of the people in that world lived up in the air as opposed to down on the ground.

My phone suddenly buzzed. Thinking it might be Deme, I half dove onto the bed where my phone was. When I glanced at the screen, however, it was my dad and not my best friend.

My heart fell for just a moment. Even though Deme had told me he'd be gone for days, I hadn't expected him to be gone *this* long. I missed him, and I was worried as hell about him.

Biting my lip, I wrestled with whether or not I should answer. Dad and I had spoken earlier, but I still wasn't over the whole being lied to for my entire life thing.

At the same time, he was my dad ...

Pressing the button to accept the call, I held the phone to my ear. "Hi, Dad."

"Hello, pumpkin." His voice was the same deep, comforting one I'd heard all my life. He also sounded tired.

"You okay?" I asked.

"Just worn out. Long day at the hospital."

I glanced at the time. It was 8:30 p.m. "Are you still there?"

"I'm walking home now. I called to see how *you* were doing."

My thumb found its way into my mouth, and I started gnawing on my fingernail. "Okay, I guess."

"You don't sound okay," he murmured.

"No, it's just ... it's a lot to take in, I guess."

"I imagine it is. The whole elemental thing took some getting used to for me as well, and I don't even happen to be one of them like you are."

That made me sigh. "I wish you had told me."

He was quiet for a moment. "You understand why I didn't, don't you?"

"Yes," I grumbled reluctantly. "That doesn't make me feel any better though."

"I understand, but ... I'm your father, and I love you. It's my job to keep you safe, no matter what."

I got it. Really I did.

"I love you too, Dad."

He paused, then said, "Huh."

I stopped chewing on my nail. "Are you okay?"

"Yeah, fine. I just thought I saw something. Never mind."

He'd said that last time I talked to him, too.

Frowning, I leaned forward. "Are you sure everything is okay?"

"Yes." His voice lowered to a barely audible murmur. "I've got a member of the Guard keeping an eye on me. That's who I saw. He's keeping himself out of sight, but that means I don't know where he is, either. I only see glimpses of him now and again."

My breath hitched. "Dad! Are you in trouble?"

"No, of course not." His voice was firm, reassuring. "Theobald insisted, as a precaution. I told him it wasn't necessary."

My chest tightened at the thought of him being in danger. "Is there any way this Dark Lord could know your identity?"

"Adrian? No, Jewel. I'm fine. Please don't worry about me. I regret mentioning it."

"Are you sure you're okay?"

"Yes. I'm home now. Safe and sound."

Releasing the breath I hadn't even known I'd held in, I said, "Okay. Just take care of yourself. Please."

"I'm supposed to say that to you," he said teasingly.

"I will, Daddy. I promise."

"Good. I was thinking I would visit this Saturday. What do you think?"

The thought of seeing my father in three days was a little nerve-wracking given the mess of emotions flowing through me. At the same time, I could use a little normal in my life right now, and seeing the man I knew as my father was probably as close as I was going to get.

"Sounds good. See you then."

Just as I hung up the phone, a knock sounded out on my door. I rose to unlock it, and when I opened it, to my surprise it was Luc on the other side. He wore his leather jacket and boots, along with a burgundy sweater and a dark pair of jeans.

"Hey there, Princess," he drawled, leaning against the doorjamb.

Blinking up at him owlishly, I said, "Hi."

He looked me up and down. "You haven't turned in for the night yet, right?"

Glancing down at my jeans and hot pink sweater, I said, "Nope. I was, um … doing some homework."

He made a face at the last word, then hesitated, scratching the back of his neck. "Listen, uh … this is probably not the best of ideas, but I thought maybe you could use a break from all this. A night out. On campus, of course. I wouldn't suggest leaving it right now, for safety's sake."

I realized my mouth had dropped open and snapped it shut. Was he seriously asking me out?

Luc shifted, uncertainty taking over his expression. "If you don't want to—"

"No," I interrupted, maybe a little too eager. "I'd love to. Let me get my shoes on."

Turning, I raced for my boots, which were on the floor beside my desk. He didn't seem to notice the book and, since he wasn't looking my way, I quickly slid one of my other textbooks on top of it just in case.

I sat down on the floor to tug my boots on, lacing them as quickly as I could. Given how conflicted he looked when he asked me, part of me was scared he was going to change his mind if we didn't get out of here soon.

When I grabbed my coat and joined him back at the doorway, he looked half regretful already. But he turned and led the way down the quiet hallway, then through the doors leading into the great room. Thea and Kai were seated across from each other at one of the wooden tables. They both had the same textbook set in front of them, which meant they must be doing a study session.

They glanced at us as we entered, and Thea's eyes narrowed a fraction.

"Hey, where you guys going?" Kai asked, giving us a friendly smile.

Luc clapped him on the back as he strode past. "Out. I'd invite ya buddy, but I know you have that big test tomorrow."

From the sound of his voice, he wasn't too upset about it.

Thea gave me a pointed stare as I followed Luc, one eyebrow lifting, and I fought back a flush. I could practically sense her emotions, and they made me hella uncomfortable. She was mostly jealous ... but a little bit worried, too. Something told me that while most of her concern was for herself, she also really thought Luc was going to break my heart.

Weird.

Since I didn't even dare unravel that land mine, I kept going. But just as I got to the stairs, Kai called after me. "Jewel."

Turning, I looked at him.

"Have you heard from your friend Deme yet?

The Professor told me he was out doing some secret important mission for the Guard."

I shook my head. "Not yet."

"Oh." He rubbed the back of his head and gave me a reassuring grin. "I'm sure he's fine. I don't know the guy well, but from what I've seen, I bet he can take care of himself."

Yeah, he was probably right, but that didn't mean I wasn't going to worry about him.

"Thanks," I said, then turned and followed Luc up the stairs.

Chapter 13

OUTSIDE THE Fellowship Hall, I snuggled deeper into my coat as we headed down the sidewalk. It was freezing cold. My nose felt like it might crack into a million pieces and crumble right off my face.

Luc noticed me shivering. "You okay?"

"I'll make it." Then I realized I didn't know where 'it' was. "Where are we going, anyway?"

"The Back Door. Have you been there yet?"

The Back Door was the college bar that sat on the farthest edge of campus. I'd seen it once or twice while heading to a nearby building, but given I wasn't old enough to drink yet, I'd never gone inside.

"I'm not twenty-one yet," I murmured. For some reason, I felt embarrassed about it.

He gave me an amused look. "No worries. I'm friends with the night manager. Besides, you can do more than drink there."

"Oh," I said, hoping he would attribute the redness in my cheeks to the wind.

"They have pool and darts. Stuff like that."

"Cool."

Throwing me a sidelong glance, Luc asked, "How do you feel your training is going?"

"I'm learning a lot." I ruefully rubbed at the sore spot on my ass from where I'd been thrown to the ground multiple times by Aeron and Sarah yesterday. "The hard way."

He let out a hearty laugh. "What about your elemental magic?"

Luc hadn't practiced magic with me for a couple of days since he had other Guard duties to attend to.

Scrunching up my nose, I said, "That's slower going."

"That's magic," he quipped. He came to a standstill and faced me. "Show me what you've got."

My eyes widened. "Here? Out in the open?"

He scoffed as if my words were hilarious and gave a pointed look around. "It's a magical campus. Where better?"

Yeah, I guess he had a point. I was thinking from my human point of view … but I wasn't human.

The usual nighttime crowd milled about campus. Glancing around, I saw quite a few students were using magic. One guy looked like he was skating atop the wind every time a good breeze hit, his feet several inches from the ground. Another held a ball of fire in both hands that a couple of friends huddled around, drawing from its warmth.

"Um … okay." I dug my hands out of my pockets and brought them in front of me. The now familiar ball of light grew in my palms.

He backed up until he stood about ten feet away. "Okay, see if you can throw it at me."

I made a motion like I was throwing the ball, but the light only dissipated.

Luc gave a crooked grin at my look of defeat. "You didn't expect it to happen the first time, did you?"

"Guess not," I mumbled. The truth was my progress when it came to magic felt slower than a snail's pace. Even though Luc and Aeron assured me this was normal when first learning magic, it still sucked. Compared to everyone else, I felt like a helpless infant.

He gave me an encouraging nod. "Try again."

Grumbling under my breath, I rubbed my hands together to dispel some of the cold, and started over. This time the ball floated a foot or so away, momentarily kicking my pulse up with excitement. But as quick as it left, it came soaring right back, settling into my palms. I threw my hands up in frustration, the light absorbing into my skin. "Argh!"

His eyes rolled exaggeratedly. "Don't get impatient. Just try again."

Throwing him a dirty look, I touched my hands together once more, palms up. The light formed, and I willed it toward him. It floated just like before. I watched it halfheartedly, fully expecting it to only go one foot and come back again like it had last time. But it kept going, slow and steady. I watched it with growing excitement.

"That's it." Luc's lips curved into a grin.

"Please. Go," I whispered under my breath.

Slowly it floated, until it struck Luc right in the chest, disappearing into his body. He spread his arms wide and threw his head back, breathing in deep as the energy nestled within the glowing orb worked its way into him. Watching him enjoy it was surprisingly sexy as hell. Almost like he had a part of me inside of him … and liked it.

And now I was uncomfortably turned on.

Luc lowered his hands, giving me a toothy grin. "What a fucking rush."

I knew firsthand how right he was.

"That was good," he added, his eyes glimmering with residual power. His hands slid into the pockets of his leather jacket. "But I'm still freezing my ass off. Let's get inside."

"Yes, please," I laughed, shoving my hands into my pockets.

We took the rest of the way to The Back Door at a half-run, arriving breathless and shivering from the night chill.

As soon as we stepped into the bar, warmth spread over me like a glove. The inside of The Back Door was dark and cozy, with soft white lights over the side of the bar housing the four pool tables and the dartboards. Glow lamps decorated the booths on the other side, and the bar top was nestled into a corner. It was late enough that there was a decent-sized crowd, but one of the pool tables was free.

"Here, let me get your coat."

Luc held out his hand, and I unbuttoned my coat before arching my back to wriggle it off my shoulders. I heard a sharp intake of breath and glanced up, only to see Luc's eyes glazed with something that looked a lot like desire.

I stilled, heat flooding my body at the thought he might actually be looking at me in *that* way. As someone sexual and not some pathetic fledgling who knew less about magic than your average five-year-old elemental.

As if he just realized what he was doing, Luc coughed and averted his gaze.

I stayed for there for a moment, frozen in place. *What was that about?*

Sure, we'd almost kissed a couple of times, our lips had even brushed, but that hungry look in his eyes ... it wasn't expected.

Not when I was me and he was, well, Luc.

Residual heat sparked between us, along with a hint of Luc's stormy scent, as I slid my coat all the way off and handed it to him. He wordlessly turned and headed toward the coat rack to the right of the door, setting my coat and his jacket on it.

A tap on my shoulder distracted me from my anxious thoughts of Luc and what had just passed between us. I glanced over to see a guy who looked like he belonged to a frat standing beside me. He was sort of cute, but he smelled like the beer in his hand had pissed all over him. Then he leered at me and stumbled to the side, beer sloshing over the rim of his glass. "Hey, sexy. Want a drink?"

"Dude," Luc's voice sounded before I could reply, "you look like you've had ten too many."

The frat guy stiffened like he was itching for a fight and glared over at Luc, but whatever he saw stopped him cold.

"Fuck off," Luc said in an amiable tone.

The frat guy stood there for a moment, swaying unsteadily, but he finally turned and stumbled off, murmuring, "Fucking guardians, think they're the shit."

Watching the drunk guy weave his way through the small crowd, spilling his beer all over the place, I asked Luc, "People on campus know you're a part of the Gaian Guard?"

"Sure. It's no secret."

Huh. I didn't know why that surprised me.

"Come on." Luc grabbed my hand, a sparking shooting from his skin to mine as he led the way to the bar. He stopped right in front of it, waving at the man taking drink orders. The guy saw him and nodded, holding up one finger.

As we waited for the bartender to finish mixing drinks, I watched him in wonder. He was no ordinary bartender. He didn't even bother to pour the drinks himself. Instead, he blew short puffs of air from his mouth that lifted the bottles and poured the liquid into empty cups in just the proper amounts. Another breath of air expertly mixed them, then zoomed them upward and set them in front of the person who'd ordered them. The guy was well-practiced in his elemental magic.

"What were those drinks he just made?" I asked, leaning into Luc.

"Looks like they were Long Island Iced Teas."

"Ooh, that sounds good." A drink named after tea couldn't be that bad, right?

Luc let out an amused chuckle. "Sweetheart, there's like twelve different types of liquor in there. How often do you drink?"

I gave him an embarrassed grin. "Not often."

One of his brows raised. "What do you drink when you do?"

"Um …" Absently twirling a lock of hair, I

confessed, "I've only ever had wine coolers."

His eyes bugged out at me. "Well then, you definitely don't want to start with one of those."

The bartender stopped in front of us. "S'up, man?"

"Not much." Luc leaned across the bar top to exchange a fist bump with him. "Dude, can you get us two Coronas?"

The bartender examined me, then jerked his head in my direction. "She cool?"

"Yeah, man. She's good."

Nodding, the bartender left to grab our beers.

Someone squeezed in next to Luc, and his shoulder brushed mine. Even through our sweaters, I felt a spark of energy come off him. It hardened my nipples, and when I glanced down, I saw they were clearly visible through the fabric. Surreptitiously, I crossed my arms. My habit of wearing soft cup bras was turning out to be a bad idea when it came to being around Luc.

When I turned toward him, his head jerked up. Fire raked my cheeks as I wondered if he'd noticed. Then wondered if it would bother me if he had …

Luc shifted, his hand absently rubbing the back of his neck.

Feeling suddenly self-conscious, I asked, "How often do you come here?"

"Once or twice a week, depending on what's going on with my duties for the Guard."

The bartender brought our beers, a slice of lime wedged onto the rim of each bottle.

"Thanks, bro. Put it on my tab." Luc bumped fists with the bartender again, then grabbed one of the bottles and shoved the wedge of lime inside it. I copied his motion, and he nodded toward the still empty pool table. "Come on, let's play."

He led the way to the table and I followed. There was a group of girls standing between us and the table, holding glasses in their hands as they chattered amongst themselves. One of the girls saw Luc and nudged another, murmuring something into her ear. They both tittered and watched as Luc passed them by, their gazes lingering on his ass.

An unwelcome burst of jealousy slid through me. I gave them dirty looks as I followed Luc, but they didn't even notice me. Truth was, I couldn't blame them. I couldn't stop staring at his ass, either. It was well defined and not flat like a lot of guy's asses were; his muscles rippled as he walked.

Apparently, I was a bit of an ass lady. Who knew?

Seeing my smirk, Luc asked, "What?"

"Oh … nothing." I took a quick chug of my beer and coughed. "Ugh, this tastes horrible."

"Welcome to the world of beer," he said, deadpan. He grabbed a couple of pool sticks from the nearby rack on the wall.

Oh well … when in Rome. Chugging some more of my beer, I made a face and then set the bottle down on one of the empty bar tables next to me.

"You'll get used to it." As if to prove his point, Luc downed half his beer in one gulp, then set his bottle beside mine. "Have you played pool before?"

"A few times. I'm not very good," I admitted.

"We all start somewhere." He handed me a stick and racked the balls. "You go first."

I started off strong, hitting a ball into one of the pockets from the get-go, but it was quickly apparent Luc was far more skilled than I was. Story of my life, it seemed. Luc distracted me by engaging me in small talk.

"So, what was your childhood like?"

"Good, I guess." I leaned over to line up my stick with a ball. "Kind of quiet. It was just me and my dad at home, and he worked a lot. Thankfully Deme and his mom lived a few doors down. She worked all the time too, to be able to afford the rent there, so Dad sprung for a babysitter for both of us when we were younger."

"That was nice of him." I missed my shot, and Luc walked around the table debating his next move.

"Yeah, I guess it was." Luc passed by me, his unique stormy scent floating over to me, and I shivered, crossing my arms again. Yup, definitely needed to invest in a hard cup bra. "When we got into our teens and didn't need to be watched as much, we spent most of our time at my place, playing video games. Or we headed to the mall after school."

Deme had liked to shop for clothes as much as I did, which made him, like, the best friend ever.

"Sounds like a good childhood."

He was right. What would it have been like if my father had told me about my heritage? If I knew I was being hunted? Would I have been nearly as carefree?

Suddenly I could understand his actions a whole lot more.

"What was your childhood like?"

Luc hit a ball, but it missed the pocket by an inch. He rose and looked at me. "Sucked, pretty much. My mom died when I was a baby."

"Like me," I interrupted, without even thinking about it.

His mouth tightened, his eyes shadowing. "Yup."

He looked strange when he said that, almost … haunted. But then, I could understand the trauma of losing someone so young.

"My father couldn't be bothered to watch me once she passed. I was shuffled off to an uncle, to second cousins. Basically, the first years of my life I went from home to home, always wondering how long each stop would last."

"Wow." My heart ached for him, for how that must have felt to a lost little boy. I found myself even more grateful to have ended up with my father. "That sounds horrible."

"Yup," he said matter-of-factly. "Between the ages of twelve and nineteen, when I came here for school, I was back with him. But even then, I felt more like an employee than his kid. He would call for me when I could be of use to him, but otherwise he pretty much ignored my existence."

"I'm sorry," I whispered.

Luc gave me a half smile, shaking his head. "That's just life."

I opened my mouth, about to ask him another question, when a girl wandered over to us. Even though it was probably twenty degrees outside, she was wearing a short black dress along with thigh-high hooker boots.

"Luc," she crooned, ignoring me completely as she stepped over to him and teasingly ran her finger down the front of his sweater. "Where've you been, baby? I've missed you."

He threw a sidelong glance at me, then backed up, gently taking her fingers off him. "Hey, Trish. Been busy."

His tone was cool, but she didn't get the hint.

"I've missed you," she cooed, ignoring his clear attempt to brush her off. "We should hang out again."

Her words made me bristle. For all she knew, we were on a date right now, and here she was, blatantly trying to pick him up right in front of me.

Then it hit me what she was referring to. From the way his cheeks tinged just the slightest, it wasn't hard to read through the lines. They'd hooked up before, and she wanted to do it again.

So much for celibacy, I thought sarcastically, recalling his earlier words to Kai.

"I don't know. I'm real busy this semester." He turned his back on her, facing the pool table. "Take care, Trish."

She finally got the hint. Stiffening, she whirled around to glare at me before stomping away, as if I was the reason he'd blown her off.

Hell, for all I knew, I was. Maybe if I hadn't been here, he would've eagerly taken her up on her offer. The thought made my stomach twist into an uncomfortable knot.

I hated feeling this way.

"Come on." Luc turned to give me a grin. "It's

your turn, remember?"

"Oh, yeah." I strode to the table, thinking over my next move. There weren't any easy ones. Biting my lip, I leaned over the table and tried to find the best position to line up my shot. After moving around a couple of times, I sighed and just went for it. As predicted, the shot went wild, bouncing off the side before rolling to the center of the table.

"Guess my pool skills are as good as my magic skills. As in, they suck."

I said it jokingly but Luc must have recognized my serious undertone, because when I rose and turned, he was right there, inches in front of me. His face was stone-cold sober. "Why do you do that?"

"Um ..." The stick dangled from my fingers as I pressed against the table, bending half backward in an unconscious attempt to escape the intensity in his gaze. "What?"

"Put yourself down," he said softly.

I was speechless for a moment, shocked he would notice something like that. That he would even care.

The heat of his body washed over me, and I took a shuddering breath. I could tell he was fighting to keep his gaze on my eyes, and I didn't need to look down to know I was aroused. That was just what he did to me.

"I ... I guess that's how I see it."

"No." He shook his head firmly, gazing down at me. "That's not who you are."

"I don't even *know* who I am. A few weeks ago, I was a regular person, doing regular people stuff. Now I'm some sort of light elemental, and a dark elemental psycho wants to use me to create his love child." I laughed, and it was a far more bitter sound than I'd anticipated. "Face it. I'm supposed to be this ... this royalty, and I'm pretty underwhelming."

He scoffed. "Are you serious?"

"It's just what I see," I repeated.

"No." He reached up and cupped the side of my face, his fingers stroking my skin and making me shiver. "No, Jewel. You're brave and strong in the face of all odds. Intelligent. You roll with the punches." His gaze bored into mine, hot and hard and full of some nameless emotion. "I *see* you, Jewel. The *real* you. And she is spectacular."

My mouth dropped open at his words, and my body shook from the intensity in his eyes. When he said that, like he really meant it, I could almost see myself that way, too. I could see what he saw in me.

Some wild and undefinable emotion passed between us. I was too wired from his proximity to identify it, but whatever it was drew us closer. It made my body tingle and a subtle radiance settle beneath my skin.

His lower body pressed into mine, and the heat and distinct hardness I felt against my stomach elicited a soft moan from me.

Holy shit.

The pool stick dangling from my fingers fell to the ground with a clank, but I didn't notice it. My fingers clawed into his sweater, and his eyes flashed with a spark of lightning as he lowered his mouth to mine.

"Well, look what we have here," said someone standing behind Luc.

The sound of Aeron's voice tore us apart. Luc shot backward like I'd suddenly become the repelling part of a magnet. His hands crossed in the front of his jeans, and my cheeks blazed when I realized why.

Our gazes shot to Aeron, who stood a few feet away, dressed in black jeans and a black sweater. He wore a pleasant smile on his strikingly handsome face, but his eyes glittered with something hard and disapproving.

"Kai told me you two were headed out. I figured you'd be here."

"Yeah, um …" Luc raked a hand through his hair, leaving it mussed. "I was showing her how to line up a shot."

"Huh." Aeron's gaze passed between us, his smile still pleasant. "Works better when she's actually facing the pool table."

My cheeks flamed even hotter, and I was pretty sure I resembled a tomato right now. A *glowing* tomato.

"I was talking her through it," Luc mumbled.

"Sure," Aeron said easily, though from his expression he wasn't buying it.

Of course, *who the hell would?*

"I figured I'd join you guys for a game."

"Yeah." Luc shifted uncomfortably, his gaze cast downward. "Sure, okay."

"I, um …" Crossing my arms over my chest again, I willed the glow in my skin to subside. "I just have to use the bathroom first."

"Good idea," Luc mumbled, shifting in his spot and spreading his legs. "I have to go, too."

From the way he was standing, I could guess why. Trying my hardest not to stare at his groin to confirm what I thought the issue was, I gave him a vague smile and followed his lead to the restroom. We didn't speak again; he just motioned to the ladies' room. But when I went inside the single restroom and turned to lock the door, I heard footsteps approaching outside, then the barely audible sound of Aeron's voice.

"What the hell are you thinking, man? Whatever's going on in that little brain of yours, you know you can't do that shit."

I pressed my ear to the door to hear Luc's response. "Fuck ... I know, man. I know. I just ... lost my head, I guess."

"Well try to think with the big one instead of the little one from now on, shit-for-brains."

"Fuck you," Luc replied without heat.

"Just make sure you don't *touch* her."

Their footsteps retreated, and I pressed my forehead to the door, grateful for the cool wood to chill the heat on my face.

Oh god. What had almost happened with Luc ... had been magical.

When he said "I see you," I really felt like he did. Like he was seeing beyond my body and deep down into my soul.

Why did Aeron tell Luc not to touch me? And why had he sounded almost *jealous* when he said it?

Aeron was sexy, I couldn't deny it. He was a few inches taller than Luc and slightly leaner. Very handsome, with bronze skin that made you wonder if he was the same intriguing shade under all those clothes. But he was also a dark elemental. I was light. Nothing could ever happen between us, and surely he must know that.

Right?

Confusion wound through me as I sighed and finally reached down to lock the door.

Chapter 14

"**NO, NOT** that way." Luc demonstrated the kick he'd just taught me once again.

It was late afternoon on the day after our bar outing, and since he was acting like nothing had happened, I was trying my hardest to do the same.

When I'd gotten back to the pool table last night, Luc and Aeron were already been playing a game, joking around like they were best friends again. Whatever moment had passed between me and Luc was long gone. The rest of the night he treated me no different than he did Aeron.

They'd both shown me some pool tricks and we'd shared a few laughs, but that was it. And after we all headed back to the bunker, Luc and Aeron went off to bed with nothing more than a cheery, "Good night."

While my night had been filled with more shadow dreams interspersed with dreams of making out with Luc, the guys had probably slept like logs.

Jerks.

And if I'd had a *teensy* little dream about me, Luc, and Aeron engaging in one very naughty threesome ... well, who could blame me? They were both hot, and I was more than a little horny. Couldn't blame a girl for what went on in the depths of her subconscious.

"Move your leg around in more of a semicircle," Luc said, breaking me out of my jumbled thoughts.

Doing my best to push those crazy dreams out of my mind, I tried to mimic his motion. "Like this?"

He gave a sharp nod. "Better."

Learning how to incorporate kicks into my fighting repertoire was a lot like learning a new language. I was doing a bunch of moves I now knew classified as mixed martial arts rather than karate. Yeah … I still had a lot to learn when it came to fighting.

Luc moved back, assuming a fighting stance, and we traded jabs back and forth. This time, when I got a fist to the face, I shook it off rather than immediately erupting into tears. Three cheers for progress.

Sensing an opportunity, I swung my leg around in the semicircle he just showed me. To my surprise, my foot connected with his solar plexus. He let out an "Oomph" and went stumbling back a few feet.

"Ooh!" I gave an excited hop in the air. "Ooh, that actually worked."

He winced and rubbed his stomach, then let out a laugh. "Yeah, it's supposed to."

That might be so, but I wasn't used to landing many hits yet. Now if only I could learn to control my powers.

A familiar voice spoke behind me, from over by the doorway. "Wow, I'm gone for one week and look what happens."

Deme.

Relief spread throughout my body as I whirled

around and ran straight for him. He grinned and held out his arms, and I jumped into them. Wrapping his arms around me, Deme spun me around.

"Where the hell have you been? I texted you like a billion times!"

Setting me down, Deme made a face. "I broke my phone right after I left. I haven't had time to stop by the mobile store and replace it."

"You asshole." I set my hands on my hips and glared at him. "I missed you like crazy. *And* I was worried. You couldn't borrow someone else's phone?"

He gave me a sheepish grin. "There wasn't any phone service where I went. No other people, either," he murmured as an afterthought.

My forehead scrunched. "Huh?"

"I'll leave you two to hash it out," Luc said. He strode toward us, shooting Deme a casual smile. "Glad you're back in one piece, man."

"Thanks," Deme replied, his voice cool. I remembered he wasn't a big Luc fan.

The moment Luc was out of earshot, I asked Deme, "How come you don't like Luc?"

"I don't know." He shrugged. "He seems like a player. He's a good guy, I guess. Just not for you."

Rolling my eyes, I stuck my tongue out at Deme. Guess I wouldn't be telling him about our almost kisses anytime soon. "Said like a real-life overprotective brother."

He made an exaggerated clicking sound with his tongue, winking at me. "You know you're lucky to have me, chica."

True. I might still be the teensiest bit pissed about all the secrets he'd kept from me, but at the same time he was as much a pawn in this whole mess as I was. My powers had been bound by his grandmother before he could even *walk*, much less understand what was happening. What else could he have said when she asked him to be complicit in keeping me in the dark? "No?"

I knew enough about his family dynamics to know refusing would have been impossible.

In the end, he was still my family. Just like my dad.

My eyes raked over Deme, drinking in the sight of him. His hair was blue now and swept to one side of his head like a funky wave. My gaze fell to the matching blue-stoned bracelet on his wrist, and my lips gave a wry twist. "Still wearing that? Your binding magic doesn't work on me anymore."

"Yeah, but, you know … habit." A smile crept to his lips. "I still made you a matching one, too."

Because we're family.

Though he didn't say the words, I heard them clearly.

"Are you allowed to tell me where you went now?" I prodded.

"Death Valley National Park."

"In California?" My brows knit together. "*Why?*"

When he let out a sigh and absently mussed his hair, I knew the answer wasn't going to be an easy one. After a long moment, he motioned toward one of the tables. "You wanna sit?"

Oh god. It was worse than I thought.

Frustration wound through me as I stomped over

to the table. "I swear, Deme, if you're going to tell me you're secretly in league with the Dark Lord or something—"

"What?" He gave a shocked laugh. "No, no of course not."

Leaning back on the edge of the table, I crossed my arms and stared at him. "Then what?"

"My ..." He cleared his throat and approached me, sitting on the edge of the table like I did, a foot or so away from me. "You know I'm an Earth elemental. Gaian."

"Yeah," I said suspiciously.

"What you don't know is that our family line also has a rare gift." At my sarcastic snort, his lips twisted. "Another one, I mean."

When he didn't continue, I prodded him with a "Yeah, and ...?"

Deme swallowed compulsively before meeting my eyes. "We're among the very few who can confer with the Fates."

"The immortal seers who prophesied that crossbreeding between the races would lead to chaos?" I let out a disbelieving scoff. "Are you telling me they're real?"

He let out a nervous laugh. "Some would argue otherwise."

Okay, that made no sense. "So, how did you confer with them?"

"There's a spot deep within the most secluded part of Death Valley, a sort of dimensional doorway."

"Like one of the doorways leading into the other worlds?"

"Sort of." He gestured with his hands. "The Fates predate the worlds as we know them. They're as old as the gods, right?"

My jaw dropped. "Are you telling me those are, like, for *real* now, too?"

Deme shrugged. "Who knows?"

With a sigh of exasperation, I motioned for him to continue.

"The Fates don't live on any of the six worlds," Deme explained. "They reside in the space between the worlds, where they have always existed. The doorway allows spiritual access to their plane of existence, but it's impossible for any physical body to pass through."

My brows crept to the vicinity of my hairline. "So how exactly do you talk to them? Do you stand on the threshold and yell, then wait for them to shout back?"

"No." Deme gave me a dirty look. "Smartass."

I was growing impatient. "Then what?"

He fidgeted. "I have to ingest a psychotropic aid to be able to communicate with them."

"Psychotropic aid …" My voice trailed off as I caught his gist, and then I understood why he seemed so nervous. "You're telling me you go off into the desert alone and do *drugs?* Like what, peyote or something?"

Deme colored. "It's only to allow spiritual access to where the Fates reside."

"God, Deme!" I shot to my feet, digging my fingers into my scalp. "That's crazy. I mean, how do you know you're talking to the supposed Fates and not just on some wacked-out acid trip?"

When his cheeks darkened, I suddenly got why he'd said some would argue the existence of the Fates. I sat back down with a *plonk*. "You don't know, do you?"

"Of course I do," he replied. "We just don't *know,* know. I mean, we don't have proof or anything, but I couldn't have imagined the whole thing."

I stared at him silently, not needing to tell him that, yeah, he very well *could* have just imagined the whole thing. Given how uncomfortable he was right now, he knew the truth.

"The Professor, he finds this to be a credible way of communicating with these so-called Fates?"

Deme gave one sharp nod. "He does."

Okay, so I would give him the benefit of the doubt. Professor Raymond might be many things—including a practiced liar, it seemed, based on his attempts to fool me into thinking I was human before—but he was certainly no fool.

"What did you go talk to the Fates about?"

Deme looked down and began toying with his bracelet. "I asked how Lord Adrian could be stopped."

I let out a shaky sigh and rubbed my hands along my face. The resulting tingle of energy along my skin reminded me just how different things were now. "What did they say?"

"Um …"

My gaze flew back to his face. "What?"

He let out a dry cough. "Well, they don't exactly speak in clear sentences."

I gave him an incredulous glance. "Are you

serious?"

"They're not even human," he said defensively. "Time means nothing to them. Mortality means nothing. They don't communicate in the way we would."

Oh, this was just too rich. "What exactly did they say?"

Deme looked away. "They said, 'When past is past, imbalance is struck, battle begins. Light or dark, savior or destroyer, the die is cast as time goes past.'"

I blinked in the vain hope it would somehow help me decipher what he just said. "What the hell does that mean?"

He threw up his arms. "I don't know!"

"Great," I muttered. "Just great."

Everything he'd told me, combined with all I'd learned over the past few weeks, suddenly combusted inside me. It made me feel like I was going to literally explode.

When Deme's eyes widened, I realized everything around me had taken on a brighter appearance. I looked down at my body to see I'd begun to glow, so brightly this time I lit up a one-foot radius around me.

I let out a scream of aggravation and a glowing orb the size of an ice cube flew out of my mouth, floating above me and quickly taking on mass until was roughly the size of a beach ball. It burst with an audible *pop*, sending a flood of energy through me. Deme gasped as it flooded into him, too.

My hair settled around my shoulders in bouncy waves, reminding me that all I'd gotten so far from my newly discovered abilities was good hair and a whole mess of problems.

It suddenly became too much. I couldn't hang around here for the rest of the day or I was going to explode again. Maybe next time there would be more consequences than a flood of energy and an improvement in my looks.

"Okay, that's it. I need a break from this insanity." I swept my shiny locks off my shoulders and whirled around, heading for the door.

"Where are you going?" Deme called behind me.

"I don't *know*," I yelled back, knowing the whole time I was being silly by throwing a tantrum like a five-year-old.

But damn, there was only so much craziness a girl could take before she totally lost her mind.

Chapter 15

IT WAS still early in the evening, so The Back Door was only half full when I wandered in.

Yes, I'd headed straight to a bar after my mini freak-out.

Part of me recognized this was not the healthiest of responses to what Deme had told me, but I needed to get away from everything for a bit. Somehow, I'd wound up here.

At least I hadn't been so idiotic as to venture off school grounds. Not by myself, not when there was some otherworldly psycho waiting to have his way with me.

I had never given much thought to the name of the bar, but now that I knew what I did, I wondered if it was some sort of nod to the dimensional doorways separating the worlds. I didn't have much time to ponder the thought, though, before the first guy hit on me. He was followed in quick succession by two more, and within forty-five minutes I'd been propositioned more than half a dozen times.

I guess drinking alone in a campus bar probably sent the message I was looking for company, at least to the drunken jerks who didn't bother to read the angry look on my face or manage to aim their gazes higher. Sometimes guys really sucked.

Perched on the barstool, I motioned to the bartender for a second drink. I breathed a sigh of relief when I'd come in and seen the same guy manning the bar. Since Luc had vetted me, he didn't give me any trouble when I asked for a Long Island Iced Tea.

He might be regretting that now.

A pained expression took over his face, and I thought he might protest. But then he moved his gaze to an empty glass and formed an *O* with his lips. Bottles clinked as they lifted, upending liquid into the glass and masterfully mixing my beverage with the air he expelled. Rather than floating it through the air, he picked it up and came over, then dropped it down in front of me. "Take it easy with these. They're much stronger than they taste."

Rather than snap at him like I wanted to, I dug a ten-dollar bill from my pants and set it in front of him.

"Thanks," I said sweetly. "Keep the change."

My cell phone buzzed, but I ignored it. It had been blowing up with texts for the past half hour. I knew they were from Deme, but I didn't feel very talkative right now. I'd text him back soon. Maybe after my next drink.

My stomach did a little turn as I sucked down most of the contents of the glass. If the first drink had taken some of the edge off, this second one was sparking a pleasant burn in my tummy. I felt a little calmer. Approaching numb, which sounded like heaven right about now.

Finding out about these Fates and listening to the nonsensical words Deme had recited threw me for a loop. I felt like the rules were constantly changing, and I couldn't keep up. I didn't even know which way to turn.

The beginnings of a headache pressed behind my temples. I shoved the glass to the side and rested my elbows on the bar, digging the heels of my hands into my head to alleviate the pressure.

"Penny for your thoughts," murmured a gruff voice beside me. I froze at the sound.

Luc.

"How did you find me?"

"Everyone's looking for you. Deme thought you might've gone back to your old dorm. Aeron searched the Fellowship Hall. The rest are out patrolling campus." Luc let out a little snort. "I'm the one who guessed the bar."

My lips gave a sardonic twist. "Guess I'm more predictable than I thought."

"Nah. I think you and I are just a bit alike. Maybe more alike than I originally thought. A bar's the first place I would've gone, too."

That made me laugh. "Maybe you're a bad influence."

He gave me a cheeky wink. "I've been called worse than that."

I'll bet.

I closed my hand over my drink, but when I raised the glass, I noticed I already drank all the liquid gold inside.

Huh.

That explained my shaky fingers.

Setting the glass down, I motioned to the bartender for another drink. His gaze flew to Luc, but when Luc gave him a nod, the bartender shrugged and began pouring me another.

I bristled at their interaction.

"What? I need your permission to drink now?"

"Easy there. He's just looking out for you." Luc dug out a bill from his wallet and set it on the counter, then snatched my glass when it floated in front of my face. "Come on, let's go sit at that empty booth."

When I rose off my stool and turned to follow Luc, I almost collided with another stool. I bit back a curse. Where had that come from?

Maybe Luc was right about the tea being strong stuff.

The bar had gotten more crowded since I'd first come in. There were only a handful of booths by the bar occupied then. Now all but one were taken. The people had gotten progressively drunker, too.

Like me, haha.

My gaze landed on Luc's retreating figure. He wore his usual outfit: a pair of dark jeans, his brown leather jacket, and boots. The curves of his ass outlined the worn fabric of his jeans, setting off a trail of lust that sent the heady power flowing beneath my skin straight to my groin area.

Damn, I needed to get a hold of myself. My hormones, combined with the sensual slide of my power and the weakening of my inhibitions from the liquor, was driving me out of control. Another drink and I might find myself jumping his bones.

We both sat down, and Luc set my glass on the

table. With a smirk, I slid it over in front of me and put the straw to my lips.

Guess I *was* living dangerously tonight.

Luc arched a brow at the sight of me slurping down my drink. "Rough day?"

I snorted. "Try rough week. Turns out finding out you're an elemental and there's a whole world of magic you never knew about isn't that easy to get over."

He leaned back, crossing his hands behind his head. "Look on the bright side. You're learning how to kick people's asses now."

That made me laugh. "If only."

My vision blurred, and I winced. Maybe I should take it easy on the tea. It might not taste like it had liquor in it, but the two versions of him I saw right now said otherwise.

I watched in silence as Luc pulled his phone out and typed something into it. When he slid it back into his pocket, I arched a brow in silent question.

"I'm letting everyone know I found you," he explained. "So they don't worry."

His tone said he was trying to make me feel guilty for disappearing on everyone, but I didn't. Not right now, when the liquor was warming me from the inside out.

Speaking of …

My left hand shook as I grabbed the straw to steady it. I started to lift the glass back to my lips, but he surprised me by leaning forward, suddenly placing his hand on mine.

"I think you should take a break, Princess," he said softly. "Those things are damn strong."

Ribbons of awareness curled around my flesh where he touched me. When I got the sudden urge to leap right across the table into his lap, I knew it was the alcohol at work.

Making a face, I confessed, "I think you're right."

Luc let go of my hand, then rose. "Come on. I'm gonna walk you back to the bunker."

My lips formed a pout. "I didn't say I was ready to go."

He let out a soft chuckle, as if I'd just said the funniest thing. "Sweetheart, you are most definitely ready."

I was about to argue again, but then he held his hand out, and the breath stole from my lungs. Could I turn down another chance to be skin-to-skin with him, even if just for a moment?

Apparently not. My hand let go of the cold glass and slipped into his before I could even process what I'd done.

Luc snatched my coat from the coat rack by the door, then helped me into it before leading me out. The sky was dark, the moon high.

I slid my hands deep into the sleeves of my coat as we walked. Crowds of students milled about the campus. Many of them were no doubt either headed to or coming back from one of the bars.

"It's seems so peaceful here," I murmured to Luc. "On campus, I mean."

He shot me a look. "It is. Generally."

Generally. That was the key word. "How do you think that guy got on campus, the one who injected me?"

Luc pulled a hand out of the pocket of his leather jacket and scratched his eyebrow. "When I fought with him, he could counter some of my powers with his. I think his abilities also allowed him to sense the barrier. From there it was only a matter of forcing his body through it."

I gave him a puzzled glance.

"Even if you know it's there, when you're uninvited it's difficult to pierce a barrier like that. Your body feels repelled from it. Think of trying to walk right into a roaring flame."

I imagined doing just that and let out a long shudder. "I couldn't."

Luc nodded. "Exactly. You'd have to be able to conquer that aversion. But like I said, some people can, and this guy could."

I shook my head as I thought over his words. "Does that mean the Dark Lord knows I'm here?"

"Not at all," he said easily. "He knows of the existence of the school and, obviously, he knows the general area. It would be an easy guess that you were hiding here or at one of the other schools like it throughout this world."

My head cocked toward him. "There are other magical schools like MU?"

He laughed, clearly finding humor in that. "Sure. There's one in the south, a couple on the west coast, and close to half a dozen in Europe. One in Africa. We're not so unique here, believe it or not."

That was hard to wrap my brain around. "How many elementals *are* there on Earth?"

"Probably close to a thousand."

"Wow." I let out a soft laugh. "And regular

people have no clue."

"Nope."

The Fellowship Hall came into view, and I made a sudden stop. My vision might be blurry, my mouth dry, and my body screaming for a mattress, but I wasn't ready to go back yet.

"What?" Luc asked, stopping beside me.

"Let's go to the observatory."

He hesitated, the look in his eyes saying he didn't know if that was a smart idea.

"I want to practice," I urged him. "I feel like I'm finally improving."

After a long moment, he nodded. "Okay. Just for a few minutes though."

A brisk ten-minute walk later, we were inside the observatory, in the domed room that showed a clear view of the night sky.

"Wanna spar? Elemental style?" Luc gave me a sly grin. "I promise I'll go easy on you."

I sucked in a breath. "Yes." It was probably just what I needed right now.

Although he'd spent plenty of time teaching me how to fight this past week, he had yet to pit his magical abilities against my fledgling ones. In fact, other than the handful of times I'd seen lighting shoot from his fingertips, he hadn't used his powers around me at all. I had to admit I was curious to see more of what he could do.

Luc grinned and unzipped his jacket, tossing it to the side. He waited for me to remove my coat before lifting his hands, fingertips raised toward the ceiling. Streams of lightning crackled off his fingertips, the fizzling sound reverberating throughout the room. An answering shock of excitement rocked my body, causing me to grin back like a fool as I faced him.

Oh, it's on.

Maybe the alcohol lent me confidence, because this time the mere moment I lifted my hands, a glowing orb easily formed between them. It was the size and shape of a crystal ball, with milky white energy practically pulsing from it.

"Watch out." Luc flicked his fingers and twin streams of lightning zapped off them, aiming slightly to the right of me.

As if it had a life of its own, my magic shot into action, the globe parting into two smaller ones and blocking the lightning before it could pass me.

The lightning ricocheted off the light, zinging haphazardly through the room. Luc and I both ducked to avoid it, but then it hit one of the walls and absorbed into it, leaving a scorched trail in its wake.

"Oops." Luc grinned, letting me know he wasn't all that upset about the inadvertent damage we'd caused. He aimed his fingers down this time and streams of lightning shot from them, shooting him into the air about four feet above me.

I stared in astonishment. "You can float on your lightning?"

He gave me a playful grin. "More like I use it as a propeller to move me through the air."

Then he snapped his wrist, sending another jolt of lightning to the right of me. I instinctively swung my hand through the air, and a tiny ray of light swept out of my fingertips, bending the lightning harmlessly out of my path.

Luc gave me an impressed look. "Your powers are getting more concentrated."

I circled around him, giving the crackling energy surrounding his body wide berth. "Do you have any other tricks up your sleeve?"

He winked at me and tapped the heels of his palms together. The lightning began to whirl around him. Faster and faster it moved, until it surrounded his body with a fizzling tornado of energy that would no doubt fry the fool who dared go near it.

I watched slack-jawed until some hidden instinct caused me to raise my hands. A ball of light formed there, and I concentrated on spreading it in front of me, flattening it like a pancake.

The light spread out until it became a glowing wall before me. I could still see through it to the other side.

Luc abruptly stopped his lightning tornado, and he dropped back onto his feet with practiced ease. "Hey, that's really cool."

I thought so too, even if it did require a bit of concentration to hold the wall in place. I let out a heavy breath. "I'm gonna lose it."

"Wait." He lifted one of his hands and, aiming his fingers just to the left of me, let loose a streak of lighting. It slammed into the wall and harmlessly dissipated. The contact stole my remaining energy from me, however, and left me reeling with dizziness that probably had as much to do with the alcohol I'd consumed as it did my powers.

Panting, I leaned over to rest my hands on my thighs. "That was hard."

"That was great," he said enthusiastically. "You can form your own protective barrier."

The world did a little spin as I straightened. I stood there, swaying, until everything fell back into place and I only saw one Luc instead of two.

He was standing a lot closer than before, and the way he was looking at me sent a shiver of excitement racing down my body.

"What is it?" I asked, self-consciously smoothing my hair.

Luc grinned and lifted his hand to my face. I sucked in my breath when his fingers brushed my cheek, smoothing away a strand of hair that had caught in my mouth. A tremor stole through me at the contact.

"You have no idea how amazing you are," he murmured. "I've never seen a light elemental form a protective wall like that."

"Really?" My inner lie detector left no doubt as to his sincerity. It sparked a pleased rush of awareness through my body, but my legs were like jelly and I felt like I was on the verge of crashing. "I couldn't hold it very long, though. It felt like it was stealing the energy from me."

He nodded. "Perfectly normal. Some abilities come more naturally, like your orb. Those will feel energizing, like they make you stronger when you perform them. Others require you to expend a large amount of energy, momentarily weakening you. You'll be back to normal within a few hours."

I'd never heard abilities explained that way before. It made a lot of sense.

"Which power comes most naturally to you?" I

asked him.

"Lightning from my fingertips," he said without hesitation. "I find myself doing it all the time, sometimes without even realizing it. The tornado wears me out though, so I totally get where you're coming from."

The earnestness in his face captivated me. Without even thinking about it, I found myself asking, "What does it feel like when you're using those easy powers? Does it feel, like, sensual?"

His lips twisted. "Like a lover's caress."

"Exactly." My body let out a little shiver, and I realized his voice was doing the very same thing to me right now. I also realized that never in a million years would I have talked to him about this if I hadn't been wasted. No doubt I'd be embarrassed about it tomorrow, but right now, hell, I was too drunk to care. And since that was the case ...

I brought my hand to his face, sliding it along his cheek like he'd just done to me. The whiskers on his face tickled my hand, but it was nothing compared to the flutter of awareness that his skin sparked. "You're beautiful, you know."

He froze, letting out a surprised huff.

"I mean it. You could be, like, a model if you wanted to."

"Jewel," he laughed, his voice containing a note of protest. His eyes hooded, however, like he was waiting for something.

"Yes?" I leaned in, closing the distance between us. My heart pounded hard and fast as the memory of last night flooded me. He'd told me he saw me – the real me.

Maybe he really did. Maybe he saw beyond what I was now … to the possibility of what I could become.

That, more than anything, turned me on.

"Jewel, we shouldn't …"

He trailed off, his eyes blazing with heat, and the residual effect of my powers collided with my hormones, giving birth to a haze of lust that had me snatching at his sweater. Before he could form the words of protest on his lips, I crushed my mouth to his.

He stiffened against me, and for a moment I thought he would push me away. But then his hands were on me, and his tongue was sliding between my lips, invading my mouth with skillful expertise.

I gasped and pressed myself into him. I knew he would be an amazing kisser. There had been no doubt in my mind. But he was even better than I imagined.

His mouth slanted over mine as my fingers wandered beneath his sweater, brushing against the hard heat of his abdomen. The muscles rippled beneath my touch, reminding me of some primal animal. A cougar, perched to strike. I moaned into his mouth, working my way up to his defined pecs.

When my back hit a wall, I broke away from his kiss long enough to see he'd backed me into the thick white column where the telescope rested. My skin started glowing.

Then his hand was in my hair, tugging my head back so he could run his lips down my throat.

I moaned, my hands resuming their wandering beneath his sweater. Every part I touched sparked a tingle in my fingertips, until I could practically feel the buildup of electricity between our bodies.

His hands crept beneath my sweater, then up to close over the mounds of my breasts. He gently squeezed them, his lips brushing my jaw, then kissing the corner of my mouth. "Do you have any idea how much these xcbreasts torture me?"

"Really?" I gasped, arching into his touch.

"Yes." His tongue snaked into my mouth and he kissed me hotly before drawing back to whisper, "Every time I look at them, your nipples are hard. They drive me fucking crazy, like they're begging for my mouth on them."

"Oh my god." The area between my thighs practically thrummed with desire as the image of him doing just that played in my head. His words alone could make me come.

He rubbed his palms all over the sensitive tips of my breasts, cupping and squeezing them.

This was too much. I needed him. I wanted to touch all of him.

Our lips met again, tongues battling each other. His kiss was like the sweetest drug imaginable. It took over every part of me, seared every last bit of my flesh.

I wanted him. God, I wanted him. More than I'd ever wanted anything.

My shaky hands slid down, cupping the hard, impossibly thick erection I felt beneath his jeans. He groaned, arching his hips into my touch ...

And then suddenly he was gone, tearing himself away from me, and I was left standing at the column all alone.

My body ached at his loss. Blinking, I frowned over at him, my voice a confused whisper when I asked, "What's wrong?"

Oh god, it wasn't the liquor on my breath, was it?

Luc made a pained noise deep in his throat, running his hands all over his face, then over his head to the back of his neck. He let out a long sigh, reaching down to adjust himself through his jeans.

I bit back a whimper at the outline of his erection beneath his pants. God, everything about him was perfect, and I wanted more. I wanted it all.

Luc let out a bitter laugh and finally looked at me. "You're drunk. What kind of an asshole would I be if I took advantage of a girl when she wasn't thinking clearly?"

I gave him a puzzled look. "But I want you to."

His lips formed a gentle smile. "Even if she wants me to."

My gaze washed over him, and I realized I wasn't buying it. There was something else. "Last time we, well, *almost* kissed, you said it was a really bad idea."

He nodded. "Still is."

"But why?"

Luc let out a sigh and ran his hand through his hair. "It's a long story."

Translation: one he didn't want to share.

"Luc," I pleaded, taking a step toward him.

He held up a hand to stop my approach. Averting his gaze, he said, "I can't, Jewel. I'm sorry. It was a really bad idea coming here."

Was he really going to leave me hanging high

and dry? I huffed out a breath. "At least tell me why."

"I can't," he murmured. "At least not tonight."

My body shook with residual lust as I watched him retrieve our coats, then hand me mine.

I slid it on, but my vision blurred when I fumbled with the big buttons. I messed with them for a few moments before giving up. Blinking back sexually frustrated tears, I murmured, "The buttons don't want to go into their holes."

Luc let out a low laugh as he zipped up his jacket. Then he moved closer to me, brushing my fingers away. As he worked the buttons closed, he murmured, "I'm sure that has absolutely nothing to do with those Long Island Teas you drank."

"Nope," I said solemnly.

Once he was done, he stepped back a respectful distance, and we headed to the door.

I waited outside, my hands dug deep into my pockets, as he locked the observatory back up. When he turned around, he murmured, "I'm sorry."

A nod was the only response I could give him.

Silently, we headed back toward the Fellowship Hall. Now that the high of our make out session was wearing off, the liquor was starting to kick in full force.

"Coitus interruptus," I murmured.

Luc gave me a sharp glance. "Huh?"

"Nothing." I wasn't making any sense. I wasn't exactly walking a straight line, either. Random patches of grass kept snagging the heels of my boots, making me stumble all over the place. Where the hell had all these potholes come from anyway?

Thankfully, we made it back without incident … and without mentioning what had happened at the observatory.

The moment Luc opened the doors leading into the Fellowship Hall, we heard a low din of voices.

Luc threw me a heavy glance. "That's for you."

The guilt I hadn't felt before finally decided to make its appearance. I slunk through the open door of the common room, blinking past my double vision. The Professor, Sarah, and Deme stood there, and they all looked worried about me.

Oops.

All three of them broke off their speech, and stark relief flooded Deme's face. "Jewel!"

He walked forward and pulled me into a quick embrace before setting me back to lob an angry glare my way. "We were worried about you, woman."

Wincing, I murmured, "Sorry."

"Miss Harris," Professor Raymond said, his voice disapproving, "we searched all over campus for you."

"Well," a soft hiccup escaped me, "you found me."

"If not for Luc's text—" The Professor cut off, a strange look coming to his face. "Are you inebriated?"

"Um …" I guiltily averted my gaze and shifted side-to-side on my feet. "Maybe?"

A sound of disbelief escaped him. "Do you have any idea how concerned we've all been?"

That made me snort, guilt momentarily forgotten. "Okay, *Dad*."

But the moment those words fled my mouth, I remembered my own dad. I remembered all the things that had happened between us these past few weeks and the fact he wasn't even my real birth father.

Tears suddenly began to swim in my vision, and a distinctly tortured expression took over the Professor. Leave it to a woman's tears to make a man uncomfortable.

Deme covered his mouth with his fist and cleared his throat. "Um, I'm going to take Jewel back to her room."

"Good idea," the Professor and Luc said in unison.

I threw Luc a dirty glance, but when Deme grasped my arm, I allowed him to turn me around and lead me out of the room. The truth was, my bed was sounding pretty good right about now.

Deme brought me outside the building and over to the secret entrance into the bunker. A flood of emotions took over me as he dug the key out of my pocket and unlocked the door. "I love you, Deme. You're like my family."

He gave me an amused glance. "I know."

I didn't even pretend I could navigate the stairs by myself. I leaned on Deme heavily as we stumbled down them, inhaling the familiar scent of his cologne. "I can't believe you're an elemental."

"You're one, too."

"Oh, yeah."

Silent tears began to fall down my face as Deme led me to the corridor containing the bedrooms. His arm around me for support, he murmured, "What's wrong, chica?"

"I don't know." I let out a hiccup. "I think I'm drunk."

Deme let out a hearty laugh. "I think you're right."

He half carried me inside my room, and I staggered over to the bed while he turned to close the door, giving us privacy.

The room spun as I struggled out of my coat and sat down hard on the bed. I swallowed compulsively and tried to blink my vision back into place, but it didn't work. My stomach gave a sudden roil. I clutched it and let out a groan. "Oh god, I think I'm going to be sick."

Eyes widening, his gaze scoured the room. He spotted the tiny waste can by the desk and snatched it up, turning it over to dump out the few scraps of paper inside before bringing it to me. "Here."

Leaning forward, I managed to get my head over the trash can just in time for the contents of my stomach to come exploding up through my throat.

Deme made a comforting sound as he held onto the waste basket with one hand, twisting my hair into a knot with the other to get it out of the way. "There, there. Get it out."

Tears rolled down my face as I puked until there was nothing left. Then I continued dry heaving, letting out an agonized moan. "Long Island Iced Tea is the devil."

He laughed softly. "Leave it to you to go big."

"Well, the occasion seemed to call for it," I managed to gasp.

We looked at each other and burst out laughing.

More tears rolled down my face as I kept laughing, clutching my stomach until, eventually, the laughter turned into deep, racking sobs.

With a soothing murmur, Deme set the waste can by the door and then sat on the bed to envelop me in his arms. "I'm so sorry, Jewel. For all this stuff happening to you. You know how much I love you."

"I know. I love you, too." I threw my arms over his shoulders, burying my face in his chest. "Sorry. I'm feeling a little emotional right now."

Deme sighed, hugging me tighter to him. "You never have to apologize to me, woman. You know that."

We sat there for several long moments before Deme spoke again. "You have no idea how much it killed me to lie to you all these years. But I made an oath, back when I was too young to even understand what the consequences would be. I made it to my *abuela*. You know what that means. You know me better than anyone."

"I know," I whispered. "I get it."

I totally did. Deme had grown up in a matriarchal family. His grandmother's word was law. More than that, he loved her fiercely and respected her wholly. Yes, I knew what an oath to his grandma meant.

A dull, throbbing pain had set in at my temples, and now that my stomach was empty, I found it hard to keep my eyes open. I let them flutter shut, only opening them at some point when Deme shifted me off his shoulder and all the way onto the bed.

"Don't leave," I murmured, still half asleep. "I don't want to be alone tonight."

"I won't," he assured me, laying down beside me.

"Good." I allowed my eyes to shut once more and gave myself over to unconsciousness.

Chapter 16

WHEN I woke up the next morning to the lingering smell of vomit, it did nothing to calm the queasiness in my stomach. Sometime during the night Deme had taken my shoes off and thrown a blanket over me. Although the other side of the bed still held the impression of his body, he wasn't in the room. I sat up with a groan, swallowing compulsively when the room began to spin again.

"Crap." An idea crept to my head and I raised my hands, willing a ball of light to form there. It was getting easier and easier for me to control it. This time I had no problem making it explode above me, showering me with a burst of energy. It made me feel marginally better, but it did nothing for my headache and my stomach still turned. "Great."

I crawled out of bed, managing to note that Deme had emptied and cleaned out the trash can while I slept. If that wasn't loyalty from a best friend, I didn't know what was. I wasn't even sure if I would've been able to return the favor, had the tables been turned.

After stumbling into the—*thank god!*—empty bathroom and scrubbing my body head-to-toe with soap and my teeth with about a gallon of toothpaste,

I dressed and headed to the kitchen. Several different voices floated out from behind the double doors leading into the great room with all the tables, chairs, and bookcases. Curiosity almost prompted me to go straight in there, but the queasiness in my stomach made me rethink that. I needed toast first.

I padded into the kitchen and slid two slices of bread into the toaster, then downed about a gallon of water while waiting for it to pop up. Part of me wanted to hurry so I could go see what was going on in the other room, but I knew if I didn't eat something first I might end up dry heaving in front of everyone. As it was, my stomach did large rolling flops as I forced the toast down.

"Oh god," I groaned. "Never. Drinking. Again."

Right now, I meant it. Although the liquor had helped to take my mind off my problems for a brief period, in the end it had been more trouble than it was worth. Nothing had been resolved, and all I had to show for last night was a headache that wouldn't quit throbbing.

After forcing myself to drink two more glasses of water, I got up with a wince and wandered through the swinging doors of the kitchen, then pushed open one of the double doors into the great room. Conversation cut off as several pairs of eyes looked my way. Swallowing hard, I took in the familiar faces of the Professor and Deme, along with Luc, Aeron, Kai, and Thea. They all sat at one of the rectangular tables, and based on their heated tones, they'd been debating something right before I walked in.

When Luc wouldn't quite look at me, my heart

fell. He regretted what happened last night. Given that I only wanted to repeat it, his reaction totally sucked.

Aeron was the first to break the silence. "Morning, Jewel. How are you doing?"

Grunting, I shuffled to the first empty seat I could find. I figured his question didn't really need an answer. They could probably see I felt as shitty as I looked. "What's going on?"

When no one immediately answered, I got the sense they didn't particularly want to tell me. My gaze landed on Deme and I raised a brow, silently daring him to keep me out of the loop. As I expected, he told me.

"We're discussing what I learned during my visits to the Fates, and we decided I should speak to my grandma about it."

Professor Raymond stiffened like he didn't necessarily approve of my being told, but I was too busy thinking about what Deme had just said to care. His grandma was old school. Like, when I say old school, she may have been around before school was invented.

Modern technology wasn't really her thing. She didn't even have a television, much less a cell phone, or even a landline. I remembered she'd gotten one once, when Deme was about thirteen years old, but she'd complained that she feared it was damaging to her ears, so she'd gotten rid of it just as quickly.

Growing up, whenever Deme had wanted to talk to his grandma, he'd have to go visit her at her apartment in the Bronx. And I guessed that hadn't changed.

"You're going to the Bronx? Like, today?"

He nodded.

I sat up straighter in my chair, fighting back a wince at the pain behind my temples. "Then I'm going, too."

"No," Professor Raymond said immediately. "It's too dangerous. Lord Adrian's men are still looking for you."

"Then give me a spell of protection or something." I didn't know if that was possible, but I was willing to bet if there was a will, there was a way.

When the Professor opened his mouth to protest again, I cut him off. "This whole situation involves me, and I want to hear what she has to say firsthand."

The Professor sighed. "There's no need—"

"I'm going and that's final." I crossed my arms for emphasis. It occurred to me I probably looked like a sullen teenager throwing a fit, but I didn't care. They weren't leaving me out this time. I would fight to go with everything I had.

For a long moment, no one spoke. Then Luc's voice broke the silence. "The president of the university is a mage, right? We could ask her to make Jewel look like someone else. And some of us could go with them, to make sure she's safe."

Happy he'd stuck up for me, I shot him a grateful look. But he didn't so much as glance my way.

Awesome.

A sudden horrifying thought occurred to me. I

remembered everything that had happened last night, but I'd been sloppy drunk at the time. Plus, I didn't have any real experience with making out. Maybe I really sucked at it.

Holy crap balls, please don't let that be it.

Trying not to hyperventilate, I forced the thought from my head as I turned to the Professor. "See? We can do *that*. Because like it or not, I'm going. I'm tired of being trapped here on campus, feeling like everyone but me knows all there is to know about *me*."

I wasn't going to sit back and let them handle everything while I buried my head in the sand. Not anymore.

When the Professor closed his eyes and let out a longer sigh, I knew I had him. "Okay, fine. But Luc, Aeron, and Kai will have to go with you, to make sure you're protected at all times."

Part of me chafed at the insinuation that I couldn't keep myself safe, but I forced myself to ignore it. I had to be practical here. Like it or not, some really creepy psycho was after me. Having extra people around to make sure he didn't get me was the safe call.

His face glum but resigned, Professor Raymond rose from the table. "I'll go contact the president and arrange for the spell."

Luc nodded, then glanced over at Kai. "Let's go check in with the other guardians before we go, to make sure there haven't been any new sightings we haven't heard about."

It didn't escape me that he hadn't met my gaze even once as they rose and started after the

Professor, disappearing up the stairs that led outside.

Gritting my teeth, I managed to wait until they'd all gone before giving in to the wave of nausea that threatened to make me heave the newly derived contents of my stomach onto the floor. Groaning, I leaned back in my chair and covered my eyes. "I don't understand why people drink. It's like voluntarily agreeing to take a fieldtrip into the fiery depths of Hell."

Aeron let out a low chuckle. "Been there."

"You should still be sleeping, woman," Deme chided.

I gave him a look that said, "I don't think so." I was going, whether any of them wanted me to or not.

Aaron's fingers drummed on the tabletop as he gazed over at Thea. "Hey, why don't you heal her?"

Oh. Yeah. I guess I sort of figured her abilities only worked for bigger injuries, like broken bones or bleeding wounds. But if she could take care of killer hangovers too, that would make my day infinitely easier.

I glanced over at her hopefully, but the bitchy look on her face killed any expectations I had of her helping me out.

Thea gave an amused scoff, her wavy blonde hair falling partially over one eye as she leaned back in her chair. "What would be the lesson in that?"

"Don't be a bitch," Aeron snapped, heat blazing in his eyes. "Just heal her, will you?"

She scowled, then threw her hands up in

exasperation when both Aeron and Deme glared at her. "Fine." She stood and stomped over to me, looking like she had just swallowed a lemon as she reluctantly placed her fingers on my temples.

I froze at the contact, unease running through me at our proximity. The hostility emanating from her was so in conflict with the honey scent of her hair hanging in my face that I didn't know whether to run away or inhale deeply. But then brilliant light surrounded my vision, and her fingertips heated to a near scorching temperature that had me sucking in my breath. Just when the heat grew so uncomfortable that I began to doubt she was really helping me, the light turned into a blinding flash and my headache vanished.

Discombobulated by the flash of light, I swayed in my chair, noting that Thea had moved away from me while the issue of not being able to see held most of my attention. I blinked several times until my vision corrected itself, then placed my fingers where Thea's had just been.

Amazing. A second ago I'd felt like I was on the brink of death, but now I felt perfectly normal. Better than normal, even. I felt well rested, though that certainly wasn't the case.

"Whoa." Momentarily forgetting her dislike for me, I shot Thea a grateful smile. "That was awesome. I feel great. Thank you so much."

Her face softened just a tad and she murmured, "You're welcome." But then her prune-face reappeared and she whirled about, stalking off in the direction of the bedrooms.

It might have been my imagination, but she

didn't seem quite so hostile anymore. Or more likely, I'd gotten something like Stockholm Syndrome out of gratitude for how good she made me feel. Either way, I decided I'd go with it. I felt too good to do anything else.

With renewed vigor, I stretched my arms above my head and grinned over at Deme and Aeron. "So, when are we going?"

Less than three hours later, I wore a whole new body as I sat on the subway train with Deme heading into the Bronx. After visiting the school's president to be outfitted with an illusory spell that made me look like someone else entirely—as well as a caution to be careful—me and Deme, along with Luc, Aeron, and Kai boarded a few different buses before finally hopping on the train heading into the South Bronx. Deme's grandma lived in a sketchy neighborhood on the Grand Concourse. I'd only been there a couple of times before, and each time I had to hide it from my father so he wouldn't worry about my safety. Deme's mother was forever trying to get his grandma to migrate over to Brooklyn, where she'd moved with Deme when he was three years old, but she always refused. The Bronx was where she'd lived most of her life, and no part of it frightened her.

Of course, knowing what I knew about her now, I could sort of see why. From what I'd found out, she was a very powerful elemental. Your garden variety street thugs were probably nothing more than a minor annoyance for her.

Although everyone had been on high alert during our bus rides, nothing had happened, and we all relaxed a fraction. Once we boarded the train, Aeron and Kai set off in different directions to patrol the other cars, while Luc retreated to the far end of the car we rode in now, his hawkeyed gaze vigilant as he kept an eye out for any trouble. That left me and Deme sitting alone in the center of the semi-crowded train car.

Deme gave me another strange look as we sat in silence, the train rocking side to side on the tracks while we sped along.

"Not used to it yet?" I asked with a hidden grin.

"No, it's crazy." He shook his head. "I mean, if I didn't know …"

Yeah, I got it. I looked totally different. Rather than my typical slender, dark-haired self, I now wore the body of a pudgy, middle-aged woman with blonde, shoulder-length frizzy hair. It was really strange. I kept reaching down to pat my generous-looking thighs, and even though I knew they weren't really there, it was totally surreal for my hands to pass straight through where the flesh appeared to be. Thankfully anyone looking my way wouldn't see anything unnatural, or so I had been assured.

"I caught a glimpse of my reflection in the window when we hopped on the train and almost shrieked in surprise," I whispered to Deme.

He let out a laugh, shaking his head.

I hadn't mentioned it, but Deme also looked very different from his normal self. He wasn't wearing a fake body like I was, but he'd washed all the color from his hair and schooled it into a bland hairstyle. The heavy eyeliner he normally wore was gone, and so were his grungy, unisex clothes. He almost looked preppy today, so opposite from what he usually looked like that I was sure Luc or Aeron or one of the others would mention it. But if they noted anything amiss, they too decided not to comment on it.

I was grateful for that. It had always been like this when Deme visited his grandma, and it always made me sad. I hated that Deme felt he had to hide who he was from anyone, much less a family member he loved so intensely.

Deme wrung his hands as he blindly stared out in front of us, lost in his own thoughts. I don't think he even realized he was doing it, but I'd seen it enough to know it was his nervous tick. He'd done it before going out on stage to play Pan in our school play, he did it whenever we went higher than three stories in a building, and he did it every time he went to visit his grandmother.

My heart wrenched for him. Now that everything was out in the open between us, I was beginning to realize his whole life had been about hiding. His grandmother had forced a promise from him to lie to me, and maybe that had set the stage for how he thought he should behave.

Well, that was no way for anyone to live, and now that I knew the truth about Deme's elemental heritage, maybe it was time for all his barriers to come down. He was an amazing person, and he deserved to be able to show that person to everyone in his life.

The subway train rumbled along the tracks, the screeching of the rails too loud in my ears as I thought this over. Should I say something?

For several long minutes, I wavered with indecision. But the conflicted look on his face was killing me.

Finally, I knew I had to address it. I had to say *something*. I took a breath, my heart pitter pattering in my chest.

"You know, I don't think she'll care," I said, my voice so soft I knew no one else in the train car would be able to hear me.

He frowned and came back to the present, sliding his gaze back over me. "About what?"

I took a deep, steadying breath. "That you're gay."

Deme reeled in shock, and his ears began to turn a deep, bright red.

For one scared moment I feared I'd made a big mistake. I spoke way too soon. Outed him before he was ready to admit it even to himself.

But then he exhaled, and as his shoulders dropped, the biggest look of relief I've ever seen transformed his features.

"How long have you known?"

The train shook on a turn as I reached across the space between us and placed my hand on top of his. "Probably just as long as you have."

Deme appeared to process my words, then shot me a grateful smile. But almost as quick, his eyes took on that faraway look once more. The corners of his mouth turned down. "I don't think abuela will feel the same. Or mamá. You don't understand how things are in my family."

"I do a little bit." I knew enough about his culture to know they were old fashioned about certain things. This might throw his grandmother for a loop. But I also knew just how much she loved him. She would understand. She had to.

"They'll always love you, no matter what. That much I know."

He nudged my shoulder with a brief smile. "Thanks."

Twenty more minutes passed before the train deposited us at the appropriate station. With me and Deme leading the way and the others following a safe distance behind, we made our way up the steps and out into the cold, dirty streets of the South Bronx.

I caught a glimpse of Aeron sliding his sunglasses on his face the moment we stepped out into the street. He'd put them on as soon as we left the Fellowship Hall too, and I'd had a good laugh over it. I mean, it was about thirty degrees outside and the sun had taken up permanent residence behind an enormous white cloud.

But then he'd informed me that, as a Netheren, he was extra-sensitive to sunlight, and my amusement had morphed into embarrassment.

Lesson learned. When it came to elementals, it was always better to ask before assuming.

My body tensed as we began walking the three blocks to Deme's grandma's house. I couldn't help it. Even though I now knew I had more than a few little defensive tricks up my sleeve, the neighborhood had always frightened me. And *that* always made me ashamed.

I might look different now, but all those feelings raging inside me were still the same. I didn't know if the others had ever been in this neighborhood, and I was more than a little curious to see what they thought.

I peeked behind me to where Luc, Aeron, and Kai followed us, but their nonchalant expressions told me they too found nothing scary about the people we passed or the decayed old buildings surrounding us.

We finally arrived at the eight-story building that served as Deme's grandma's house for the past fifty years. I gave Luc another quick glance and he finally looked at me, giving me a sharp nod before casually leaning against the side of the building right next to the entrance. As we had discussed prior to leaving, Aeron and Kai also took their spots outside.

Only Deme and I were going up to see his grandma. Deme didn't want to bombard her with too many strangers, and while my face might not be familiar to her, she'd at least already met me.

"Stairs," we said to each other the moment we stepped inside. Though I'd only been there a couple of times, I remembered how finicky the elevator was.

Laughing, Deme led the way.

His grandmother lived on the second floor, in Apartment 2F. I remembered the heavy metal door being red, but it had been painted green sometime since I'd last been here. Deme knocked on it, and we waited for what seemed like forever for his grandmother to shuffle her way over to the door and peek out the eyehole.

"Quién es?" she barked out.

Deme turned and shot me a wry look I easily read even though he hadn't said anything out loud.

Why bother looking out the peephole if you can't see?

I stifled a laugh as he turned back to answer, "Soy yo, abuela. Demetrio."

"Ay, Deme," she cooed, "mi hijo."

The rattling of chains sounded out from the other side of the door. I counted three different sets before the first of the two deadbolts began to unlock. His grandmother might not be afraid of this neighborhood, but she wasn't stupid either.

The door finally flung open to reveal Deme's grandmother. All of four-foot-ten and a hundred pounds soaking wet, she had a round tummy accentuated by the muumuu she wore. Her ash gray hair hung in wiry rivulets almost to her shoulders, and she wore large, tortoiseshell glasses that made her eyes look half the size of her entire face.

I didn't know how old she was exactly, but I placed her anywhere between eighty-five and a hundred years old. She looked like a typical grandma, complete with slight hunch in her back, but only a fool would miss the ancient wisdom in her eyes. Now that I saw her for what she truly was, I knew I'd *been* that fool all along.

She folded Deme into her arms, even as her gaze met mine. Pulling back, she began speaking in her heavily-accented English for my benefit.

"Deme, it's been too long since you came to

visit. You know I worry."

Deme fidgeted and dropped his gaze at the mild scolding. "I'm sorry, abuela. You know I just started college upstate. It's been a crazy few months."

"I know." She said it as if she knew exactly what he'd been up to. Stepping back from the doorway, she addressed both of us. "Come in."

I followed Deme inside, and we waited for his grandmother to close and lock the door. Once she turned back to face us, Deme motioned toward me. "Abuela, this is—"

"I know," she interrupted calmly, gazing at me. "Es Jewel."

I threw Deme an amazed glance before whispering, "How did you know?"

"Part of my elemental powers," she answered evenly. "I can see through glamours."

She turned and headed down the short hallway toward the kitchen with its tiny attached dining space. "Quieres café?" she called behind her.

"Coffee?" Deme asked me, lifting one brow.

I shook my head. "No, thanks." With the bomb she'd just dropped on me, I felt wired enough already.

"No gracias, abuela," Deme said to his grandmother as he led me to her small round table. A sense of déjà vu hit me as we settled on the padded wooden seats. I'd sat here before on the other two occasions I visited with Deme, sipping on coffee or tea while the two of them caught up. This was a very different sort of occasion, though.

Deme's grandma poured herself a cup of coffee

and grabbed a spoon from her silverware drawer before turning and shuffling over. She set the cup and spoon on the table, then slowly sat on one of the vacant chairs. Deme immediately rose to scoot her chair in for her.

She dropped a couple of cubes from the sugar container in her cup, along with the spoon. Her eyes were on me the entire time, even as she took her fingers off the spoon and it began to stir the sugar all by itself.

My eyes bulged and I looked over at Deme, who shrugged. Guess he'd seen this parlor trick before, but for me it was a total surprise.

"So, Jewel," she said bluntly. "I see you've learned the truth about your heritage."

Chapter 17

I GAZED at Deme's grandma as her words washed over me. There was something so matter-of-fact about her tone, as if she'd known I would someday uncover the truth. For some reason, it reminded me that she'd been the one to bind my powers in the first place. A glimmer of anger wound through me, making me mutter, "No thanks to anyone else."

Deme bristled at my tone. "Jewel."

His grandmother didn't seem the least bit offended, though. Her gaze was direct as she closed her fingers around the cup. The spoon flew out of it and set itself gently onto the table beside her. "You were in much danger as a bebé. Helpless. It was my moral duty to protect you however I could."

Her even-handed explanation drew the fire right out of me. She was right, of course. I didn't have to like what they'd done to me, but I understood on a basic level they were protecting a defenseless child the best way they knew how.

"Well, now I know. My powers were released."

When she lifted one gray brow, I understood her silent question.

"Someone from Netheren broke his way through the campus barrier and injected me with something that wiped away the binding."

She made a soft noise in her throat as she lifted her cup. "Lord Adrian knows your identity now? This is why you are here disguised in another body?"

Deme brushed his hair back on his forehead, absently mussing the hairstyle he'd so carefully created. "We don't know if he's figured out exactly who she is yet. The Guard has received reports of similar attacks in other safe zones, so it seems like he's just targeting those who fit a certain profile."

My gaze flew to Deme. I hadn't heard that, but it made a lot of sense.

His grandmother nodded. "Sí, young women around her age who reside in safe zones and have dark hair and brilliant blue eyes. How many of those could there be?"

"Less than a dozen all over the world," he murmured, his gaze far away.

"Then it is only a matter of time until he figures out who she is," Deme's grandmother said.

Her no-nonsense tone sparked a tremor through my veins. My power unfurled beneath my skin, as if gearing up to keep me safe.

I honestly hadn't considered he would eventually uncover my identity. I'd sort of figured the Dark Lord had been blindly stumbling around when he'd sent the man in black after me. But now I knew that wasn't anywhere near the truth.

He was *close.*

"How do we stop him?" I whispered.

She looked at me as if I was dense. "Don't get caught."

Deme interjected before I could say anything

else. "Abuela, I went to el Valle de la Muerte."

Despite my limited understanding of Spanish, I knew he was telling her about Death Valley, about his experience with the Fates.

"Sí?" Her hand trembled as she lifted the cup to her lips for a long sip. "What did they tell you?"

He briefly looked over at me. "I couldn't make sense of their words."

"This is normal," she said dismissively.

Deme's lips twisted into an ironic smile. "They said, 'When past is past, imbalance is struck, battle begins. Light or dark, savior or destroyer, the die is cast as time goes past.'"

Her eyes took on a distant glaze and she set her cup onto the table with a rattle. "Hmm ..."

When several minutes passed without her moving or speaking, Deme gave me an impatient look. "Abuela? Does that mean anything to you?"

"Podría ser," she murmured.

He glanced over at me and translated, "Maybe."

Another long pause had me perched on the edge of my seat. I wanted to shake her by the shoulders and scream, "What, old lady? What is it?" But I knew that would help absolutely no one. Instead I dug my fingernails into my hands and pursed my lips, anxiously waiting for her to say something.

"It's unclear," she finally pronounced. "But if my hunch is correct, this is another piece to the chaos prophecy."

"The chaos prophecy?" I asked, scratching my eyebrow. I remembered the Professor mentioning it, but I couldn't remember the exact words.

Deme read my face. "The prophecy copied from

the Book of Fates before it was lost to our kind. It said, 'Should two elements ever be joined, any progeny resulting from such a union will become the seventh element: chaos. Chaos shall reign supreme.'"

I leaned toward Deme's grandmother. "These Fates were referring to that prophecy?"

"Perhaps. But if so …" She trailed off, the glazed look creeping back into her eyes.

My temper was growing short now. "If so, then what?"

"If so, then the prophecy as we know it is incomplete," she said. "It doesn't represent a destruction of worlds, as we thought. At least not necessarily."

Deme's forehead scrunched. "Then what does it represent? Because it seems pretty doomsday to me."

"It represents a choice," she answered, giving a definitive nod. "That's all I can say about it now."

Her gaze moved over to me and something akin to curiosity sparkled there. "Are you learning to control your powers?"

Startled by the sudden change of topic, I nodded. "I'm working on it."

"Good." Her look became appraising. "You have much strength in you; I sensed it even as a bebé."

"Um … thanks?"

"Abuela," Deme asked, "is there anything else you can tell me?"

"No, mi hijo. There's a limit even to my abilities. Now, tell me about school. How are your grades?"

With those words, it seemed she was done

discussing it. No matter how many times he tried to redirect her, she kept going back to Deme and his college experience. So, after another forty-five minutes of conversation, Deme told his grandmother it was time for us to leave.

She didn't press the matter, merely nodded and began to rise from her chair. Deme scrambled to his feet and helped her to stand all the way.

As she shuffled over to the front door, she said, "Be careful, Deme. There is terrible unrest right now con los elementales."

"I will, abuela," he said dutifully. When she paused at the door and turned to him, he wrapped his arms around her for a big hug. "You take care of yourself, too. I'll be back as soon as I can."

"I know." She gave him a reassuring smile as she pulled away. "No te preocupes; your mamá comes to see me almost every day."

Then she turned to me and, to my surprise, her arms closed around me as well. Although she'd been friendly the last two times we met, she never initiated physical contact before. Her grip was surprisingly strong, pulling me toward her. She whispered in my ear, her words barely audible. "Stay always to the light."

When I pulled back to give her a questioning look, she gave me a direct nod, then turned to unlock the door.

Outside her apartment, we waited until all her deadbolts clicked shut and the three sets of chains rattled into place before heading toward the stairwell. I couldn't stop thinking about that spoon stirring all by itself, so the moment I ascertained we were totally alone, I asked him, "Your grandma does magic?"

"She can manipulate metal," Deme said with a shrug. "Most earth elementals can."

I lifted both my brows. "You too?"

He gave me a sheepish shrug, and I took that as a yes.

Well, count my mind blown. There was so much I needed to learn about the elemental world. But first I needed to finish learning about myself.

Deme looked over at me curiously. "Hey, what did my grandmother whisper to you right before we left?"

I thought back to her words and hesitated. For some reason, I felt compelled not to share. I didn't know why, but the words seemed liked they had been meant just for me.

I gave him a tight smile. "She told me to watch out for myself."

"Oh." Taking me at my word, he gave me a nod and then started down the stairs.

Luc, Aeron, and Kai were outside the building just where we'd left them. Luc was frowning into his cell phone when we walked out.

"Something wrong?" I asked him.

"Nah," he said, his expression distant. "I've been trying to reach the Professor. His office phone isn't ringing, and his cell phone keeps going straight to voicemail."

"Could he be teaching a class?" I asked.

Luc shook his head. "Not for another two hours."

"Maybe his battery's dead," Deme said.

"Yeah. Maybe." He didn't sound like he believed

it, but he schooled his face into a grin anyway, looking at Deme. Or rather, *not* at me. "Did you guys get your riddle solved?"

Frustration was evident in Deme's tone when he said, "Not quite. Just more mysterious words."

"Ain't that how it always goes?" Smirking, Luc nodded his head toward the direction of the train station. "Come on. Let's get back to campus and let the Professor know what you found out."

The return journey was uneventful. Luc, Aeron, and Kai resumed their watcher duties on the train, leaving me and Deme to sit by ourselves again. Since Deme seemed lost in his own world, it gave me plenty of time to mull over what his grandmother had said to us.

According to her, the chaos prophecy didn't represent destruction, but rather a choice.

What did that mean? And why did her hawkish gaze appear to be holding on to secrets when she looked at me?

She said I was strong, and god, how I wanted to be. But right now, the last thing I felt was strong. More like confused. Uncertain. Weary.

The sun crept low on the horizon by the time we hopped onto the final bus that would take us back to MU. We were a few minutes outside of campus when my phone rang. I dug it out of my pocket to see it was my Dad calling. He was supposed to be visiting me on campus tomorrow, but maybe he'd decided to come early.

Answering, I said, "Hey Dad, what's up?"

"Jewel." His voice was low, worried. "Is everything okay?"

The edge in his tone made me sit up straighter. "Yeah. Why?"

He hesitated for a moment. "I think I'm being followed."

"What?"

Deme leaned forward, murmuring into my ear. "What's wrong?"

Holding up a finger, I waited for my father's response.

"I don't know. Just glimpses here and there out of the corner of my eye. A bad feeling."

Absently biting down on a fingernail, I whispered, "What are you going to do?"

"I spoke with Theobald earlier today. The guardian who's been tailing me is here with me now. We're at my house packing some things, and then we're going to a safe house a few hours away."

"Good." My voice trembled when I said, "I want to see you."

"You will. I believe Theobald plans to gather you and some of the other guardians and meet us out here."

Relief flowed through me. I didn't want him to be going through something like this alone. Not when I was the cause of it.

"I have to go, pumpkin, but I'll see you soon."

"Okay, Dad." I squeezed the phone tightly. "Be careful."

"You, too. Love you."

"Love you."

After hanging up, I relayed what my father had told me to Deme. He looked worried, but he said, "Don't worry, Jewel. He'll be fine."

I appreciated his attempt to reassure me, but I couldn't help my anxiety.

The bus was starting to pull into its stop in front of campus. I rose and made my way to Luc, who stood by the door, before any of the other passengers could get up. I quietly told him what my father had told me and he nodded, his gaze alert.

"Okay. Let's keep our guard up. We'll find the Professor and figure this out."

After the bus stopped, we all disembarked. The soft atmospheric buzz of the barrier protecting the school wafted over to me. It looked so peaceful on the other side of the barrier, not more than two hundred feet ahead. The green of the lawn was just a tad more brilliant, the colors of the changing autumn leaves slightly more vibrant.

The moment the bus pulled away, something strange crept into the air, darkening the sky just above us. A harsh breeze began to blow, as if we were about to be hit by a sudden storm.

Before I could even process it, whatever this strange thing was spread over the campus, making my eardrums pop and adding a bite of chill to the air.

Luc and Deme, who stood on either side of me, immediately tensed. Electricity shot from Luc's fingers, discharging harmlessly into the ground as he scanned our surroundings. He didn't even seem aware of it. "We're under attack!"

Shock rooted me to my spot. "What?"

"Get her out of here!" Luc yelled to Aeron.

Before I could do more than blink, Aeron propelled himself in front of me, wrapping his arms protectively around my waist. Despite the shock and confusion winding through me, I couldn't help but note he smelled like incense. But then I caught a glimpse of Luc lifting his hands high, drawing streams of lightning from each of his fingertips with such ease and power, that I realized he'd been holding back when it came to sparring with me.

Kai sprang into place beside him, a swirling whirlpool of water forming right in front of them, while Deme opened his hands, palms down, and the ground in front of us began to churn and bubble upward.

"What's happenin—"

I cut off with a surprised cry as a large group of men in black appeared from the woods to the right of us, seemingly materializing out of thin air. They looked like blurry, black blobs as they raced toward us. I couldn't even tell how many of them there were.

Pure stark terror electrified my body, which began to glow brightly.

"Stop glowing," Aeron hissed urgently.

"Why?" I didn't even know if I *could* stop. Every inch of my body felt as if the power beneath the surface wanted to explode. It was the most disconcerting feeling, like I was about to spontaneously combust. Considering we were under attack, it wasn't a bad thing.

Was it?

Instead of answering me, Aeron wrapped his arms tighter around me, and suddenly my glow was masked in a syrupy darkness. Leading me away from the others, he broke into a run. Everything around me blurred, and then we were standing inside campus, a hundred feet away from them.

Luc and Kai hurled lighting and ribbons of water at the guys in black, while Deme formed hard bricks with the earth he'd churned up. With every flick of his wrists, the bricks would connect with some of the men in black, knocking them to the ground.

As I watched in helpless horror, a stream of lightning struck one of the men in black. He screamed and burst into a cloud of gray inkiness. But then two guys stepped forward and began casting dark shadows that swallowed up every bit of energy they touched.

Discombobulated, I swayed in Aeron's arms. How had we run so fast? "What's happenin—?"

My words cut off as he moved again. The world blurred once more.

Another shocked blink revealed we were now closer to one hundred-fifty feet away.

"The barrier is down around campus," Aeron said, his voice low. "We're under attack."

The barrier? Had that been the cause of the weird popping in my eardrums?

A shout sounded from where Luc and Kai stood, and I glanced back to see two more people had joined to fight the mass of guys in black. That did nothing to ease my fears, though. It looked like there were still twenty guys compared to the few we had.

"Oh my god, there's too many of them." Without even thinking about it, I tried to wrench out of Aeron's arms. "We have to help!"

"No! There are more guardians on the way."

Even as he pulled me back to him, three more fighters jumped in to aid Luc and Kai.

"But they're still outnumbered!"

"Jewel." He shook me until I met his gaze. "We can't let them get you under any circumstances."

The truth of his words settled into me as he again hugged me tight. The world dematerialized, only to reappear a mere moment later. Then it happened again, and again.

In what seemed like seconds, we were all the way across campus just inside the doors of the Fellowship Hall.

At last Aeron set me free, gently holding onto my elbows so I could regain my sense of balance. I stared at him blankly while the world righted itself. "What just happened? How did we get here so fast?"

"I can sift through space," he said. "My body just sort of slides through it. Not far, just a few dozen feet at a time. Anyone I'm holding onto comes along for the ride."

"Whoa," I murmured. Then I remembered the darkness that had surrounded us. "What about the black stuff that masked my glow?"

Sensing my vision was settled, he let go of my elbows. "It allows me to shade myself and those around me in darkness."

A disbelieving laugh crept from my throat. "Is that why the guys who attacked us looked like black blobs?"

"Yes. Most dark elementals have the ability. It makes it more difficult for the enemy to strike us down."

A fresh wave of fear hit me as I thought about Deme out there in the fray, along with Luc and Kai. "What are we going to do? We can't just leave them out there!"

"Jewel." His hands settled over my shoulders, his gaze calm. "They're fighters. Don't worry about them."

The truth of his words penetrated me. He was right, of course. As members of the Guard, Luc and Kai were probably well equipped to handle battle. "But there are so many of them. And Deme! He's not one of the Guard."

"There might be more Netheren, but we have the advantage of having elementals from different worlds. Our abilities are much greater when we work together. They don't stand a chance."

His matter-of-fact tone gave me pause.

"And believe me, Deme can take care of himself. His bloodline is powerful. Look at his grandmother. You don't get to be an old elemental like her without having immense strength."

"Really?" I whispered. His words made sense. Beyond that, I so badly wanted to believe them.

Aeron gave me a reassuring smile. "Truly."

The soft pound of shoes against the wooden floors alerted us that someone was racing toward us from deeper inside the building. Aeron tensed and pushed me behind him, just as a figure rounded a corner and came into view.

Aeron's shoulders softened in relief. "Professor!"

Professor Raymond wore his usual button-down dress shirt and slacks, which made it all the weirder to see him running toward us like he was on a track field. He held a briefcase in one hand and used the other to push his glasses back on the bridge of his nose. "They've breached the campus!"

There seemed no point in acknowledging such an obvious statement, so instead I shouted at him, "What are we going to do?"

"Get outside." He waved us toward the door we'd just come in through. "He should be there by now."

"Who?"

Neither of them bothered answering. Instead, Aeron grabbed my wrist and raced through the door.

There was no one outside, but I could see through the darkening night that the battle had extended onto the campus. It now reached the other side of the expansive green lawn. There were even more dark elementals than before, but also more students fighting alongside the guardians.

My heart pounded frantically in my chest as I watched. It did look like we had the upper hand. While some of the Netheren seemed able to block or dissipate powers, and they clearly had the advantage of the growing nighttime, there were simply too many different things coming at them—air, light, water, fire, and earth—for them to fight them all.

The Professor halted behind us, just as Payton came running from the side of the building that housed the entrance to the bunker. His bright red mohawk glimmered under the outdoor lights as he raced toward us.

He screeched to a stop in front of the two steps leading into the building and looked up at us. "Ready?"

I guess he was who we were waiting for. But I didn't understand what we were going to do now. I looked around, as if that would solve the mystery. "Ready for what?"

Payton gave me a cheeky grin. "For this."

With those words, his face started to transform. His jaw lengthened and grew triangular, along with his nose. I gasped as his bones popped, forming grotesque angles, and red scaly patches began to cover his skin.

"It's okay," Aeron murmured, hooking an arm around me and pulling me close when I began to tremble.

Payton's form continued lengthening and widening, his clothes tearing and falling to the ground in scraps as he dropped to all fours. A tail formed, then long, jagged claws on his arms and legs, which had transformed into large appendages that were twice as long and tall as I was. He let out a snort through huge nostrils and settled onto his haunches with a twitch of his tail.

Some distant part of me realized my jaw was hanging in pure amazement, but I couldn't close my mouth any more than I could will my heart to quit its panicked racing. "It-it's a-a …"

"A dragon," Aeron finished for me, his voice even, as if he'd witnessed this miraculous transformation before.

I covered my open mouth with my trembling hands. "Wha-what is happening here?"

Professor Raymond stepped next to me, the warmth of his body stifling the cold night air. "Mr. Previtt hails from the dragos clan on his home word, Pyrem. They can transform into dragons."

I breathed out in disbelief. "Dragons?"

"Dragons," Aeron said.

Holy freaking crap! I mean, I knew it was a dragon. I could tell just by looking at it … *him*, I mean. He looked very much like one of the dragons you might see illustrated in an old mythological story. He had red, leathery scales and wings, a large triangular snout with jagged, distended teeth, and he was, oh, about *twenty feet tall!*

My mind couldn't process what I was seeing.

When he looked down at us and exhaled a ring of smoke, I instinctively shrunk back. He looked regal and terrifying all at once. Even though I knew he was Payton, my body still told me to run away. That was why, when Aeron grabbed my elbow and tried to urge me forward, I dug in my heels.

"What are you doing?" I asked, fighting back the panic that froze my limbs.

"He's our ride out of here."

I tore my gaze away from the dragon long enough to shoot Aeron a disbelieving glance. "Are you crazy?"

"There's no danger, Miss Harris." As if to prove his point, Professor Raymond moved around me and stepped toward the dragon. It lowered its wide, flat tail, allowing him to step onto it, and slowly lifted him into the air and onto its back. He settled astride the hulking beast and looked down at me. "He may look fierce, but he is still Mr. Previtt inside. He won't hurt you."

The dragon snorted as if in agreement, and another ring of smoke wafted from his enormous nostrils.

Yeah well, I understood it logically, but just one of his dagger-like teeth looked like it could easily tear me in two. They expected me to actually get *on* that thing?

"I ..." I backed up a few steps. "I'm okay."

"Miss Harris." The Professor sounded short of patience. "The sooner you are clear of this place, the safer everyone on this campus will be."

His words hit me right where it hurt. I glanced toward where the battle was still going strong. Though I couldn't see them, I knew Deme and Luc were in there somewhere. Hopefully not injured.

They were there because of me. Because they were protecting me.

Guilt tore through my chest. Objectively I knew it wasn't my fault this was happening, but it still felt like it was. If it weren't for my presence here, the dark elementals wouldn't have attacked. Which meant I had to do whatever it took to keep *them* safe, even if it meant riding on the back of a terrifying dragon.

My body shook as I allowed Aeron to lead me to the dragon. Its tail dropped to the ground right beside us, and we stepped on. It was so massive there was plenty of space for us, but I still grabbed on tight to Aeron when the tail started to move.

Although we were lifted slowly and with practiced ease, every last inch of me was cognizant of the fact we were getting higher and higher, and all that stood between me and a large drop was a few feet of scaly flesh.

Sensing my fear, Aeron wrapped his arms around me. "Almost there."

I gratefully buried my face in his chest, but it was no more than a few seconds before we shifted and I felt my body falling. I let out a squeal that died when I realized I was lying on my side atop the dragon.

"Here." Aeron grabbed my hand and shifted us into a seated position. "Toss your leg over the other side."

My body trembled as I scrambled to get into place. I hooked one leg over the side of the dragon, facing forward. That's when I realized just how massive he was. Professor Raymond sat at the very front, I was in the middle, and Aeron was behind me. Yet even though three of us were on the dragon, there was probably two feet of space between me and the Professor.

"Hold onto the scales," the Professor said over his shoulder. "Like this." He grabbed the scales nearest to his hands and dug his fingers beneath them.

Somehow it felt wrong to be digging under his scales like that. One wrong move and I might be twisting off part of his back.

At the same time, I wasn't too keen on falling off, so I did as he demonstrated. To my surprise, the scales seemed much sturdier than I'd expected, while also retaining a soft, buttery feel.

"Are you sure this is safe?"

"Safer than here," Aeron said bluntly. He settled

in closer behind me, so I felt the security of his legs on either side.

"Thank you," I whispered gratefully. The only thing more terrifying than getting on the back of the dragon was the fear I might go flying off once it started moving.

No sooner did I have that thought than the dragon's ragged wings began to flap, creating wind as it rose into the air. I stifled a shriek and dug my knees into the sides of the beast.

Muscles shifted against my thighs, and I realized the large body beneath me was quite warm. I don't know what I had expected. I guess something more reptilian. But no, this creature was all sinew and heat. I didn't even feel that cold, though it was close to freezing outside.

The dragon circled in the air before a growling sound reverberated through its body, and a stream of fire shot straight out of its mouth. It landed several hundred feet away, where it dissipated into the cool night air. My heart clenched at the sight as pure wonder overtook me.

I can't believe this is happening!

I dared a look downward. We were now flying over the sight of the battle. Many of the dark elementals had stopped fighting. Though we were far up in the sky, I could see the fright and wonder on their faces as they stared up at us. Even amongst people who were accustomed to special abilities, the sight of a fire-breathing dragon flying through the sky was obviously a rare occurrence.

Campus disappeared, and we flew through the forest. The fear and urgency of the past few minutes fell away as darkness blanketed us. It seemed so peaceful up here, leaving me to process that the dragon I currently rode on was Payton transformed.

A dragon. He can turn into a freaking dragon!

What else was out there I had yet to discover? Something told me a lot.

Such a wild, crazy world I'd stumbled into. One that had been my birthright before circumstances had stolen it from me. For the first time, I realized there was no use ruminating on the past. It wouldn't change anything. The present was all there was left.

Chaos. That was what the Dark Lord wanted. And for some reason, he wanted to use me to get it.

I wasn't going to let him.

"Where are we going?" I had to yell to be heard over the roar of the wind.

"A safe house to the northeast," the Professor shouted. "Best to settle down as much as you can. It will be several hours."

As minutes turned into a half hour and the residual adrenaline began to leave my body, I was suddenly exhausted. I found myself slumping over and startled awake, scared I'd go tumbling off the side if I fell asleep. When it happened one more time, Aeron's arms closed over my shoulders.

"Get some rest," he murmured. "I'll watch over you."

My body was so worn out I couldn't protest. With a soft thanks, I let myself fall back into his chest and shut my weary eyes.

Chapter 18

A JOSTLING lurch jarred me awake. Momentarily disoriented, I panicked at the sight of the massive red leather wings spread out on either side of me. My fingers clenched, crushing against soft leather. I glanced down and saw it wasn't leather I held onto, but scales from the winged beast.

A scream rose in my throat, and then I remembered.

The battle. Payton turning into a dragon. Our escape.

I didn't know how much time had passed since I'd fallen asleep, but we'd come to a stop and the sky was still dark.

The dragon's tail lifted and then bent so the wide, flat surface rested just below our feet. Professor Raymond slid his leg over the side of the beast and hopped onto the tail. It began to lower, slowly dropping him to the ground.

I blinked the sleep from my eyes as I looked around. We were stopped in front of a rambling wood house painted in peeling, grayish-white paint. The house was massive, with four stories that grew progressively narrower, like the tiers of a cake. The very top level looked to be some sort of a rectangular turret.

Far in the distance, behind the house, was an imposing group of craggy mountains. When I allowed my gaze to wander all around, I realized there was nothing more to see. Just inky black forest.

"Where are we?"

"The safe house," Aeron replied. "At the base of the Adirondack Mountains. It's secluded here. There's nothing else around for miles."

The tail returned, and Aeron steadied me as I swung my leg over the dragon and dismounted. He hopped onto the tail right after me, and we began our slow descent.

Now that the panic of the battle had faded into the background, I wasn't quite so terrified at what was happening. In fact, it was kind of cool to be lowered in the dragon equivalent of an elevator.

I thought of Deme having to do this and almost laughed. Given his fear of heights, he probably would have fainted before the tail even began to move.

Then I remembered where he was, and my amusement faded. For all I knew, he could be dead right now, dead because he was protecting *me*, and here I was fighting back laughter.

The beast gave a snort, and I turned to watch as it twitched and jerked. Bones began to crack, joints popped, and the whole thing started to shrink. Amazement struck me once again as scales morphed into tan flesh, claws turned back into fingers, and the snout shriveled. Finally the dragon was gone, leaving Payton in its place.

He was down on all fours, his gaze on the

ground. His red mohawk shone in the moonlight, and his body shivered from the residual effects of his shift. When he gave a final shudder and rose, I was still so caught up in the wonder of his transformation that it took me several long seconds to realize he was stark naked.

"Oh. Sorry!" My face flamed as I whirled away from him, keeping my eyes glued to the dilapidated house.

"No worries," Payton said, amusement coloring his tone. There wasn't a hint of embarrassment in his voice.

But then, based on the glimpse I'd gotten, he had absolutely nothing to be embarrassed about.

Professor Raymond set his briefcase onto the ground in front of the door and clicked it open. He grabbed a set of clothes from the very top and tossed them toward Payton. I made sure to keep my gaze tight on the Professor as he continued rummaging through his briefcase.

"Come on." Aeron grasped my elbow and led me up the flight of five stairs leading onto the ramshackle porch. Trying to scrub the memory of Payton's solid, nude form from my mind, I glanced around again.

This is our safe house?

Based on the decrepit state of the porch, this house looked like it had been abandoned decades ago. I couldn't imagine staying here for minutes, much less using this place as a safe house.

"Aha," the Professor said, just as a newly dressed Payton joined us on the porch. He took an old skeleton key out of his case. It was fitting; the thing looked as creepy as the house. He closed the briefcase back up and rose with it in one hand. With the other he set the key into the door and murmured, "Aperit." Then he turned the key and opened the door, leading us inside the darkened house.

"What was that?" I asked him.

"Protection spell," the Professor replied. "The chant is a password which unglues the lock allowing me to turn the key."

He flipped a switch, and I turned to focus on our surroundings. My mouth dropped open as I looked around.

Unlike the outside, the inside was updated and luxurious. We stood inside the entrance to an open-floor first level. The walls were painted a muted grey that lent an air of coziness to the otherwise large space. To the right was a dining area with a rectangular wood table, and further back was a large kitchen, complete with mahogany cabinets and a marble-top island. To the left was a great room that held several overstuffed micro-suede couches and a gaming table. There was also a large flat screen television mounted on the wall.

"Wow. This is unexpected."

"That's what makes it such an effective safe house." The Professor strode to the dining table and set his briefcase atop it. "A mage bespelled the outside to look rundown and abandoned. Unless the person looking at it can see through glamours, which is quite rare, they will never suspect the house is occupied, or even safe to enter."

He led us to the staircase, which was directly to the right of us beside the dining area, and we climbed the stairs to the second level. Several doorways were set into the walls. Professor Raymond began to walk the hallway, turning the knobs as we passed so we could peer into each room.

"There are half a dozen bedrooms on this level, as well as two bathrooms. There are four more bedrooms on the third level. The top floor contains an empty room that is perfect for training."

Each bedroom looked about the same. They contained a full-size bed decorated with a gray comforter, a small flat screen television mounted to the wall opposite the bed, and a side table holding a lamp. Not quite as luxurious as below, but certainly good enough considering what this was: a hideout.

After taking a look at each of the bedrooms on this level as well as the bathroom, and absently noting when I glanced in the mirror that my glamour had worn off, I turned to face the others. "So, what now?"

"Some of the Guard will be joining us here," the Professor said, looking preoccupied. "The remainder will be stationed nearby."

A sudden thought occurred to me. "My father! He called to tell me he was being followed, that he was going to a safe house."

"He's with Grimm, one of my guardians. They're headed here as we speak."

"Oh, thank god."

Professor Raymond nodded. "Now if you'll excuse me, I'd better start calling the remainder of my Guard." He turned and walked to the stairs, taking them down to the first level.

Feeling lost, I stumbled into the nearest room and shrugged out of my coat, then sat heavily on the bed. Absently, I noticed Payton turn to follow the Professor downstairs.

Nibbling on my lower lip, I allowed my gaze to catch Aeron's. "Do you think they're okay?"

"Yes." His answer was unequivocal. He entered the room and came to sit right beside me, his smoke and cinnamon scent washing over me. "I promise you, they all know how to protect themselves."

"Yeah, I guess you're right." I gave him a shaky smile. "I just can't stop thinking about them."

He nodded, understanding glimmering in his dark brown eyes.

"Do you think they figured out who I am?" I asked him.

One of his brows arched. "Given they attacked in such great numbers, I'd say they did."

My mind raced with the implications. "What's going to happen to the university? Will it be shut down?"

Aeron shook his head. "No, the institution has been around for decades. They'll add more barriers, maybe do a relocation spell, but I can't imagine it'll be shut down for too long."

I gave him a puzzled glance. "Relocation spell?"

"Earth magic. Someone powerful enough could physically move the school and surrounding areas, so the Netheren no longer know its exact location."

My mouth dropped open at the thought. "But what about the humans who think it's just a regular school?"

"There are none of those." Aeron's lips twisted.

"If you're at the school, it's because you're elemental or somehow involved with the supernatural."

Ah, so that had been another one of Professor Raymond's lies. I guess he'd known just what to say to reassure me. Given I couldn't sense his lies, I'd believed him.

My newly heightened sense of hearing picked up a knock on the door downstairs. Someone opened it, and what sounded like several people entered the house. A low din of voices started up, and I jumped off the bed with a mixture of excitement and anxiety. "Could that be them?"

Given their lack of dragon transport, I didn't see how it was possible for everyone to be here so quickly. Part of me feared the Netherens had somehow discovered our hideout. When Aeron tensed and shot to his feet, that fear increased. But then I heard the distinctive rumble of Luc's voice, and my heart gave a relieved little flip.

"It's them!" I raced out the door and toward the stairs.

Aeron was right at my heels, his voice still laced with caution. "Hold on. We need to make sure."

But I couldn't wait. I needed to see them.

I started down the stairs, and my searching gaze landed on Luc standing right at the entrance. Kai, Thea, Sarah, and Deme stood beside him. Though they all looked windblown, none of them had any cuts or bruises. Their voices were low as they spoke to Payton.

Relief poured through me, making my knees go weak. When pressure began to build behind my eyelids, I realized just how scared I'd been that something was going to happen to them.

Deme saw me standing there, and his face softened. "Jewel!" He raced toward me, meeting me at the base of the steps. His arms wrapped around me. "I'm so glad you're safe. I was so worried about you."

I uttered a soft laugh as my cheek rested against his chest. "I was going to say the same thing to you! Tell me what happened."

"Nothing you didn't see. There were a lot of them, but given our combined abilities, we were able to fight them back. Especially once the other students joined us."

I suppose there was a benefit to the Netheren having attacked a magical school. The kids on campus were at least moderately equipped to deal with a battle of that sort.

I pulled back. "What happened then?"

"They stayed around long enough to give us a few bruises, then retreated." He shrugged. "Thea healed us, and we headed here."

Thank god. I couldn't help but think of how much worse it could have gone. "How did you guys get here so fast?"

"Oh." He laughed, and his gaze floated over to Sarah. "Sarah is an air elemental. She turned into a tornado and whipped us here on her air current."

I choked out a laugh. "You're joking."

But the half impressed, half terrified expression on his face said he wasn't.

"You actually *flew* in the air? For me?" I squeezed his shoulders. "Look at you, conquering your fear of heights."

"Not conquering. More like barely living through it." He closed his eyes, looking briefly like he was going to throw up. "You owe me, woman. Big time."

I guess I did.

When I gazed over at Sarah with new appreciation, she gave me a cheeky grin.

"Looks like I have a lot to learn about elementals," I said to Deme.

"It's a whole new world," he agreed.

There was a sudden lull in the conversation, and when I glanced over at Luc and the others, they were focused on the kitchen area. Their solemn expressions instantly made me freeze up.

I followed their line of vision to where Professor Raymond stood. He held his phone to his ear and based on the horrified look on his face, he'd just received some bad news.

He glanced at me and a foreboding crept upon me, tightening my throat.

Instinctively I took a few steps toward him, but when I noticed the tears leaking from his eyes, I stopped.

Professor Raymond cleared his throat and murmured into the phone. "Okay. I'll send someone there as quickly as I can."

He pressed the button to end the call and slid his cell phone back into his pocket, his gaze on me the entire time.

Suddenly I knew I didn't want to hear what he had to say. I backed away, shaking my head.

Sorrow and sympathy bled from the Professor's

pores. "Miss Harris."

"No," I whispered. Because I knew. I knew without him telling me what he was going to say.

I shook my head even harder, backing away even more, until I made contact with something behind me. Deme's hands steadied my shoulders, offering me support. Right now, they felt more like restraints.

I didn't want to be here anymore.

"Miss Harris." Professor Raymond's face threatened to crumple, and he paused to wipe the moisture from his cheeks. "I just rang your father's phone and his housekeeper answered. She arrived at your home a few minutes ago to deliver a meal."

"No." I slapped my hands over my ears. If I didn't hear it, maybe it wouldn't be true.

"She saw his body as soon as she entered," he said, his voice cracking. "I'm sorry, but he's dead."

Chapter 19

MY HEART gave a furious clench when he uttered the words I'd so desperately wanted to avoid. The power inside my veins curled itself deep inside me, as if it were trying to smother me from the inside out. Agony wound through my limbs, electrifying my muscles. Threatening to double me over.

Lowering my hands, I all but choked on my breath as I looked at the Professor. "How?"

He closed his eyes. "She found him on the floor  the foyer, the door partially open. He was lying beside another man."

"Grimm," Aeron murmured.

The Professor nodded bleakly, explaining, "He was an Earth elemental. Powerful … he should have been able to sense it before anything bad happened …" He cleared his throat. "She called 911 as soon as she found him, but they weren't able to resuscitate either one of them. Neither man had a mark on him."

Grief and disbelief morphed with fury.

"No," I bit out. He knew what I was really asking. "*How?*"

Professor Raymond opened his mouth to respond, then hesitated.

In the end, it was Aeron who responded. "Lord

Adrian can drain the essence of life with the touch of his hand."

My breath released in one long shudder. Another wrench of pain twisted in my gut, bringing with it an instant burst of nausea. I cupped my mouth and choked back a wretch.

My father—the only one I'd ever known—was dead. And he'd been killed because of me.

When my legs threatened to buckle, Deme caught me. He led me to the dining table, then pulled out a chair and deposited me onto it. He knelt to look me in the face.

I stared back at him, watched his lips move, but I couldn't make anything out over the ringing in my ears. My vision blurred, then doubled, and somewhere in the recesses of my mind I knew I was on the verge of passing out. I was totally okay with that. I welcomed the respite unconsciousness would bring.

But, lucky me, everything came back into focus instead, buffeting me with sorrow. Pain tightened my throat and I swallowed repeatedly, hearing the Professor say to Aeron, "I want you to go there and confirm what happened. Sarah, please accompany him."

"I'm going, too."

I tried to shoot out of my seat, but Deme dragged me back down, his red-tinged eyes boring into me. "Are you crazy?"

At the same exact time as Deme, the Professor said, "Absolutely not."

"There's no fucking way," Luc growled.

I took several breaths. "I want to see him."

"No," Deme and Professor Raymond said in unison.

Blinking past the haze of tears in my eyes, I whispered, "I don't want him to be alone."

Professor Raymond sighed and stalked toward me, squatting beside Deme to meet my gaze. "I know how you must feel. Timothy was my friend. I know you would give anything to be there with him right now. But I also know he would want you to be safe."

His voice cracked, and he paused to clear his throat.

"Timothy was practical above everything else. What do you think he would want you to do?"

The Professor was playing dirty, and he knew it. I wanted to protest, wanted to insist that I go. That I see my father one more time. But I honestly didn't know if I would be able to handle it. Seeing those washed-out blue eyes without a hint of life in them ...

Oh god, I was going to lose it.

Even though I knew he was dead and it didn't really matter, the thought of my father being all alone was too much to bear. Someone who knew him should be there. Someone who loved him. If not me, then ...

I looked over at Deme. "Will you go? You knew him."

Like true family, he seemed to understand what I meant. Deme squeezed my hand and gave me a solemn nod. "I will."

"Thank you. I think I need to be alone for a while."

Mindless of their concerned gazes, I rose and stumbled toward the stairs. Part of me was surprised my legs could hold my weight. They seemed to be made of rubber, but they carried me. Moments later I was closed behind one of the bedroom doors, staring blankly at the wall. I lost track of how much time I spent there. Enough to dully take note of Deme coming into my room and embracing me. Whispering words of comfort.

Enough to hear him, Aeron, and Sarah leave for their mission. The front door clicked when they left, and there was a subsequent murmur of hushed voices.

They were talking about me, yet I couldn't bring myself to care. My mind raced with thoughts, things I hadn't yet dared articulate.

What could have been hours passed before there was a knock on the door. Before I could respond, it opened and Luc slipped inside. He shut the door behind him and wordlessly came over to where I sat on the bed, sitting down beside me. "Want to talk?"

I shook my head.

But he didn't leave. He just sat there, leaving me to my silence, until the thoughts I tried so hard to suppress became too much to bear. Silent tears traced down my cheeks. "This is all my fault."

Luc gazed at me, sympathy radiating off him. "Come on, Princess. You know it's not."

His words rang with truth, but I couldn't accept it. "If it wasn't for some stupid dark elemental who has a thing for me, he would still be alive."

Luc reached out and grabbed my shoulder. "Jewel—"

A sob tore from my throat. "My father died because he dared to take me in."

"Stop." He snatched me into his arms, holding me tight. "Your father loved you. He would have given anything to protect you, even his life."

"I can't … I don't know if I can take this."

He rocked back and forth, comforting me with the warmth of his embrace. His hands smoothed over my hair. "You'll be okay, Jewel. You're strong. Your father knew it."

Giving into the swell of emotions inside me, I clenched my fingers in his shirt, and let the tears fall.

Chapter 20

A KNOCK sounded on the door to the bedroom I'd claimed as mine. I didn't even bother taking my eyes from the television screen. "Go away."

Deme's voice filtered through the other side of the door. "Come on, Jewel. You've been closed away in there for days. Let me in."

I didn't want to. I didn't want the inevitable conversation that would come with his visit, bringing up memories I was having so much trouble keeping locked away. "Come back later."

"I have ice cream," he sang. "Chocolate Chocolate Chip Haagen Dazs. Your *favorite*."

He really did know me well. Those were just about the only words that could get my attention. Since we were close to an hour from the nearest store and we hadn't had any ice cream before, I knew that he or someone else must have gone to special lengths to get the ice cream for me. I appreciated it. It was the one thing that could always make me feel marginally better.

I let out a sigh and smoothed out the shirt and boxers I'd found in the drawer of the bedroom dresser. Since we'd fled campus with nothing but the clothes on our backs, I'd been reduced to wearing somebody's borrowed clothes while my one outfit did its daily round in the washer and dryer.

Not that I cared. Other than the occasional bathroom trip, I hadn't left my room since I learned about my father's death.

It had been five days since he'd died. Five miserable, long days of pain coming and going in waves.

After Aeron, Sarah, and Deme had returned with the news that my father had in fact been murdered rather than dying of natural causes—Aeron could smell the Netheren magic on his body—we'd gone into full lockdown mode, which was fine with me. It gave me an excuse to closet myself away in my room.

At least the television distracted me. Occasionally, while watching an engaging program, I'd forget what had happened. But then the memory would hit me like a rogue wave, and the pain would double me over once more.

No, I couldn't be out in polite company right now.

Yet that didn't really apply to Deme. He'd seen me at my worst over the years.

"Fine," I finally called out. "But I'm not sharing."

"Deal." He opened the door and stepped inside, then shut it behind him.

I took my eyes off the screen to watch as he made his way over with the pint of ice cream and two spoons in his hands. He'd found some clothes in his room, too. A shredded black shirt depicting some sort of heavy metal band rested over his torso.

Not entirely his style, but he looked good in anything. His hair was wet, and it looked like he'd purposely combed it straight upward.

"You look entirely too good for someone who's hiding out," I murmured.

He grinned and tossed himself back onto the bed beside me. "Always good to be prepared."

Crossing his bare feet at the ankles, he handed one of the spoons to me. Then he pried off the lid and the plastic seal beneath it, and dipped his spoon inside.

"I told you I wasn't sharing," I said without any heat.

"You know all bets are off when it comes to ice cream."

True. I dug my spoon in and brought it to my mouth, practically moaning at the delicious explosion of flavor on my tongue.

Why was it that ice cream made all the world's problems seem a little less tragic? At least, until it was gone.

Deme glanced at the commercial playing on the television, then nudged me with his shoulder. "What are we watching?"

"*Breakfast at Tiffany's.*"

He gave an excited, "Ooh! One of our favorites."

Yes, we had loved it ever since we first saw it back at my house when we were fifteen. We'd kept our eyes glued to the screen the whole time, so much so that Dad had laughed at us when he'd walked by the living room.

The thought of him sparked a fresh wave of tears. I bit back a sob.

Deme dropped his spoon to wind an arm around me, pulling me into his chest. He held me silently, until at last my sorrow lessened to a manageable dull pain. I drew back.

"Every time I think I'm starting to feel better, something happens to make me think of him and I start crying all over again."

He nodded as if that made perfect sense. "Of course. He was your dad."

I stayed nestled in his arms as we watched the movie. After a while, I whispered, "How am I ever going to get over this, Deme?"

"One day at a time, chica." He pressed a comforting kiss to the top of my head. "One day at a time."

My fist flew, connecting to warm flesh with a loud *crack*. Luc's head snapped to the side, and when he looked back at me, a thin trail of blood flowed from his mouth down his chin. He wiped it away and gave me a feral grin that told me maybe he enjoyed the pain a little.

His fingers crooked toward me, egging me on. "Harder."

Anticipation built within me as I geared up for another attack. My loud cry echoed through the room as I whirled into a spinning kick.

He blocked my leg before it could connect with his side, and I went down to the ground. But I was only there for a second before I sprung back to my feet and regrouped. This time I feinted left before whirling to the right with a roundhouse that connected with his solar plexus. He let out a pained *oomph* as he went flying, landing on his back.

Like me, he was only there a moment before he made a move that landed him back on both feet.

Luc let out a chuckle as he came back at me, clearly trying to guess my next move. "You're getting good."

"Thanks." I came at him with a series of kicks and punches that left us both breathless as we each took turns hitting, then blocking.

In the days following my father's death, Luc kept me busy with round after round of sparring. Mostly we used magic, until I began to hone my control over my light. Now that I had some level of discipline over it, I realized it could be a pretty useful weapon. If I concentrated just right, I could refract magical attacks right back onto the attacker. The flip side was that one wrong move sent the magic ricocheting dangerously all around me.

After we'd practiced magic over and over again until I'd wanted to drop dead from exhaustion, Luc moved on to hand-to-hand combat. He wanted me to be prepared for every scenario, he said. While I knew that was true, I also knew he was trying to keep me distracted, and I appreciated it.

The safe house was growing more stifling by the minute. Professor Raymond spent almost every waking moment on the phone with his contacts from the Guard, trying to figure out our next move. But in the meantime, it had left the rest of us cooped up and restless.

So, yeah, bring on the fighting.

As the Professor had advised, the top floor was perfect for sparring. Large and devoid of furniture, it boasted windows on all four sides. The result was a breathtaking view all around us.

Luc landed a kick to my side that left me reeling for breath. He paused, his breathing heavy. "Want to take a break?"

"Yeah." Panting, I headed to the closest wall and slid down it until I sat on the ground, pressing my hand to my tender side.

He sat down next to me. "You okay?"

I made a face. "Nothing Thea can't heal." At least she and I were on better terms now. I wouldn't say friendly, but she'd lost her air of pure hostility after the campus attack and my father's subsequent death. Since I didn't think I could handle any more emotional stuff right now, I really appreciated the small gesture on her part.

Luc rubbed at his jaw where I'd landed a hit minutes ago. A speck of dried blood still coated the corner of his mouth. He threw me a crooked grin. "Your right hook is pretty impressive."

"Thanks to you."

He nodded, looking pleased with himself.

I let the silence continue for a few minutes before I gave voice to the question that had been growing stronger in my mind over the past several days. "What are we going to do, Luc?"

He gave me a sideways look. "What do you mean?"

"All this. We can't expect to hide out forever." When he looked as if he would argue, I added, "This is no way to live, just waiting and praying I don't get found. And why the hell does he want *me* so bad anyway? What makes me so special?"

Luc snorted at the last part, though he looked less than amused. "Netherens are vain."

"Aeron is Netheren," I pointed out.

"Proves my point," he said deadpan.

I laughed.

He grinned, continuing. "From what I've heard, no one is vainer than Lord Adrian. Just like the god who created him, some would say. When he makes up his mind about wanting something, he'll let nothing get in his way."

"But why?" I just didn't get it. "Wouldn't it be a million times easier for him to kidnap some other random elemental?"

He looked at me like I'd grown two heads. "You're a daughter of the first house. The ultimate in Aetheran royalty. Probably the only match for him in his eyes. What makes you think someone as vain as him would settle for anything less?"

The Dark Lord had already proven he wouldn't, hadn't he? He'd gone to war with the aether dimension over my mother. And close to two decades hadn't cooled his desires.

My heart sunk as I whispered, "What hope is there for me? I can't hide out forever." That was no sort of life.

"You're right," Luc said bluntly. "Which is why he needs to be disposed of quickly. It's what the Guard has been trying to do ever since he was sighted."

That was news to me. I looked over at him questioningly.

Luc sighed, scratching at his eyebrow. "Look, the way Professor Raymond tells it, things were quiet after your mother was killed in the battle. Lord Adrian retreated to his world, though he kept sources out there looking for you. But his world is dark and dangerous, and anytime spies were sent to Netheren most of the time they didn't come back. So the other elementals, I guess they just let things lie. As long as you were under the radar, there was a status quo, uneasy as it might be."

"But now he found me," I murmured.

"Yup. Which is bad"— he made a face —"but it's good, too. Because now that he's ventured out of his world to search for you, he's made himself vulnerable. Which means if we can catch him, we can put him down."

"I wish that made me feel better."

Instead it only reminded me of what I'd lost. Not only my freedom, but the life I'd known. My reality.

My father.

The thought of him brought fresh tears to my eyes, and I furiously blinked to keep them at bay.

Luc noticed and he pulled me into his chest for a soothing hug. "You're gonna be okay, Princess."

Between him, Deme, and Aaron, they'd done a good job of keeping my mind occupied ... and of letting me fall apart when I needed to. I appreciated it more than I could express.

I let myself fall into the comfort of his embrace, drinking in his storm-and-spice scent. My magic responded, weaving itself around me and caressing my flesh like the warmth of a blanket. It always responded that way to him. Like it thrived off the energy pulsing off his body in almost palpable waves.

Awareness woke within me. I fought to tamp it down as I lifted my head to meet his gaze. "Thank you."

His face was close to mine, our lips mere inches from each other, and I couldn't help but recall what had happened back at the observatory. Though it hadn't been that long ago, it felt like years in terms of all that had happened in between.

Luc's gaze flicked briefly down to my lips, as if he was remembering the same thing. He dragged his eyes back up to mine, murmuring, "For what?"

"For everything," I whispered back. "I don't know if I could've gotten through all of this if it weren't for you."

A ghost of a smile tugged at his lips. "I think you would've been fine. You're stronger than you think."

The scent of his breath, a cross between minty toothpaste and the metallic tang of blood, kissed my lips, reminding me just how close we were. I shuddered despite myself, and when Luc's gaze flicked down, I found my body responding to him. My nipples stiffened into hard little buds.

Luc tensed, and for a moment I thought he would close the distance between us. I prayed he would. Not only could I use the distraction, but well …

I still wanted him. Desperately.

Instead, after a heavy pause, his jaw tightened and he removed his arm from around my shoulder. Rising to his feet, he turned to give me a hand.

"Come on, break over. Let's try those kicks again."

Chapter 21

SEVERAL DAYS later, I was back in the big empty space on the fourth floor sparring with Aeron. Day was already giving way to night, and bright orange and purple streaks wound through the sky as the sun disappeared. It was a pretty sight, not that I focused on it too much.

Sarah and Deme had been with us at first, and we'd all practiced our elemental magic on each other. But they'd gotten hungry twenty minutes ago and went downstairs to eat. Since nobody but Deme needed to eat real food, I called B.S. on the whole hunger thing. More likely they were restless and feeling the strain of our confinement. But then, you didn't have to actually be hungry to have an appetite.

Since my appetite had pretty much left the building once my father had been killed, I'd decided to stay up here to work on my skills. Aeron suggested moving on to fighting rather than doing more magic. Lately I was primed for a good fight, so his idea was a big GO on my end.

A sharp job hit my right cheek, and my head flew back.

"Pay attention," Aeron said, giving me a smug grin.

"Ass," I spat back, only half joking as I came at him hard. We spent the next several minutes trading kicks and punches. I was starting to get good at blocking, so my confidence level was high.

After I hit Aeron with a roundhouse to the stomach, he staggered backward with a grunt. I came at him with a left hook, but he recovered quickly, lunging to the side and grabbing my wrist. I jerked forward and he spun me around, expertly jerking my arm behind my back as he stepped behind me.

"Ow." I arched back against him, fighting the stab of pain in my arm.

Aeron loosened his grip. "You okay?"

His warm breath kissed my ear; his chest was so close to my back that his smoky scent washed over me. There was something about it … something almost arousing.

It smelled almost familiar in a way, though I knew that made no sense.

Letting go of my arm entirely, Aeron set his hand on my shoulder. His chest pressed against my back. "You all right, Jewel?"

Suddenly realizing he'd asked me that twice, I cleared my throat and moved away. "Yeah, um … let's take five."

"Sure."

Aeron headed over to the far wall where we'd earlier set our water bottles on the floor. I followed him, and he bent to grab both our bottles from the ground. His shirt rode up to expose the skin on his back, and I absently noted his bronze rippling muscles. His body was a beautiful color.

When he straightened and turned around, it hit me that I'd been staring. Ogling, really.

I averted my gaze, fighting back a hot blush. The truth was, being in such close proximity to Luc every day had me in a near constant state of arousal. And honestly, the plethora of toned male bodies wandering the halls of this house didn't help much, either.

As if he sensed the direction of my thoughts, Aeron's mouth widened into a lopsided grin. He held my bottle of water out to me, and I took it gratefully.

"Thanks."

"No problem." His chest heaved as he uncapped the bottle and lifted it for a huge gulp, draining most of it. He capped it again as I drank my own water.

The moment the bottle left my lips, the back side of his fingers slid across my cheek.

I stilled, wondering what he was doing, but when a glimmer of regret shone in his eyes, I realized he was touching the spot where his punch landed moments ago.

"Sorry about that."

"Don't be." I'd stopped fretting about bruises days ago. Besides, if I was ever in a real life or death situation, I didn't expect my opponent would take it easy on me. "Like you said before, I need to know how to take a hit."

He let out a low laugh, flipping his hand so his palm cupped my cheek. "I'd say you've learned that lesson well by now."

"It's an important one to learn," I retorted with a smirk. "You were right. After a while, you barely notice the pain anymore."

I had even begun turning down most of Thea's offers to heal me. As long as nothing was torn or broken, I was good. I was still living and breathing at least.

More than I could say about my father.

The thought of him brought that now familiar burst of pain back to my chest. Sensing my change of mood and the reason for it, Aeron let his water bottle fall to the ground and set his other hand on my opposite cheek, cradling my face.

"Hey. You're okay."

My breath had gotten caught in my throat without me realizing it. I sucked in sharply and gave him a shaky smile, setting my hands over his. "Thanks. For everything. I don't know if I would've made it through these past few days without you, Deme, and Luc."

The corners of his lips tilted upward. "I'm here for you. Never doubt it."

Something undefinable lit in the chocolate depth of his eyes. For some strange reason, I suddenly recalled the words he'd uttered to me the very first time we'd sparred.

My kiss. It's not always poisonous.

The smile faded from my face as I stared at him, matching his serious gaze.

I didn't know exactly what was happening right now, but it was confusing the hell out of me.

His fingers tightened on my face, and for one strange second I thought he was going to kiss me. But when he leaned forward, his lips only brushed my forehead.

I shuddered at the contact, and—

Luc's voice cut through the empty space. "Am I interrupting something?"

He sounded pissed, and when I jerked away to see him standing at the top of the stairs, the flash of his eyes told me he was.

"Just practicing," Aeron replied, his tone cool as he bent to retrieve his water bottle and uncapped it for another sip.

"I hope that's all it is," Luc said, his eyes flashing heat, "because I'm sure I don't need to remind you that you're a dark elemental and she isn't."

I gasped at his boldfaced insinuation.

Tensing, I looked from him to Aeron, whose fist had clenched his open water bottle causing liquid to ooze from the top.

"Maybe it's me who should be reminding you of other things," Aeron said, his voice low and hard. "Certain *obligations*."

A low thump settled in my chest. I glanced at Aeron. "What does that mean?"

The two guys stared at each other for a long, loaded moment. From the way Luc stiffened, I knew he was afraid of whatever Aeron might say. But then Aeron took a breath and raked a hand through his hair, breaking their tense stare-down.

"Listen, this is ridiculous. We were only practicing."

"Good," Luc murmured.

Aeron turned, giving me a look filled with some unreadable emotion. "I'm gonna head downstairs."

"Okay. I'll be down soon."

First I wanted to have a talk with Luc.

Striding to the stairs, Aeron bypassed Luc, then headed down. Luc didn't say anything, just watched me with a tight jaw.

I waited until Aeron's footsteps had retreated before speaking in a low, angry voice. "What the hell was that?"

"I'm just looking out for you, Princess."

The tone of his voice said something else entirely.

He was pissed.

"I can look out for myself," I retorted, slicing a hand through the air for emphasis.

He snorted, shaking his head as he stepped toward me. "Listen. I know how charming Aeron can be. But you've heard about the prophecy. Elemental races can't mix."

Was he kidding me with all this? The guy had rejected me—several times—and he thought he could get all up in my business?

Now *I* was pissed.

"I have enough brains in my head to make my own decisions. Besides, you shouldn't care what I do with my sex life. It's not like you care about me that way."

"I don't … are you fucking serious?"

My laugh was low. "You've rejected me like ten times already."

Luc shook his head at me in disbelief. "You have no clue."

"I'm just facing facts here," I said bitterly. "If you really wanted me, you would have done someth—"

"Damn it, Jewel!"

He crossed the distance between us in several quick steps, his arms clutching my shoulders. His lips crushed mine, his tongue dominating my mouth with expert flicks and dips that had me clutching his shirt.

My body responded instantly, fierce need curling low in my belly. I let out a moan and the world fell away, leaving nothing but the sensation of this one unbelievable kiss.

Writhing in ecstasy, I was barely aware of pressing deeper into him, of his arms wrapping around my waist and tugging me closer. My back hit a wall, and he undulated against me, stealing a gasp from my lungs.

Holy hell. I had *never* been kissed like this before. His body was so hard against mine, his skin so hot. I didn't know if my heart could take it. My legs certainly couldn't. They wobbled and then gave, and suddenly I was sliding down the wall, Luc following me to the floor without breaking the kiss for even a second.

My fingernails raked Luc's neck as I deepened the kiss, sucking his tongue into my mouth with reckless abandon. He groaned and sank back onto his heels, simultaneously lifting me by the waist and easing me onto his lap, with my knees on either side of his legs. I hissed at the exquisite pleasure of his distinct hardness rocking into the juncture of my thighs.

His skin pulsed beneath my fingers, prompting me to slide my hands down to his chest and then beneath his shirt, where I connected with the silky steel of his abdomen. I reveled in the feel of his heated flesh beneath my fingertips, working my hands all the way up to his bare chest. Another moan tore from my lips as he sucked my tongue back into his mouth.

I had lost all control. My skin had lit to a fierce, pulsing glow. I didn't care.

All I wanted was to keep feeling this way.

His flesh vibrated with power while he kissed me senseless, hands sliding over the curve of my backside. I could feel their heat even through the thick denim of my jeans, and I gave a brief curse at the fact they were still on, preventing me from feeling his touch on my bare skin. He gave a slow, hard roll of his hips, rocking his hardened length against me. I tore my mouth away to free my soft cry of ecstasy.

"Jewel." His voice sounded different. Gruffer. Sexier. My head fell back, and he pressed kisses down my neck and over the black sweater I wore. "We should stop."

"No," I panted. "We shouldn't."

"They're all downstairs," he murmured between kisses.

I arched my back, pressing my breasts toward his face. "I don't care."

It didn't bother him enough to stop either, because he dug his hands beneath my sweater and dragged it up and over my head, leaving me clad in nothing but my jeans and black bra. His normally storm blue eyes were dark and fiery, his pupils fully dilated as he his gaze raked over me. "You're beautiful."

There was no awkwardness, no embarrassment, even though this was the farthest I'd gone with any guy. All I felt was deep, harsh desire and a need to go much, *much* farther.

Thinking he had the right idea about us wearing less clothes, I rose onto my knees and slid my hands beneath his shirt, tugging it upward. He lifted it over his head and dropped it by my sweater, and I suddenly had unfettered access to all the silky heat of his chest.

Our lips met again, tongues tangling recklessly as I raked my fingernails over his skin, reveling in the feel of him.

He pressed my hips into him as he rocked against me, and they settled into a rhythm of their own, instinctively grinding into him with a movement that sparked a deep groan from both of us. He tangled one hand in my hair, yanking it back so our lips broke apart, and began trailing wet kisses down my neck to my cleavage.

When his lips closed over the cup of my bra and he sucked my nipple into his mouth through the thin fabric, I let out another cry and dug my nails into his hair, encouraging him to continue the sweet torture he inflicted on me.

I had no idea it could feel this good. The discovery was like being fed sweet nectar of the gods. Intoxicating.

I never wanted it to stop.

One of my hands moved between us to palm the hard heat nestled between my thighs. It burned through the fabric of his jeans, making me wonder what he would feel like with no barrier between us.

Intent on finding out, I slid my shaky fingers to the button and attempted to undo it.

"Wait."

Luc's hand closed over mine and he pulled back, his face a mixture of desire and agitation.

"*Fuck*. We should stop."

I let out a deep groan. "Not again."

"There are things you need to know about me," he pressed. "About back home. Responsibilities I have."

Despite what he said, I could see how much he wanted to continue. Conflict warred on his face, urging me to keep going. I sure as hell didn't want to stop, and the last thing I wanted to do right now was talk.

I fumbled with the button, finally undoing it, and tugged the zipper down before sliding my hands beneath his jeans and his underwear. His hardened heat brushed my fingers and he groaned loudly, rocking up into my hand.

His fingers dug into my hips almost painfully as he rested his forehead against my cleavage. I took that as my cue to continue, closing my fingers around as much of his girth as I could manage.

Though I'd never done anything like this before, it seemed like I could do nothing wrong. I slid my hands up and down tentatively and was rewarded with a second long, hard groan.

Luc shuddered and then he was yanking at my bra strap, tugging one cup down so he could close his mouth directly over my breast. I cried out at the feel of his lips and tongue on me as he scraped his teeth against the delicate flesh. Stars exploded in my vision, and my heart let out a thud so loud it sounded like an explosion. My power showered out around us, settling back over me like rain during a summer storm.

He stiffened against me and I moaned, pressing myself closer to him.

"Jewel." His hand reached down and closed over my wrist, stilling my movement.

There was a second raucous thump, and this time I realized it wasn't coming from within me.

My eyes flew open to meet Luc's. It was then I heard the screams and yells all the way down on the first level.

We had a mere moment to exchange glances of shock and horror before yet another boom sounded. The whole house shook, and what looked like fireworks burst outside the wall of windows surrounding us.

The expression on Luc's face was horrifying. "*Shit*. We're under attack!"

Chapter 22

LUC MANEUVERED me off him and reached for our clothes, throwing me my sweater and yanking his shirt on before I could fully process what was happening. He jumped to his feet, absently tugging his jeans back into place as he raced toward the stairs. "Come on. Hurry!"

Adrenaline coursed through my veins, but the shock of changing course so rapidly made my body sluggish and slow to respond. I wrestled with the sleeves of my sweater before finally getting them to go on straight and then tugged the sweater over my head.

"Come on," Luc called from the top of the staircase.

My heart raced as I sped toward him, grabbing his outstretched hand. It was only then I noted that the sunset had given way to full dark sometime during our frantic rendezvous.

The screams below died down to nothing just as suddenly as they'd started. I didn't dare contemplate what that meant.

Instead, I focused on getting down the stairs in one piece as Luc took them at breakneck speed. The third and second levels seemed to be empty as we sped past them.

We got to the top of the stairs leading to the first level, and Luc came to a dead stop. I banged into him from behind, almost sending the both of us careening down the stairs. Thankfully he caught himself, holding his arm out to the side to prevent me from bypassing him.

Something in his body language told me to stay absolutely quiet.

He silently motioned for me to step back, then did the same before dropping to his knees. I realized he wanted us to stay hidden by the wall at the very top of the stairs, and my stomach wrenched.

This couldn't be good.

I peered over his shoulder. From our position, we could barely see the downstairs. Only the dining area and a hint of the entranceway was visible, and what I *could* see was pure mayhem.

The front door looked like it had been blasted through with explosives, and the entranceway had been reduced to nothing more than rubble and ash. Frigid air wafted up the stairs from the part of the house now exposed to the elements. My breath caught when I saw something half-buried in the wreckage. I looked harder, and it hit me what it was.

Professor Raymond.

His head was turned to the side, facing my way, but he was completely still and covered in a gray cast, as if he had literally been frozen into stone.

Some weird sort of energetic shift came from beyond the front door. It made my ears pop and the tiny hairs on the back of my neck stand on end.

What the hell is that?

Someone stepped past the rubble that had once been the front door, materializing out of the darkness. Every muscle in my body clenched.

It was a man. Tall, imposing, and very handsome.

He had skin the color of mocha and hair the color of pure darkness. It was straight and silky, and he wore it longer than most men. The sides were tucked behind his ears. He wore black slacks and a turtleneck, but his aura told me he wasn't just some random Netheren. No, there was something in his glittering black eyes and hawkish gaze that spoke to his considerable power.

Adrian. The Dark Lord.

Every part of me screamed this was him. It was like I knew him somehow. There wasn't an inkling of doubt in my mind who he was.

As his gaze raked over the destruction on the lower level, Luc and I shrunk back behind the protection of the wall, only risking occasional peeks. When I chanced another look, a second man had entered the ruins of the first level. He had his palms facing outward, and a black shadow emanated from them. The color of the shadow grew lighter as it went farther out, but this was where the strange energetic shift came from.

That was when I understood. The man with the shadows arcing from his palms was a Netheren mage, and somehow his shadows had literally petrified everyone. Yet his power must only extend so far. By some random burst of luck, Luc and I had stayed clear of it on the upper levels.

Had anyone else managed to escape?

Lord Adrian's shoes crunched through the rubble as he stepped over to the Professor and squatted. He brushed bits of dirt and debris off Professor Raymond's face. Then his lips curled in derision. "I remember you from decades ago. I take it you are the one responsible for the girl's abduction?"

The Professor couldn't respond, of course. He'd been turned into stone.

His face hard, the Dark Lord rose and aimed a kick straight at the Professor's cheek.

Scared I would cry out, I clapped a hand over my mouth. Luc nudged me back out of sight, but not before I got a good look at the Professor's face. His body hadn't moved from its fossilized position, but his cheekbone appeared to be shattered, and blood oozed from a large gash.

Oh my god.

Something told me he had felt every bit of that.

Luc's leaned back against my chest, and I understood he was comforting me and urging me to be quiet at the same time.

I peeked again, just in time to spot several other men in black stepping past the rubble and into the house.

The Dark Lord nodded at them. "Go check the other floors."

Quicker than I could process, Luc shot to his feet. He whirled and grabbed my hand, propelling me up and into action.

My heart clenched in terror as we raced down the hallway of the second level, moving as fast as we could without making the floorboards creak.

He led me to the rear bedroom on the right,

silently opening the door and shoving me inside. We heard footsteps slamming up the stairs a second before he clicked it shut behind us.

"Oh my god, Luc," I whispered. "What are we going to do?"

He let go of my hand and headed for the windows facing the back of the house. "We have to get you out of here. They'll be here any second."

Anxiety swirled inside me as I followed him. "Do you think anyone else got away?"

"Given that we haven't seen anyone else, I doubt it." His voice was grim.

"We can't just leave them here at his mercy. What's he going to do to them?"

Luc unlocked the window and slid it open. "That's not important right now. Let's get you out of here, then we'll summon the rest of the Guard."

"No, what about Deme—?"

"Save it." He sat on the ledge and reached out his hand.

"But ..." I glanced between him and the darkness outside. "We're on the second floor."

He wrapped one hand around my waist and fell back into the open air. I stifled a shriek as we went tumbling out the window, wrapping my arms around his neck. I had the discomfiting sensation of freefalling, but then Luc aimed the fingers of his free hand downward and streams of lightning arced from them, slowing our descent. I recalled the way he'd floated on his lightning back at the observatory. That was what we did now, using it to drop us gently to the ground.

When Luc set me to my feet and released me, I

willed the pounding in my heart to recede. "You could have warned me."

He grabbed my hand, and we zoomed into the forest at the back of the house toward the mountains in the distance. "I thought you remembered. Can you tamp down the glow?"

It was only then I realized the adrenaline had kickstarted a glow over my body. Focusing hard, I reeled it in until it was nothing more than a dull sheen.

Lord Adrian's booming voice floated from an open window at the rear of the house. "Where's the girl? She's not here!"

We broke through the edge of the woods and ran for cover behind a thick copse of trees. Suddenly this remote location made a whole lot of sense for a safe house. The Netheren had the edge as far as it being dark, but I doubted they would be able to spot us through the dense cover of the trees, even with the small amount of light my body still emitted.

Even though I knew I shouldn't, I screeched to a halt. Luc kept going for a moment, practically jerking my arm from the socket.

He turned to face me, his storm blue eyes flashing in the dark. "What is it? We need to keep going."

"But Deme," I whispered. And Aeron and the Professor. "He'll kill them."

His voice hard, he said, "We don't know that."

"But we—"

"Stop," he growled, his hand squeezing mine, his voice low and furious. "Getting you out of here is all that matters right now. Got it?"

The distant sound of the Dark Lord's voice cut through the forest. ""The girl must be here. Find her now!"

"Go." He turned, but the rustling of trees up ahead stopped us cold. Luc tensed, shoving me behind him.

Fear stole my breath, making me shake as a figure started to emerge from behind a tree. But then I saw a bright red mohawk, and the tightness in my body eased a fraction.

"It's Payton," I whispered.

"Thank fucking god."

Keeping a death grip on my hand, Luc started toward Payton, who wore only a pair of jeans, no shirt or shoes. When they were within arm's reach, Luc snatched him in for a hug.

Payton returned it, then pulled back to give me a look of stark relief. "Glad you got away."

"How did *you*?"

He nudged his head toward the deep woods. As one we turned and broke out into a run, heading toward the mountain in the far distance.

"I was upstairs on the third floor about to take a shower," he said as we raced through the woods. "There's a tree branch right next to the window in the bathroom, so when I heard the explosion I hopped on it and shimmied down. I didn't want to reveal myself by shifting."

Good idea. There was no way his dragon self could remain inconspicuous.

We continued running for several minutes before Payton asked, "Do either of you happen to have a cell phone?"

"No." My phone was abandoned somewhere on the fourth floor, where I set it down before I started sparring. I hadn't given it a moment's thought as we'd raced down the stairs following the explosion.

"Mine is in my room," Luc said.

"Damn. Mine too." Payton looked over at Luc. "You're taking her to one of those cabins by the mountain, right?"

"Yeah."

"Good. I'm going to keep running until I'm far enough away, then shift and go get the rest of the Guard."

Thank god. Throwing Payton a worried glance, I said, "Do you think they'll make it back in time to rescue the others?"

The solemn look he gave me destroyed any hope I had of that happening.

"Later." Payton nodded to Luc, then broke off, zagging to the left and disappearing through the trees.

With my heart breaking into a million pieces, I kept racing forward with Luc. But the memory of the Dark Lord's voice tore through me like an echo, until it became a ringing cacophony of sound that threatened to break me.

Even though we might have a chance at getting away, I couldn't forget we'd just left the only family I still had behind.

Chapter 23

"**IT'S NOT** your fault, Jewel."

It was probably the hundredth time Luc had said it in the past three hours, but it didn't feel any closer to true this time around. I let the wooden blinds fall back into place and shoved away from the window.

After we fled the safe house, we ran through the forest for over an hour before finding this place nestled into the side of the mountain. The log cabin was tiny, maybe three hundred square feet total, with nothing more than a small kitchen, a round, two-seater dining table, and a tiny living room with a hunter-green loveseat and recliner. At the far end of the living room, a door led to an even tinier bathroom with a shower and pedestal sink. The only source of entertainment was a stack of books and magazines on the small coffee table in front of the loveseat.

This was one of several mini hideouts that had been built surrounding the main safe house, Luc had told me. Sort of a backup in case the shit ever hit the fan.

Which it had.

Even though Luc didn't expect Lord Adrian or any of his henchmen to find us given the stark quantity of forest there was to search, I couldn't help but occasionally peer out the window to see if anyone had tracked us. And I couldn't stop thinking about the people we'd left behind.

Everyone had sacrificed so much to keep me safe. Deme, my father, the Professor. Even the remaining guardians. And now they would most likely pay with their lives.

Who was to say my life was more important than theirs?

I felt guilty for what happened. So damn guilty. I knew it wasn't technically my fault. All I'd done was be born the daughter of the woman Adrian desired … and in her death had somehow *become* the object of his desire. Yet I still couldn't help but think they would be safe now if it wasn't for me.

That was what really got me. If the Dark Lord wanted to kill me out of some misplaced sense of revenge, that would be one thing. I would trade my life for all of theirs in a heartbeat. But no, he didn't want me dead. He wanted to use me as a breeder to create some sort of mythical seventh element.

Which made things infinitely more complicated.

Oh god. My heart broke for everyone we left back at the safe house.

I faced Luc, who sat perched on the loveseat, and asked the question that had been haunting me ever since we fled. "How do you think they found us?"

He shrugged, leaning forward so his elbows rested on his thighs. His storm blue eyes glinted with repressed anger and worry. "Got me. I would say maybe someone was tracked back here, but if that was the case, I would have expected him to strike days ago. So, I have no clue."

That was the thing that nagged at me. It just didn't make sense that he'd found us here. I mean, the world was huge. We could've gone anywhere. Wouldn't it sort of been like finding a needle in a haystack?

A wave of guilt and sorrow poured through me as I paced the room. The power winding its way through my veins sizzled and crackled, as if going haywire. My body was still hopped up on adrenaline, and part of me felt like I needed to go blast a hole through something. Preferably the Dark Lord.

At the same time, I was frozen with terror for Deme and the others.

I leaned on the edge of the dining table and rubbed my hands over my face, praying the right answer would appear. "What are we going to do?"

"Wait for backup," he said firmly. "Once Payton reaches the rest of the Guard, they'll come with reinforcements. They could be here in as soon as a few hours."

I'd asked the same question before and gotten the same answer. I didn't like it any better now than I did then.

"They'll be dead by the time reinforcements arrive," I muttered, my face still hidden in my hands.

If they weren't already.

"You don't know that." His voice was hard, but then he let out a long sigh. The couch springs creaked as he rose and crossed over to me.

His hands slid over my wrists, slowly peeling my palms away from my face. "We can't worry about them. We need to keep you safe."

Although his expression was impassive, I knew he had to be hurting just as much as I was. "They're your friends, Luc. *My* friends."

And in the case of Deme, the only family I had left.

"We can't just leave them there at his mercy."

A flare of pain lit his eyes before he locked down his expression. "What choice do we have?"

All the air left my body in one sudden rush. "I can't live like this forever, Luc."

"I know, Princess." His hands wound through my hair, and his eyes fluttered shut as he pressed his forehead to mine. "I know. I'm sorry."

"Isn't there anything we can do?" My voice bordered on pleading, but I was too distraught to care. "Maybe we could bargain—"

He pressed a kiss to my mouth to quiet me and murmured against my lips, "We can't risk you, Jewel. No matter what. You've seen what lengths he'll go to get to you."

Yes, and now, after seeing him, I knew. For whatever deranged reason, he'd decided he wanted me. And he would stop at nothing until he had me.

Nothing.

"I'm scared, Luc," I admitted.

"I know." He kissed me again. Soft. Almost desperate. "Me, too."

An image of Deme flashed through my head. Then Aeron. I was so frightened for them. For myself.

Based on everything that had happened these past few weeks, it seemed a foregone conclusion it was only a matter of time before the Dark Lord caught me.

I clutched Luc's shoulders, and he pulled back to give me a quizzical glance.

"I'm just scared," I whispered.

Anger and concern flashed in his gaze, and an instant later his lips were on mine again. He gave me a sweet, shuddering kiss that melted away some of my fear. When his hands slid down my back, caressing me, I came to a realization.

I'm falling for him.

No. I had already fallen.

Somewhere along the line, my little baby crush had morphed into full blown desire and longing for this man.

And now, with Payton seeking help and the others captured, we were the only ones left …

Pulling back, I let my gaze wander over his face. Drinking in every single detail, like the tiny cleft in his chin, the five o'clock shadow that had slowly crept onto his jaw during the past day, and the stormy blue of his irises.

Man, I loved his face. I wanted to carry the memory of it with me always.

Luc gave me a smile that reached all the way up to his eyes. A streak of lightning sparked in them. "What is it?"

It seemed silly to desire him at a time like this. Disrespectful to the friends we'd left behind. At the same time, I couldn't help but wonder what the future held.

For all I knew, the Dark Lord might capture me tomorrow. And what if he did?

I didn't want the memory of my first time to be one of horror. Of being forced.

I wanted to know, just once, what it would be like to be with someone I truly wanted. What it would be like to be with *him* …

My heart rammed against my ribcage as I pulled his head back to mine. Our tongues met, tangling erotically, and the passion that had overtaken me earlier returned. This time it was a slow burn, punctuated with fear and grief, rather than a sharp explosion of lust.

His scent, like cloves mixed with the smell of the air just before a rainstorm, washed over me, intoxicating me with its headiness. My hands slid down to his waist, and I opened my legs, urging him between them.

He broke off our kiss, but I didn't give him the chance to retreat any farther. Instead I clenched my fingers in his shirt and tugged him closer, gazing right into his eyes so he could read the desire in my expression. "I want you."

Luc hesitated, the longing in his eyes battling with the conflict on his face. "Jewel, you don't really mean that."

"You know I do," I murmured honestly.

"It's just … there's things you don't know about me—"

"I don't care," I bit out, interrupting him before he could say anymore. "We could all be dead tomorrow."

"Don't say that," he admonished.

But it was true.

"I just want to know what it's like to make love

with you," I whispered, letting my eyes show just how much I wanted this. Wanted him. "Just once. *Please*."

My last word was his undoing. He whispered my name, agony wrenching his face, and crushed his body to mine. Our lips met again, and this time there was no resistance, no hesitation. Only the fuel of our passion rising between us, threatening to set us both ablaze.

I slid my hands under his shirt, reveling once again in the incredible feel of his bare skin against mine. His muscles bunched beneath my fingertips and power vibrated throughout his body, like lightning encased in the hard heat of his flesh. I wanted so damn much to feel him against me.

With quiet desperation, I stopped kissing him long enough to tug his shirt off his body. He let out a low growl when I did the same with my sweater, leaving me clad once again in nothing but my bra and jeans.

His arms wound around me, fingers kneading my back as he kissed me senseless. He trailed his kisses down my neck to the swell of my breasts, his tongue sweeping beneath the soft fabric and searing my nipple with a long, hot lick.

When his fingers crept upward to fumble with the clasp of my bra, I helped him undo it, then let it go flying off. I wanted no more barriers between us.

"Damn, you're gorgeous." Luc let out a low, appreciative moan as he cupped my breasts. He lowered his head down to them, gracing one hardened nipple with the molten heat of his tongue before moving to the other, then back again, as if he wanted to devour me whole.

Ecstasy tore through me, making me cry out at the intensity of how he made me feel. Somewhere along the line, my skin had begun to glow again. The power beneath my veins raced throughout my body, as if I was a circuit on the verge of overloading. Almost as if my body recognized it had found its match.

As if it longed for our joining as badly as I did.

"I want you," I repeated in a whisper.

His only response was a feral growl. He slid his fingers down to the waistband of my jeans, and I had a moment to take in his lust-stricken face, his dilated pupils all but overtaking the iris, before his lips closed over mine again.

He ravaged my mouth with such savage hunger that I cried out, feeling as if my whole body would melt into his from the heat of his passion. When he started to tug at my jeans, I lifted my hips so he could yank them down past my legs.

He made hasty work of removing my boots and socks so he could slide my jeans and underwear down my body. Caught up in our kissing, he failed to completely remove the second pant leg. It dangled carelessly off my foot.

I didn't care. I just needed him.

I reached for the button of his jeans, but before I could undo it he slid his lips down my body, past my breasts and stomach as he knelt onto the ground.

Alarm penetrated my haze of lust, and my legs tightened. Against my better intentions, my lack of experience was starting to intrude. "What are you—?"

His hands closed over my knees, prying my legs open, and he made a thick sound of appreciation deep in his throat. His eyes blazed a deep black-blue as he gazed at me. "Like I said, fucking gorgeous."

Then his mouth was on me, and every thought went flying from my head. A little scream tore from my throat as he licked and penetrated my flesh, driving me all but insane with ecstasy. My back arched and my palms slapped back against the table, rocking it with the force of my action. While I objectively knew what oral sex was, nothing could have ever prepared me for the actual experience.

It was incredible. Amazing.

So mind-shattering that, rather than close my legs as instinct had initially dictated, I spread them further open and wriggled my hips, writhing at the intensity of the sensation.

A wave of ecstasy exploded over me, tearing a ragged cry from my chest, and for a moment I lost all awareness. All thoughts of anything but the pleasure wracking my body in sweet, tortuous waves disappeared.

Luc let out a groan as he worked his way back up my body. His mouth met mine, and the salty-sweet taste coating his tongue aroused me more than I could have imagined. His hardness brushed against my hypersensitive flesh, and I grabbed him through his jeans, briefly thinking I should return the oral favor. It would be another first for me, and something told me I would like it very much.

But his fingers brushed mine aside, fumbling with the button of his pants, and I realized he was too far gone for that.

"Jewel," he murmured, his voice sounding almost pained.

"Yes." I helped him tug his jeans past his hips, urging him on. "Now."

While part of me was frightened of the unknown, it wasn't enough to stop. Not in a million years.

My fingers closed over the thick head of his erection, enjoying the silky feel of his flesh. He dug into the pocket of his jeans, took out his wallet, and opened it with shaking fingers. The part of me that could still think was grateful he'd remembered the condom, because I was so aroused it wouldn't have even crossed my mind.

Leaning forward, I slipped my tongue into his mouth, reveling in my newfound power as every stroke of my hand tore a groan from his lips. My hips moved in time with his groans, my body eager and more than ready for what was to come. I moved my hand away as he rolled the condom on, and then his fingers were there at my core, one and then two sliding into me. Testing my readiness.

"Now," I repeated, my tone taking on the urgency I felt.

His fingers dug into my hips, pressing into them with almost painful intensity. He kissed me deeply, the erotic tanginess on his tongue making me moan. Then he was there, pushing into me, and my body clenched instinctively.

I broke off our kiss, burying my face in his neck, and dug my fingernails into his shoulders to mask my sudden uncertainty. He pressed forward, and a twinge of pain made me bite back a whimper. He heard it, though.

He stopped, letting out a tortured gasp as he pulled back. He seemed to use every bit of his control to hold still as he met my gaze. Sweat beaded on his forehead and a glimmer of doubt shone in his eyes.

"Have you ... done this before?"

That was the last thing I wanted to talk about now. If anyone was going to be my first, I wanted it to be him.

"Shush." I wrenched his lips back to mine, rolling my hips to urge him forward. It worked. His tongue drove into me as he pushed deeper inside, inch by slow inch, not stopping until he was fully seated within me.

I trembled at the residual pain combined with the erotic feel of his body invading mine. Recognizing I needed time to adjust, he stayed motionless sheathed within me, letting me know with the deep thrusting and parrying of his tongue what he would soon be doing to my body.

The pain faded and I moaned, shifting my hips in a silent plea for him to move.

As if he understood every twitch of my body, he obeyed, pulling back just a bit before shoving in again. I moaned against his mouth and he repeated his motion, pulling out farther this time. Then again, and again, until he withdrew nearly all the way and thrust back in with a deep slice of his hips.

My head fell back and I cried out, digging deeper into his shoulders as ecstasy began to build within me once more.

Luc began to move in a circular pattern that I naturally matched, arching deeper into me with every thrust. My cries grew louder and hoarser, urging him to increase his pace. Every move, every thrust, felt like it would break me into a million pieces. Then he would move again, and it would start all over.

Did it always feel like this? So intense? So overwhelming, as if by claiming my body he was claiming every single part of me?

I hadn't considered it before, but I couldn't help but wonder now if my heightened senses also included touch. With every hard pump of his body, the feel of his thick length deep inside me threatened to drive me over the edge. I couldn't get enough. It was like the strongest, most dangerous drug. With the first taste, I was addicted.

"More," I moaned, my voice nothing more than a garble tearing from my throat. It was then I became conscious of the fact my fingers had begun raking down his back, egging him on. Encouraging him to drive deeper and harder into me.

"Jewel," he panted as he wrapped his arms around my back, holding me tight so he could lift my hips off the edge of the table. He slid one hand under the curve of my ass to fit himself tighter to me.

My legs locked around his waist as he thrust faster and harder, his mouth meeting mine for deep, wet kisses that mimicked the urgency of our movement below. Friction built within me, and I tore my mouth away to let out a shuddering cry.

God, I was so close. *So freaking close.*

He wound his hand through my hair, snatching it back to nibble my throat. "Harder?"

"Yes," I half hissed, half shouted, squeezing him tighter with my legs. It was exactly what I wanted.

I was almost *there.*

He obeyed, grinding his hips to mine with such savage pleasure that, at last, I went screaming over the edge of ecstasy. The orgasm that erupted within me was so strong it sparked an explosion of stars in my vision. My skin pulsed and throbbed where we connected, leaving me a shuddering, quivering mess in his arms.

His eyes darkened to pools of black, and his breath puffed as he pressed me so tightly to him it stole my breath. He drove into me even more rapidly, using his free hand to yank my hair back so he could plunder my mouth with deep kisses. He stiffened and groaned against my lips, convulsing as his release overtook him.

We stayed like that for a long time, pressed together as if we were one. Finally, he set me back onto the table with a trembling groan, slipping out of me with aching tenderness while continuing to caress my back and hips. Aftershocks rocked my body, leaving me a boneless heap.

Barely able to hold myself up, I watched through a dreamy haze while he kicked off his boots and socks so he could finish removing his jeans. I suppose I should have been embarrassed we didn't wait until all his clothes were off, but how could I?

Our lovemaking had been explosive and magical and more than I ever could have dreamed. I would always treasure this experience, no matter what the future held …

No. I wouldn't think about that right now. I

wouldn't allow any horrible thoughts to ruin this special moment.

Once he was fully naked, he swept me into his arms and carried me over to the loveseat, settling me into the plush cushions before heading to the bathroom to clean up.

Half out of it from the overload of my senses, I lay there until he returned with a small white hand towel. Proving himself thoughtful to the core, he set one knee on the couch and used it to clean me up. When he took it away, I noticed the tinge of blood on it, and awareness returned like a slap to the face.

My cheeks flamed as I sat up, curling into a ball. I tried to think of how best to explain why I'd chosen here and now to give him my virginity.

"Listen, um—"

He took pity on my floundering, leaning forward to give me a deep, passionate kiss. When he drew away, he murmured, "I'm the luckiest guy in the whole entire multiverse."

My cheeks flushed at his words. Breathless, I watched him toss the towel into the waste basket in the kitchen. Then he came back over and settled onto the loveseat, pulling me on top of him so I laid against his chest. The couch was so small that his legs hung over the edge, but thankfully it was wide enough to comfortably hold us both.

He hugged his arms around me, and I slowly let myself relax against him once more. My fingers trailed over his muscular chest while the inside of my knee slid up against his groin.

Luc's hands slipped into my hair, playing with my silky locks. He kissed the top of my head.

"Thank you. For letting me be your first."

Dampness crept to my eyes, and I blinked hard until it dissipated. Finally, I whispered, "You're welcome."

He let out a throaty laugh and tightened his arms around me.

Chapter 24

I STOOD in a dark, vast wasteland. Even though it was almost pitch-black, I could see clearly with my natural night vision. There was nothing else out here. Nothing but an arid breeze that stirred the air and ruffled my clothing.

When I looked down at the ground, I saw cracked dirt and packed sand. Nothing grew here.

These were dead lands.

A shuffling sound started behind me, and my spine stiffened. Terrified of what I would see, I slowly turned.

A man in black stood in front of me. His straight, silky hair was tucked behind his ears.

"Adrian," I gasped, taking a few involuntary steps backward.

"At last we meet." He inclined his head in acknowledgment, his gaze poring over me. "You're beautiful. Just like your mother."

Nausea filled me at his words. I swallowed hard, my fists clenching. "I know I'm dreaming."

"Yes." He gave me a secretive grin. "And no."

"Wha-what do you mean?"

"This," the Dark Lord motioned all around him, "is the Shadow Lands."

The Shadow Lands. I looked all around me.

Swirling, twisty tendrils of smoke floated here and there. I thought the name was more than appropriate.

"Do you know why you're here?" he asked.

"No. Why?"

He looked at me for a long moment, as if he was waiting for something. When I only lobbed him a confused stare, he looked almost disappointed. "Never mind."

Okaaay. After taking another quick look around, I asked him, "Is this a real place?"

"Yes." One of his brows quirked. "Though you're not really in it."

"I don't understand," I said softly.

His pearly teeth flashed in the darkness. "It's a rare Netheren skill. With a little bit of magic"—his voice grew dry—"and unfortunately quite a lot of concentration, I coaxed your soul into astrally projecting here while you slept. This is a sacred Netheren place, one where I could confer with you without either of us having to be physically present … since you didn't happen to be where I thought you were."

He said the last part as if he was disappointed in me for running away.

Yeah well, suck it.

I didn't dare say my thoughts aloud, though.

"I would have brought you here to the Shadow Lands ages ago, but unfortunately, you were impossible to find when your powers were bound."

"Well, excuse me for not being more excited about all *this*," I muttered, motioning to the wasteland surrounding us.

Adrian sighed, his gaze tight on me. "Yes well, bringing you here also required a sacrifice, I'm sad to say."

My throat tightened with horror. "You didn't …"

"A beautiful, tall blonde who evaporated into a stunning ray of light."

"Thea," I gasped.

"I had debated starting with the man who stole you from under my grasp, but …" He shrugged. "Ladies first."

Grief and disgust threatened to choke me. "You *bastard.*"

"If you'd been at the house," he said in a reasonable tone, "I wouldn't have had to resort to violence."

I took an unthinking step forward, and he held up a placating hand. "You can still save the rest."

His words stopped me cold. I licked my suddenly dry lips. "How?"

"Although I may not know you personally, I knew your mother. Based on my knowledge of her, I'm willing to make a few assumptions about you."

That he even dared talk about my mother made me want to punch him in the freaking face, but I forced myself to stay still. "What?"

"I'll bet you have formed relationships with these people who have been protecting you."

Fearful I would give my hand away, I didn't respond.

"Just like your mother, I believe you'll do anything to save those you care about. So, I'll give you a choice. I'm still at the house, as are the remainder of your friends. Something tells me you aren't far away."

His gaze searched mine, as if he sought confirmation of what he'd just said.

I held my breath.

When he didn't find what he was looking for, his lips tightened, and he continued. "I'll wait here for you until daybreak, no later. Come join me, and I swear no harm will come to you. In exchange, I'll let your friends go. Unharmed."

"If I don't?" I whispered.

"If you don't show up, or if you're one minute late, or call in reinforcements"—his face hardened, and his voice grew commanding—"I'll kill them all."

"No," I whispered. My heart started pounding in my chest, a deep, rhythmic beat that stole my breath.

"Until daybreak," he reiterated.

The beat floated all around me now, and I realized it wasn't actually my heart I was hearing. Rather, it was the steady ticking of a clock.

"Their lives are in your hands."

His voice sounded farther away now.

The ticking grew louder, invading my dreams.

Luring me awake …

A sharp gasp escaped me as my eyes shot open.

I was in an unfamiliar place, the memories of the dream all too sharp.

Something shifted beneath me, and I remembered I'd been lying on the couch with Luc. Without intention, I'd fallen asleep. From the steady thump of the heartbeat beneath my ear, Luc had as well.

The last thing I remembered was curling up with him on the couch, enjoying the comfortable silence in the aftermath of our encounter. He'd been stroking my hair with one hand, while the other trailed lazy circles down my arm.

It had been so comforting, the wind down such a marked contrast to the intensity of the prior few hours, that I'd decided to close my eyes for a few seconds. I must have passed out almost immediately.

The dream floated back to me, and I knew at once it had been no ordinary dream. It, along with Lord Adrian's ultimatum, had been all too real …

My pulse thumped frantically as I considered his offer. I didn't want to become his captive, and I knew none of my friends would approve of me giving myself over to him in exchange for their lives. He intended to use me to breed a child of chaos, and the thought of that was reprehensible.

At the same time, could I really let them all die when I had the chance to save them?

Suddenly, I knew what I had to do. It was the only way to save my friends. To help the people I loved.

And, god willing, I would be able to accomplish it without giving Lord Adrian what he wanted.

But there was no way Luc would ever agree. Not in a million years. I couldn't count on him for this one, which meant I would have to sneak away. My heart wrenched at the thought. At the knowledge that once I left, I would likely never see him again.

Dread and uncertainty twisted my insides. I didn't know if I could go through with it. But then, what other option did I have? Lord Adrian had said he would execute the others at daybreak.

It suddenly hit me that it had taken us over an hour to make our way here from the safe house.

Oh god, was I too late?

Despite my inner turmoil, I made sure to lift my head slowly off Luc. It would do no good if he woke up. He would never allow me to go. I craned my neck to search out the clock I still heard ticking, and found it hanging on the wall by the kitchen. My panic receded when I saw there were a few hours left until daybreak.

I still had time.

It took ten precious minutes to extricate myself from Luc's grasp without waking him. Every time I moved an inch he would moan and shift. By the time I slipped from the loveseat onto the floor, I was practically sweating from the effort.

Luc let out a little groan, and his head shifted toward me. After confirming he was still asleep, I took the opportunity to just look at him. His thick, dark lashes fanned out above his cheeks, and the nostrils of his long, straight nose almost flared as he breathed. His lips were full and slightly parted; he was sexy as hell. The rest of his body matched the face. Broad shoulders, a muscular chest and thighs, flat, defined abs, and—as I'd learned earlier—beyond generous proportions elsewhere.

He was, in a word, breathtaking.

Funny how different he looked in sleep. More youthful. At peace. Part of me couldn't believe what had happened with him. The way he'd made me feel.

It had been better than I'd ever dreamed.

So stay, that deepest, darkest part of me urged. *Enjoy him some more. The rest of the Guard will show up eventually. Luc said so himself. What could you do than entire army couldn't?*

But I couldn't listen to that part of me. It was selfish. It wanted him, damn the consequences. Damn everyone else.

No. I couldn't wait. The Guard wouldn't show up on time. Even if they did, they wouldn't be able to save the lives of those I cared about. There was no one who could help me in this. In the end, it was totally up to me.

So I would go.

I had no choice.

Unfamiliar soreness settled between my thighs as I rose and searched out my clothes. I tried not to dwell on the memories it sparked. My hands shook when I untangled my underwear from my jeans. I slid them on as quickly as I could.

By the time I got to my bra, my nerves had built up so high that my skin had begun to glow. I concentrated on willing it back inside me. I would need every bit of stray energy I could muster.

After dressing in everything but my boots and coat, I tiptoed into the kitchen and opened the drawers, searching for the stainless steel knives I'd spotted earlier. I picked up the sharpest looking one and stabbed the tip into my finger, testing it. Blood welled immediately, spilling down my finger in a long, thin line.

I sucked in a breath at the jab of pain and slid my finger into my mouth, trying not to give into the rising panic.

Ohgod, ohgod, ohgod.

Could I really do this?

What choice do you have?

Moisture pooled beneath my eyes, and a few stray droplets slid down my cheeks. I swept them away and focused on the memory of Deme's face. Of Aeron and the Professor. That would get me through this.

As quietly as I could, I slipped the knife into the deep side pocket of my coat and then slung it over my arm. I held my boots in my hand as I slunk toward the front door.

The locks turned without sound, thank goodness, and the door gave a soft creak when I opened it. I glanced back at Luc. He shifted almost imperceptibly, making my throat tighten in fear, but then a soft snore escaped him.

Something soft and poignant settled over me at the sight of him sleeping so soundly. I hoped he would remember this night as fondly as I did. Well, the earlier part, not what was to come. I hoped it had meant something to him, at least a little bit.

With one last longing glance, I stepped outside, then shut the door behind me.

Once I was several yards from the cabin, I settled onto the cold ground to slip my boots on, then added my coat. I buttoned it up and slid my hands inside the pockets. My right hand brushed the frigid metal of the knife. I focused on the slippery-cold feel of it, using it to give me strength as I started back in the direction from which we had come.

Lord Adrian would think I was giving in to him.

That would be my advantage. Once I had what I wanted from him … well, he would be the one surprised.

The minutes ticked by as I followed the path back to the safe house. The woods were dark and eerie. I hadn't noticed it before, when Luc was with me. Now that I was alone, it was all I could think about.

Branches crackled beneath my feet, making me jumpy, and the occasional howl in the distance made the tiny hairs on my arms stand on end. But I kept going. When the cold began to seep through my coat, I snuggled in deeper and concentrated on the memory of Luc's heated body against mine, his skin crackling with unspent energy.

What seemed like hours passed before the lights of the safe house finally came into view. I'd begun to run the last twenty minutes, half afraid that I wouldn't arrive in time. Soon the sun would begin its ascent into the sky.

I brushed through the dark forest until I was there at its edge, facing the rear of the house once more. It was silent, no signs of life anywhere, and for a long, frightened moment I feared the Dark Lord had changed his mind. He had killed the others and left.

Then I saw the cluster of objects laying on the ground beside the back of the house. It took me a moment to realize what they were, but then I made out familiar features coated by a grayish cast.

Deme!

He lay on the ground beside the others. My gut wrenched as I made out Aeron's figure. Kai. Sarah.

The Professor. They all lay frozen in place, their bodies the color of cool gray stone.

One of the henchmen appeared beside the cluster and entered the clearing that constituted the backyard. His rigid posture and the sharp swiveling of his head told me he was patrolling. Keeping watch over the others.

Waiting to get sight of me.

My body broke into a full-blown shiver. I told myself it was from the cold and not from fear, but I knew it was a lie. I was terrified of what was to come.

It's not too late, that selfish part of me spoke. *You can turn around. Go back to the cabin. To Luc. Wait for the Guard to show up. The Dark Lord might not do anything to them. Why give up the leverage when he might be able to use them in the future?*

But I recognized that for the lie it was. Lord Adrian was not the type of man to make idle threats. I didn't know how I knew that, but I did. Just like I knew he was expecting me to show up.

Taking a deep, fortifying breath, I pushed through the last bit of forest and into the clearing. Grass and twigs crunched under my boots, and the henchman whirled to face me, his body taking a defensive posture.

Uncertainty wound through me. What the hell was I doing here? But I pushed it back and concentrated on making my voice hard as nails.

"I'm here to see Lord Adrian."

Chapter 25

THE NETHEREN henchman slowly straightened, but before he could stand tall, another figure appeared from around the side of the house.

My heart stuck in my throat as I saw Lord Adrian striding toward me. He ignored his man, his gaze drinking me in as he came to a stop no more than ten feet away.

Since he was unabashedly assessing my appearance, I took the opportunity to do the same to him. Though history put him well into middle-age, he still retained the raven-haired locks of youth. The laugh lines that marred his face and the crow's feet that settled around his eyes did nothing to detract from his attractiveness. In fact, they made him look even more distinguished. And he was tall, a fraction over six feet if I guessed correctly.

Don't let his looks fool you. He killed your father.

And he was responsible for my mother's death. Hell, for all I knew, he might have killed my real father, too.

Adrian gave me a warm, genuine smile. I returned his look with confusion. He looked surprisingly happy to see me, and I didn't understand why.

I mean, I totally understood he got his shits and giggles by dominating people and, well ... here I was.

But still.

"You are more beautiful than I imagined, Lumina."

Lumina? Huh?

I frowned at him. Was he looking for someone else? "My name is Jewel."

He gave one sharp shake of his head. "That was the name you were given by a human. Your Aetheran name was Lumina, given to you by your mother, Elena."

When I noticed my mouth gaping, I snapped it shut. It made sense Dad would change my name when he adopted me, given I was technically in hiding and all, but I'd never given it any thought. The fact that it was Adrian—the man responsible for his death as well as my mother's—who told me my birth name was more than a little ironic.

"Whatever." I dismissed his words. "I'm Jewel now, and I'm here to make you a deal."

"Spoken like true royalty." Lord Adrian let out a soft chuckle, and the glimmer in his eyes told me he was pleased. "What sort of a deal would you like to make?"

My heart slammed against my ribcage, and I caressed the handle of the knife in my pocket as I gazed over at the pile of bodies lying on the cold ground. "Are they okay?"

"Yes. They're impervious to cold in their petrified state, so you don't have to worry about them freezing any extremities."

That made me snort. "Why'd you drag them out here anyway?"

He looked at me as if the answer was simple. "So you'd see them if you were hiding out in the woods."

Ah, that made sense. He'd wanted to make sure I remembered why I was supposed to be trading myself in. It was a tactic to ensure I didn't chicken out.

"I assure you they're safe," he said easily. "Once the magic wears off, they'll be back to normal."

I heard the silent *if* in his tone. *If* they were still alive, he meant.

"What you said earlier." My voice shook, and I took a deep breath before continuing. "About me exchanging myself for the others …"

"Yes?"

Something about his expression made me choose honesty. "Am I a fool for taking you at your word?"

"Wise of you to ask." His eyes shone with appreciation, his voice pleasant when he said, "No, you're not, not if I make an oath. I know you were raised human and probably don't understand much of your own kind, but you'll find the same to be true of all elementals."

He slid his hands into the pockets of his slacks like we were having a friendly conversation instead of negotiating for my freedom. It confused the shit out of me. I didn't understand him at all.

His words rang with truth though, and it made me ask, "Why is that?"

"There's a soul price to be paid for breaking an oath, one that most find too high to bear," Adrian explained. "It's true of all living things, even humans. They just aren't aware enough to feel the dissonance when they contemplate doing so."

The veracity of his words swept over me. I remembered talking to both Deme and Luc about oaths, how serious they'd been about the things they had promised. Now I realized why.

"There's a lot you should have learned about your kind, Jewel," Adrian said softly. "I only wish you hadn't been raised human, so you would know."

Thoughts of my father swirled in my mind. The knowledge I stood mere feet from his killer made me want to throw myself at him and scratch his eyeballs out. Slowly and with much pleasure.

But I couldn't give into that fury. *Yet.*

I briefly glanced to where his henchman stood as I chose my next words. The last thing I wanted to do was betray my thoughts. "Do you swear to me that if I make the exchange, then no matter what happens, even if something happens to me, you'll let them go? Alive?"

He gave me a puzzled look. "Are you in some sort of danger?"

My laugh was instantaneous. Was he fucking kidding me? *He* was the danger.

"Answer the question," I said, gritting my teeth.

Even though he looked like he didn't understand, Adrian nodded. "I swear. I don't have any burning desire to hurt them. Well, the man who stole you, perhaps. But you're what matters most, so yes, I'll let him go too, if that's what you desire."

"It is." I briefly slid my hands from my pockets

to make an open-handed gesture. "Here I am. So now keep your end of the bargain."

Something almost predatory glinted in his eyes. He turned to his waiting henchman. "Get the others and carry her friends inside. I've sworn they'll be freed, and no harm will come to them."

The man nodded and bent to retrieve one of the petrified bodies—Sarah—before carrying her toward the front of the house.

Fear sliced through me in anxious waves as I turned back to face Adrian. "Is there a trick? Are you going to come back and kill them later or something?"

A soft laugh trickled from him. "No trick. That would go against the spirit of our bargain."

Again, his words rang with truth.

I bit my lip, hoping I wasn't making a huge mistake. "Then you don't mind if we wait right here until they're all safely inside, do you?"

"Not at all." He grinned as he gazed at me, rolling onto the balls of his feet.

The intensity of his gaze made my skin crawl, so I kept my eyes off him and on his men as they came around the side of the house and lifted my friends one by one, carrying them back to the house. But even though I didn't look at him, I was all too aware of his presence, of the heavy power emanating from his body. It interacted with mine, sparking a wave of energy under the surface of my skin and a dull glow over my flesh.

My heart began to pound louder and harder, fear at what I was about to do coalescing with absolute rage over what *he* had done to those I loved.

When the last of my friends was carried away, I realized I had to know. "Tell me, Adrian. Why me? I mean, what's so important about me?"

Adrian inhaled sharply, his eyes widening as if those were the last words he expected to hear. He stared at me as if truly seeing me for the first time.

"So," he murmured at last. "You really don't know. None of you. I'd suspected it, but I wasn't sure what Elena might have confided."

I shook my head, confused. "That doesn't make sense."

When he didn't immediately respond, a burst of anger tore through me. "You killed my father, you bastard! At least you can tell me *why* I mattered so much that you'd harm an innocent man!"

"That man wasn't your father!" Something that looked like rage flashed in his eyes. He took a breath and visibly reigned in his temper. "I didn't want to kill him; I only wanted to discuss you."

"Yeah, right," I snorted.

"It's true," he said, and damned if his words didn't ring with veracity. "The moment I walked through his front door, the elemental guarding him attempted to murder me. I killed him in self-defense, but before I could turn from him, your father stabbed me in the back."

My breath caught. "He stabbed you?"

Adrian's lips twisted into a sardonic smile. "Yes. If not for the healer I hired …" His voice trailed off, and he cleared his throat. "At any rate, he attacked me and I defended myself. I'm sorry for your grief."

The very last sentence was the only part of what he'd just said that didn't ring quite true. I didn't know how to take it. My mind was a confused jumble of thoughts right now.

Finally, I whispered the question I wanted to know most. "Why does it have to be me?"

He opened his mouth to respond, but suddenly a raging wind began to blow across the clearing. I peered around, confused.

Were we being hit by a freak storm?

Adrian glanced upward and stiffened. His voice sounded annoyed when he said, "Damn."

I followed his gaze up to the sky over the forest, which was beginning to turn pink with the first streaks of light. My sight landed on what looked to be a huge flying blob in the sky right above the tree line. I stared at it, confused, until the shape began to separate and become clearer.

At the center was a massive dragon, and surrounding it were close to a dozen winged creatures. No, not creatures. People. *Winged people.* Floating beside them were several man-sized tornadoes that rustled the treetops, a few whirlpools, and something that looked kind of like a smaller, squatter version of the dragon Payton had become. A figure rode atop the dragon that was Payton, and though they were still too far to make out features, I instinctively knew who it was.

Luc.

Aether. Air. Water. Fire. And that was just what I could see.

Luc's earlier words came back to me*: He doesn't stand a chance compared to the combined power of all the other elementals.*

A brief flame of hope lit in my chest, then died

immediately. They were still too far away.

"It seems the cavalry has arrived," Adrian said dryly. He turned to me, reaching for my arm. "Time to go."

"No!" I shouted, sliding my hands from my pockets. One of them held the knife, but before I could do anything with it, the familiar glowing ball of light formed right between my hands and instantly flattened out in front of me. Shocked, I stared down at my creation.

My protective barrier.

Other than that one drunken night with Luc, I hadn't been to recreate the invisible wall. I'd begun to think it was a fluke.

Adrian's hand collided with the invisible barrier and bounced off harmlessly, sending him careening back a few places. He regrouped, his expression changing from grim to murderous. "What are you doing?"

"I would have thought that was obvious." Since it wasn't, I elaborated. "Stopping you."

His body tightened, his eyes a raging pool of black fire. "We had a bargain."

"For an exchange," I bit out, my palms shaking with the effort of holding the barrier in place. If I could just keep it up until the Guard arrived. "I kept my end of the bargain. I didn't specifically say I would *go* with you."

An incredulous expression swept over his face. After several tense moments, he began to laugh, looking almost amused. "Just like your mother. Always relying on semantics."

Yeah maybe, but I sure as hell didn't want to be

a pawn in his wacked-out game.

Since I didn't want to be dead either, I was going to play every card I had.

Before I could think up a response to his words, his hand swept out and carelessly swiped through the air. A black, formless shadow emerged from it, colliding with my protective wall. It almost looked like the shadows I'd dreamed of, but I had no time to ponder that because the shadow crept over my invisible barrier and it instantly died, zapping most of my strength along with it.

My hands dropped to my sides as I panted for breath, eyeing him with growing fear.

He'd flicked my protective barrier away like it was a pesky bug. How could I ever hope to compete with his magical strength long enough for everyone else to arrive?

Agony twisted my insides when I realized I couldn't. I only had one card left, and barely enough strength to play it.

All I could do was pray he wouldn't thwart that one so easily, and that I didn't wimp out.

Come on, Jewel. Come on. I took a shaky breath, trying to steel my nerves.

He held his hand out again, as if truly expecting I would take it. "Come, Jewel. It's time to go."

"No," I snapped.

Temper flashed in his eyes, and he reached for me again.

"No!" I staggered back, putting several feet of distance between us.

When he lunged for me, I jerked the knife to my throat.

Adrian stopped short, his face blanching at the sight of me with the sharp end of the knife pressed against my flesh.

The intensifying winds blew his hair back from his face. His voice was grim when he said, "What are you doing?"

I pushed it lightly into my skin, wincing at the pain and gasping at the sensation of blood droplets trickling down my neck. Praying for strength, I spat out my answer. "Wondering if you can magically swipe my knife away before I slit my own throat."

The truth was, I didn't know. Based on how easily he'd taken down my barrier, I knew he was powerful. The question was whether he could manipulate objects as quickly and effortlessly as he did magic.

To my shock, he looked genuinely horrified and confused. "Why would you do that?"

"Are you … are you serious?" I gripped the handle tighter, inwardly cursing my sweaty palms. "Maybe because I'd rather be dead than forced to be your breeder!"

"My breeder?" His brows crept toward his hairline, his lips curling with undisguised aversion. "Is that what they told you?"

"Uh … well, yeah." His disgusted tone caught me off guard. "They said you want to use me to create the seventh element. Chaos."

A sharp gust flew into the clearing and I staggered a few steps, somehow managing to prevent further slicing my neck.

Concern wracked Lord Adrian's face and he stepped toward me, but stopped when I brought my other hand up to the back of the knife, steadying it.

"They told me you want to use me," I continued, glaring daggers at him, "like you wanted to use my mother. As some sort of elemental cross breeder. But she died before you could get to her, so now you're after me."

"Ah." Understanding crept to Lord Adrian's face. "Let me guess. You were informed that I wanted you because you're the most royal of your species, right? Or perhaps out of revenge due to being thwarted by your mother?"

I didn't respond, but my face said it all.

Right on both counts.

Lord Adrian glanced upward, and when his face tightened, I guessed the Guard was a lot closer.

Please. Please. Please. Let them be close.

"Well, they were right … and wrong."

My forehead scrunched. "Huh?"

"Allow me to enlighten you. I don't want to"—his mouth tightened—"to *breed* with you. My goal in seeking you is not to create this prophesied seventh element."

My grip slackened on the knife as I gazed at him in confusion. "Then what—"

"So many lies." He gave a soft, snorting laugh and peeked up again, then redirected his gaze to me. "So many mistruths."

"I-I don't … understand."

Adrian's dark gaze bored into me. "I've been looking for you all these years, Jewel, because *you* are my daughter."

My heart dropped to my stomach, and without even realizing it, I lowered the knife. "What?"

"*You* are the seventh element. A child of aether and nether, light and dark. You are *Chaos*."

I gazed at him in bemusement as his words penetrated my mind. A dull roar started in my ears and sharp pain pounded my skull. The knife dropped to the grass with a muffled thump, forgotten.

Focused on his face, on the truth I heard in his words, I barely noted the wind picking up, the sound of flapping wings nearby.

"You're lying," I whispered.

His lips gave a sardonic twist. "If you're anything like your mother, then you know I'm not."

He was right. Not only could I feel it, but now that he'd revealed the truth, I saw what had been staring me right in the face the whole time.

Oh, shit.

I looked like him.

Same hair, same shade of skin, same jaw structure. Only in our eyes was there a marked difference.

Adrian noted the recognition on my face. He gave me a slow, serious nod. "Will you come with me?"

Gasping, I stared at him. What he had told me changed almost everything, but it didn't change one very important fact. Whether he was my birth father or not, he'd killed my real father. He'd killed Dad.

"No." My voice shook, but I didn't care. "I will *never* go with you."

Disappointment lined his face. He turned and motioned to his men, who'd all headed into the clearing sometime during our conversation. I'd been so caught up in our talk I hadn't even noticed.

Adrian's men began striding into the dark woods, their bodies blurring into darkness as they activated their abilities to meld into the shadows.

He turned back to me, his gaze washing over me with something akin to sadness. "I would never want you dead, so you win this round. But the time will come when you seek me out. When you embrace your true destiny. You might still feel like you're human, but you're not. You're Chaos, ruler of All, and you have no equal save me. You belong by my side."

Sharp denial rose in my throat, but when I opened my mouth, no words came out.

Adrian turned and stalked toward the forest. He paused at the edge. "You should know I loved your mother. Very much."

With those shocking last words, he disappeared into the darkness, blending in with the inky black shadows of the forest.

Astonishment reverberated through my body as I watched the spot where he disappeared. A gust of wind at my back told me the flyers were finally making landfall, but I didn't turn around to watch them. I just stood there, staring at the dark forest, until a large man with wings folded against his back approached.

He set a hand on my shoulder, shaking me to get my attention. "Where did they go? Lord Adrian?"

"They …" My voice failed me, and I lifted my shaky hand, pointing out the spot. I silently watched as he went crashing into the forest, trailed by an army of people. They were combing it for the Dark

Lord and his men.

They wouldn't find them. Not tonight. I didn't know how I knew ... but there was a lot about myself I didn't know.

After what seemed like two dozen people slipped past me and into the forest, a familiar pair of hands snatched me and whirled me around. Luc crushed me to his chest, robbing me of air.

"Jewel. *Shit.* I was so worried." He pulled me back to slide his hands down my shoulders, then shook me. "How could you leave me like that? Are you crazy?"

Still in shock, I stared at him. "I ..."

His jaw went slack as he looked me over. "Is that blood on your throat? What the *fuck*?"

I shook my head. "Never mind."

It didn't matter. Not anymore.

Luc grabbed me tight again, murmuring low words of comfort as he hugged me to him and slipped his hands through my hair, then down my back.

It took me a long moment to realize he was reassuring himself as much as me.

Slowly, I wound my arms around his waist and held him tight. Right now, he was the only thing in my world that seemed real.

We stayed like that for a long time, just listening to the sounds of people searching through the forest, calling out to each other in growing frustration when they found nothing.

Finally, he pulled back to meet my eyes. "What happened?"

"I ... Thea's dead."

He drew a ragged breath. "What about the others?"

"They're inside," I whispered. "He said he didn't hurt anyone else."

Pain darkened Luc's eyes, and he momentarily closed them.

"Let's go check on them and make sure they're safe. I'll explain everything later."

There was going to be a lot to explain.

Luc nodded, seeming to understand I needed some time. He grabbed my hand, leading me from the cold clearing back toward the house.

Chapter 26

STARING AT the pointed toes of my high-heeled shoes, I wriggled my feet to counteract the numbness that had set in.

They weren't mine. Sarah had brought them to me—along with the business-like black sheath dress I now wore—and they were a tad too small. I didn't ask where they came from. Given everything else going on, I didn't particularly care.

I'd been here for hours, waiting for someone to come tell me what the hell was happening.

Oh my god. How long is this going to take?

Nerves had long ago given way to anxiety edged with boredom and grief for Thea. She'd given her life for me, and I would never forget.

After the Guard had failed to find Lord Adrian or his cohorts in the forest, they'd returned to make sure the Professor and the rest of our crew were okay. They were still petrified, but someone had reassured me the effects of the magic would wear off in a day or two. Several vans came to whisk us away to a new location, and exhaustion set in the moment I crawled into the seat. When Luc settled in beside me, pulling me in close, I'd rested my cheek on his chest, then fallen promptly asleep. With the exception of the one bathroom break I'd taken, I slept most of the way. Turned out a showdown with the enemy who ended up being my father was beyond exhausting.

Many hours later, we'd made it to our destination: some place smack in the middle of rural Florida. It was another magical university, I'd learned, and the location of the headquarters of the Southeastern American Gaian Guard.

After being shown to some empty rooms in one of the campus dormitories, we were given a few hours to shower and rest. I took advantage of the alone time and napped some more. But then Luc came into my room, kissing me gently awake and informing me the others had woken. We had to go meet with Professor Raymond at the office of the Dean of the Classics Department.

It turned out he was the Commander of the Southeastern Guard, and even though his office was large, it was still crowded with all of us packed in there. He and the Professor asked me to explain what had happened with Lord Adrian.

Still half in shock, I informed them of what he'd told me. I hadn't given much consideration to the consequences of making such a revelation, but the astonishment on everyone's faces made one thing abundantly clear:

They had no idea I was Adrian's daughter – that I was the seventh element.

It was just as bad as I thought it would be. The one thing I hadn't expected was Luc's reaction when I shared the news. He reeled as if I'd struck him. I'd gotten a brief flash of something pained in his eyes before he closed them and bowed his head, looking truly defeated.

After several long minutes of tense silence, during which the Professor and the other Commander stared at each other communicating silently, the Professor turned to me and cleared his throat. "Jewel. You realize this changes everything."

"Yes," I murmured, digging my fingernails into my skin. I did know, but I didn't know *how* things would change.

After another pointed glance at the Commander of the Southeastern Guard, Professor Raymond said, "We'll have to notify the Interworld Council."

That was when I'd learned about the Council, a group of people who governed relations between all the elemental worlds with the exception of Netheren. The Council had been created as part of the Interworld Treaty, and they basically controlled anything having to do with the multiple dimensions.

Which meant they controlled *me*.

What I hadn't realized was that I would be ushered back to the dorm room I'd been given and placed under lock and key. Four guardians had been posted outside my door, including the burly winged guy who'd shaken me back at the clearing when my father had vanished. He looked like Gerard Butler from the movie 300, but with regular clothes on. He honestly scared the crap out of me.

For several tense hours, I'd waited in solitude, pacing restlessly between the bed and small dining table. Then Luc had come.

The moment I saw him, I wrapped my arms around him. He placed his hand on the small of my back, but his embrace was loose. Cold. Pulling back, I flinched at his emotionless gaze. "Luc, what is it?"

"I have to go back to Aethera to fill Lord Devon in on what's happened." At my blank expression, he elaborated, "He's your uncle, your mother's younger brother. With her death, he became the official ruler of Aethera."

I nodded. At one time learning I had more family would have shocked me, but given everything that had happened the past day … well, I guess I was numb.

Luc let go of me and took a step back. His eyes didn't quite meet mine we he said, "The Council will be here in two days to meet with the commanders of the Guards. They'll decide what to do then."

That was when the gravity of my situation hit me. "Luc, am I … am I in danger?"

He hesitated, still avoiding my eyes.

My stomach dropped to my feet, and I lifted my shaky hands to my mouth. "Are they going to, like, kill me or something?"

Startled, he finally looked at me. "No, of course not. I would never let that happen."

If his words were meant to be reassuring, they weren't. Especially when he looked so unattached, like he'd given up on me already.

"Then what?"

He reached out and briefly squeezed my shoulder. "I don't know. I'll be back for the meeting."

With those words, he'd turned and left.

Now, here I was, two days later, still numb as I waited to hear what the Council and the Guard had discussed.

After waking this morning, I'd been visited by Sarah. She, along with Aeron and Deme, had thankfully kept me company the past few days. Since I'd been on lockdown, they'd taken turns visiting my room, bringing movies and games for us to play. I appreciated their attempts to keep me distracted.

Sarah had brought me the dress and heels, telling me I should look good for my introduction to the Council. "Never hurts, right?"

I'd let her dress me up and do my hair and makeup. With my now-perfect skin I didn't really need any, but hell, what else was I going to do to pass the time?

Shortly after noon, the 300 guy came into the room and announced it was time. With him at my front and a half dozen guardians surrounding me, I'd been ushered to another building on campus that served as a small lecture hall. There, I'd learned I would be waiting out in the lobby while the Council and the Guard discussed the situation.

So here I was. Waiting.

The guardians who had been assigned to me manned the perimeter of the building, while 300 stayed within ten feet of me at all times. At first it unnerved me, especially when I'd grown too anxious to sit and had begun to pace throughout the lobby, with him hot on my heels. But after the first hour, I began to ignore him.

At last the door leading into the lecture hall

opened. I tensed, thinking I was going to be called in, but instead Deme slipped out, clicking the door shut behind him. He was dressed to the nines in black pinstripe pants, matching vest, and a green dress shirt. His hair had been spray-painted green to match, though it was respectfully slicked to the side.

"Deme!" I raced to him, throwing my arms around him. "I didn't know you were in there."

He nodded, pulling back. "Yeah, they've been calling all of us in through the side door, one by one, to testify on your behalf."

"Testify?" My pulse tripled its speed. "Am I on trial or something?"

He, along with the others, had been reassuring me that nothing bad was going to happen, but I sensed the doubt in their voices. The truth was they didn't know what would happen to me. No one did.

Because nothing like this had ever happened before.

I was the first—the *only*—seventh element.

Deme frowned and grasped my shoulders. "Of course not. You did nothing wrong."

"Then what?" I stomped my feet. My nerves had frayed to the point of breaking. "What is happening?"

"Jewel." He sighed, squeezing me. "They're just trying to figure out what to do. You have to understand what sort of position they're in. According to the prophecy, chaos shall reign supreme."

"But they know I'm not evil, right? I don't want to rule anything." My voice was raising now, bordering on panic, but there was nothing I could do to stop it. "I just want to be normal!"

"I know, Jewel," he murmured reassuringly. "That's exactly what I told them, and they know I know you better than anyone. You're going to be okay. All right?"

I took a deep breath, willing my heartbeat to calm down. "Okay."

He glanced at 300 and then said, "Listen, I'm not supposed to talk to you right now but—"

"What?" I snatched at his vest, crunching the delicate fabric beneath my fingertips. "Why?"

"Stupid Council rules," he muttered. "But I asked for a few minutes. I wanted to explain what's going on. I didn't want you to worry."

Too fucking late!

"Enough," 300 growled, moving to stand right by us.

Deme flinched, giving him a look that wavered between fear and admiration. He turned back to me and snatched me in for a quick hug. "Love you. Talk to you later."

With that he let me go and headed toward the exit.

"Bye," I murmured, watching him go. As much as I appreciated him filling me in, it sort of also felt like I'd just lost a best friend.

What the hell was going on in that room?

I was saved from further wondering because the door to the lecture hall opened once more. This time it was Professor Raymond. He held the door open for me, looking somber. "The Council wants to see you now, Miss Harris."

My muscles tensed, stiffening my gait as I

headed toward him. When I was close enough to him, I murmured, "Is everything okay?"

He gave me a brief reassuring smile that didn't meet his eyes. "They want to ask you some questions."

O-kaaay.

Taking a deep breath, I entered the hall, barely taking note that 300 followed several paces behind me. Florescent lighting flooded the front of the room which had auditorium style seating for about fifty people.

My heart clenched in fear when I saw almost half of those seats were occupied. I'd known they would be. Aeron told me they'd requested the presence of the commander of every Guard contingency, including Professor Raymond. But still, knowing it and seeing all these people here were two different things.

To the very front was a rectangular table behind which sat five people, two men and three women.

The Council.

Aeron explained to me yesterday that the Council consisted of representatives from five of the six worlds. All but Netheren, of course, who didn't play nice with anybody. They voted on matters of import concerning the worlds, and they were the ones who would decide my fate.

Mouth dry, I forced one foot in front of the other, walking down the center row until I stood directly in front of the table. I gazed at them one-by-one, idly wondering which one of them was from my home world of Aethera. Then my gaze met a pair of familiar turquoise eyes, and my heart stilled for a beat.

When I let out a soft gasp, the man with the turquoise eyes gave me a half-smile. "Hello, Lumina of Aethera. I'm Lord Devon, and I'm your uncle."

I realized my mouth gaped open like a fish and snapped it shut. Luc hadn't told me my uncle was actually a *member* of the Council.

Gee, thanks for the warning, I thought sarcastically.

Realizing he was waiting for an answer, I cleared my throat. "Nice to meet you. I—I go by Jewel now. Jewel Harris."

He nodded, though he didn't look particularly pleased by my response. I allowed myself a quick moment to study him. His skin was several shades lighter than mine, his hair a golden blonde. Other than our eyes, we didn't look much alike.

I look more like my father.

The realization hit me hard, threatening to take me down.

Holy crap, Lord Adrian, the Dark Lord, was my *birth father!*

I hadn't even allowed myself to think of that over the past few days. I swayed, and Lord Devon frowned. "Are you okay?"

"Yes, I-I'm fine."

The councilwoman sitting at the center of the table, a beautiful lady with flowing mahogany hair and bright green eyes, spoke. "Miss Harris, you are here today because you had an interaction with Adrian of Netheren several days ago, correct?"

I nodded, fighting back a scowl at her words.

You know that's right.

But I only said, "Yes."

"I'm told it began with a dream. That he visited you while you slept and said he'd astrally projected your soul into a place called the Shadow Lands."

"Yes." I noticed I was fidgeting and clasped my hands together. "That's right."

She exchanged wary glances with the other Council members, and something tightened in my chest.

"Is that ... bad?"

The councilwoman shook her head, looking bemused. "We've never heard of an ability like this before, not even among Netherens. We didn't know he had the ability to astrally project, or to force others to do the same."

"Oh," I answered in a small voice. They didn't sound too happy about it, and since I didn't have anything else to say on the topic, I figured I'd better just keep my mouth shut.

Taking a deep breath, the councilwoman said, "This is how he initiated the exchange for the prisoners?"

I nodded. "He told me he'd let them go if I went to him."

Her brows knit together. "When you met him in person, what did he say to you?"

I got what she was asking. My heart was jackhammering in my chest now. "He said I'm his daughter."

"The seventh element?" she prodded.

Making sure my voice was steady, I answered, "Yes."

There was a collective gasp through the crowd, though I didn't know why. I wasn't sharing any fresh news. They all knew this already. Maybe knowing it and hearing it straight from the source were two different things, though.

The man sitting on the councilwoman's other side shifted and spoke. "You understand the dilemma this puts us in, right? You know of the prophecy, how it defines the seventh element."

Oh shit. I was starting to get the feeling I was in deep doo-doo here.

Still, there was no denying it.

I nodded. "Yes. Chaos."

My uncle made a sound deep in his throat. He murmured, "Chaos shall reign supreme."

"But I don't want to rule anything," I said in a rush. "I don't want chaos. I-I don't even like it when my room gets messy."

The green-eyed councilwoman waved her hand in the air. "That doesn't matter. The point is, Adrian will seek to control you, to use you to gain supremacy over the other worlds."

Yup. I was in *real* deep.

"I ... I don't want that," I whispered.

One of her thick, perfect brows lifted. "What's to stop you from deciding to join him? You are his daughter."

"No." I shook my head in vehement denial. "No. I don't even know him. He's responsible for the death of my mother. He killed my father, my *adoptive* father. I would never join him."

The councilwoman sighed, setting her elbows on the table and interlacing her fingers. "You believe you wouldn't, but how could we guarantee such a thing? His blood flows through your veins just as much as your mother's."

"I …" Tears came to my eyes, and I furiously blinked them back. "I'm nothing like him."

Yet even I recognized the doubt in my voice. Because how could I know that? I didn't know him. For all I knew, we could be very much alike.

She shifted in place. "What sorts of abilities have you manifested?"

"Um …" I took a shaky breath. "A glowing orb that refracts magic. I-I've managed to turn it into a protective wall a couple of times."

She made a sound of assent in her throat. "What else?"

"I can tell when someone is lying. Um …" Sensing she wanted an exhaustive list, I tried to think of all the changes that had happened to me throughout the past few weeks. "Heightened senses. I'm stronger, faster, better hearing. I can see just as well in the dark as light."

A hiss settled through the crowd, and the councilwoman's eyes narrowed. "A Netheren ability."

A gargling noise escaped my throat. "It … it is?"

I hadn't known. I'd sort of just assumed everyone else could see in the dark as well as I could.

"Anything else?"

Her sharp tone dragged the truth out of me. "Once I … I made shadows dance across my room."

A collective gasp sounded throughout the hall.

"I'm not sure if it was a fluke or not," I

continued in a rush, a pleading note entering my tone. "It only happened once."

From the marked silence that fell over the room, it didn't matter. It was another Netheren ability, and it made them fear me.

The members of the Council exchanged more pointed glances, and though they didn't speak, it seemed as if they were in the midst of silent discussion.

After several tense moments in which my muscles tightened to the point of aching pain, Lord Devon spoke up. "Lady Jewel, the Council has decided that you are to accompany me to Aethera, as the special guest of the first house. You will reside in comfort at my palace."

Surprise flooded me as I blinked at him. They'd already decided my fate? Given they hadn't conferred at all before he announced it, I guessed the answer was yes. They had decided what they were going to do with me before this meeting had ever happened.

Yet, it didn't sound so bad ...

"You are to remain there indefinitely under the strict watch of the Aetheran Guard," he continued, his voice harder. More authoritative. "Security will be increased to include more guardians from each of the other elemental worlds."

His meaning finally hit me, and I gasped. I wasn't a *special guest*.

Palace or not ... I was a prisoner. The guardians would be there to make sure I didn't escape as much as to ensure I was safe from Adrian's grasp.

"But—"

Dismissing me, Devon turned to the other Council members. "You have my assurance that Lady Jewel will remain under strict guard at the Palace."

"No," I gasped without even realizing it.

They ignored me.

Another councilman chimed in. "As earlier decided, Aeron Dunn will also be held by the Gaian Guard under suspicion of collusion with Lord Adrian of Netheren."

"Wait, what?" I gasped. "No. He didn't!"

I might not know Aeron well, but I knew he wasn't in league with Adrian. No way.

Then how did he find the safe house, that voice inside me asked. *A needle in a haystack.*

No. It wasn't possible.

Yet even as I thought it, doubt crept in.

"He was one of the people caught in the mage's spell," I half whispered. "If he was in league with the Dark Lord, wouldn't he have escaped with him?"

But they ignored me.

"And so it is decreed," the green-eyed councilwoman said. She thumped her fist on the table with resounding finality.

"No," I cried out. "Wait."

But before I could move more than two paces, 300 came up behind me, snatching my arm and dragging me back toward the exit.

The Guard leaders who were in the audience began to stand and murmur amongst themselves. Most of them ignored me, but the occasional man or woman threw me either a mistrusting or sympathetic glance. No one, it seemed, knew what to make of me.

Including myself.

Professor Raymond stepped in front of me just as we reached the exit. 300 stiffened, and for a moment I thought he would protest. But then he let go and took a small step back, giving me a moment with the Professor.

"Professor," I whispered, inching toward him. I hated the pleading note in my tone, but I couldn't help myself. "What am I going to do?"

He hesitated, and I could see the internal battle ranging within him. At last he said, "They'll treat you well, Miss Harris. They assured me of that."

I simply stared at him.

He made a halfhearted attempt at a smile. "I've been to your uncle's palace. Trust me, there are worse places to reside."

"But I'll still be a prisoner," I whispered.

Pain flashed in his eyes, and he reached out to give my arm a brief squeeze. "I'll visit you regularly. Your father would have wanted that."

"Would he have wanted me to be imprisoned?" I replied, unable to hold back the bite in my voice.

"He didn't know what you truly are. None of us did. There are no examples for this. No precedent to fall back on. And let's not forget Lord Adrian still wants you, albeit for a different purpose than we originally assumed."

He gave me a sympathetic shake of his head. "No, I'm afraid this is for the best."

My eyes welled with tears at the finality in his tone.

"Be well, Miss Harris."

With those words, he turned and left. Fear and worry swirled inside me as I watched him go.

Hours later, I was back in the dorm room. The first thing I'd done when they took me back was strip off the dress and too tight shoes. As I'd slipped back into my own clothes, my mind had raced with thoughts.

I was being shipped off to an unfamiliar world to live with family I'd never met before.

As their glorified prisoner.

What was going to happen to me?

He's my father. My real father. Oh god. Oh god. Oh god.

My body shook from the maelstrom of emotions raging inside me. I willed myself to calm, because breaking down wouldn't do me any good now. But I couldn't help but wonder, how did he come to be my father? He said he loved my mother. Could she have possibly loved him back?

I sat on the bed, pondering that thought.

No, I finally decided. That wouldn't have made sense. If she'd loved him, there would never have been a battle between light and dark. More likely he'd stolen her away, as he had tried to do to me. Forced her. She'd gotten free and fled back to her people, only to lose her life fighting him after I was born.

"I can't believe this is happening," I whispered. Everything was one big mess.

The guardians outside my door had been doubled, but they allowed Sarah and Deme to come through to visit with me. Sarah offered words of reassurance before slipping me a sad smile and leaving with the outfit she'd lent me. Deme told me he would be campaigning the Council, to find a way to get them to free me.

I knew he would do everything he said, but I didn't hold any illusions about them granting me my freedom.

Now that I was alone again, I could focus on the fact I had yet to see the one person I wanted to see most.

Where are you, Luc? What's happening with you?

At long last the door opened, and Luc slipped through. His body was tense, his expression guarded, and his eyes were rimmed with dark circles, but I didn't care. Right now, he looked like the most beautiful thing in the world.

"Thank god!" I rushed for him, throwing myself into his arms.

They wrapped around me, and he squeezed me tight for one all-too-brief moment before he pulled away.

His frown reached all the way to his eyes. "Jewel, I don't have a lot of time, but I needed to come in here and see you before we leave for Aethera."

"We?" A tiny ribbon of hope flared in my chest. "Are you going to be part of the Guard assigned to me?"

Because if so, then maybe I could cope with the

loss of freedom. Maybe it wouldn't be so bad at all.

"Sort of." He flinched and his lips twisted wryly. "Not really."

"Huh?"

He let out a long exhale and propelled me backward to sit on the bed, then squatted in front of me with his hands on my thighs. "Listen, that stuff about Aeron is bullshit. There's no way he's in league with Adrian."

A shaky laugh escaped me. "Thank god you think so, too. I mean, it's crazy!"

He gave one sharp nod. "They're only saying it because Adrian tracked us down, but they're just grasping at straws because of Aeron's heritage. I know him. He's innocent."

I closed my hands over his. "What are we going to do about it?"

"I'm gonna petition the Gaian Guard to have him taken to the palace at Aethera," he murmured. "At least he'd be treated better there. He would have friends there."

And so would I.

I squeezed his hands gratefully. "What about you? What will you do there, if not be part of my Guard?"

He flinched and his eyes lowered.

My gut clenched at the condemned look I'd seen in his eyes before he drew them away. I lifted one hand to slide my fingers under his jaw, forcing his gaze back up. "Luc. What is it?"

"There's stuff I should have told you before, Jewel," he whispered, agony bleeding onto his face. "At first it didn't matter much, and then, later, I was scared."

My fingers shook as I lowered them. "Luc, you're frightening me. What is it?"

"Political unions are common in Aethera." His gaze darkened. "Arranged marriages."

My heart began to hammer against my ribcage. "Tell me."

"I'm from the second house. Very high up, politically speaking. Second only to yours." His eyes fluttered shut. "Ever since the age of twelve, I've been betrothed."

His words shattered me. Broke through me like glass. "You're engaged?"

His eyes opened, raked into mine. "Her name is Alina. She's Lord Devon's daughter."

Shock all but paralyzed me. "She's—"

"Your cousin."

A scream built in my throat. I swallowed it as I pushed him back, shooting to my feet so I could retreat to the far side of the room.

"My cousin? You're engaged to my *cousin*?"

His face looked haunted as he rose and nodded. "Her father thinks it's time to make our union official."

The truth hit me like a ton of freaking bricks. "That's why you're going back. To get married. To be with her."

He dragged a shaky hand through his hair. "Jewel, I don't have a choice. Things aren't like here on Aethera. My father made a pact with hers. An unbreakable oath."

His words echoed what Adrian had said to me, but his explanation didn't matter. Not to me.

All I heard was he was getting married. To a cousin I'd never met.

And he wasn't going to put a stop it.

My whole body trembled from a combination of rage and sorrow. I wanted to hit him, to burst into tears, to take refuge in his arms and beg him to tell me it would all be okay.

It took every bit of strength I had to stand there. To keep my composure. I wouldn't let him see me fall apart.

Instead, I raked him with a contemptuous glare. "Did you ever plan on telling me?"

"After we …" He winced. "After what happened at the cabin, I thought maybe I could talk to your uncle. If it was a political alliance he wanted, then …" His voice trailed off.

I stilled as I made sense of what he'd said.

Oh my god.

He had considered asking his uncle if I could replace my cousin in the betrothal. He wanted to be engaged to *me*.

Luc cleared his throat. "But then we found out you're the seventh element. That changes everything …"

Suddenly, I understood what it was he *hadn't* yet explained. What I myself hadn't considered in all the craziness of the past few days.

Mating was forbidden between the elemental races. As half light, half dark … I had no elemental match.

I didn't belong anywhere.

It took a colossal effort not to break down, not to give into the sobs that built within me. I turned to face the small window looking out onto the campus. "Get out."

"Jewel." His voice sounded tortured. "You have to understand, I never meant for any of this to happen. I never meant to fall for you. Certainly not to …"

"To fuck me," I supplied emotionlessly, not wanting to sugarcoat it.

"No," he whispered. "I've known about my duty for years. I've seen her once or twice since we were betrothed, but only briefly. I don't know her, not really. But I knew what the future held, so I always made sure to keep my … my relationships casual."

I snorted. "Fuck buddies, you mean."

He made a strangled sound and approached. "Jewel, I'm so sorry. Please."

When his hands closed over my shoulders, I wrenched out of his grasp. "Don't touch me!"

How unfair that he could still smell so deliciously good, look so amazingly breathtaking, even while breaking my heart.

Luc threw his hands up in the air and turned away. Willing my emotions to harden to granite, I watched as his hands snaked down his neck. He dropped them to the side and then took a deep, fortifying breath.

When he turned back to me, he'd steeled his face into an expressionless mask. "I wanted to tell you this because she's here. She came through the portal with her father. You'll meet her when we leave to go back to Aethera."

Another dagger through my heart. I didn't think it could be any more shredded than it was, but I guess I was wrong.

"Don't worry." I let out a harsh laugh. "I won't tell her about us. It was clearly a mistake anyway."

His eyes shuttered. "Jewel."

"Just go," I murmured, cursing the crack in my voice. "Please. Go."

His breath came out in a long shudder, and then he nodded. Turning, he strode to the door. He paused with his hand on the doorknob, not looking back. "We're leaving in three hours."

I waited until he left, until the sound of his receding footsteps faded into nothingness, before giving into the tears that clogged my throat. Throwing myself face-first onto the bed, I allowed them to come.

No. No. No.

Everything was all wrong.

What a mess my life had become. Just a month ago, I'd thought the worst thing that had ever happened to me was my mother's death. Now I knew what true pain was.

I'd lost my father, my freedom, and my identity all in one aching chain of events. And now, thanks to Luc's betrayal, thanks to my own heritage, I'd lost the first man I'd ever loved.

Don't forget your virginity, that snarky voice inside me cackled. *You lost that, too. Not that you could ever hope to repeat the experience.*

"Shut up," I yelled, dragging a pillow over my head as if it could drown out the sound of my own mind.

The worst thing was I couldn't fully blame Luc. He'd tried to tell me several times, hadn't he?

Pulled away from me. Resisted.

I knew something was wrong, but I didn't listen. To him or to my gut. Instead I'd urged him on, tempted him when I should have waited for his explanation.

Because, despite everything, I wanted him.

Now, I knew what I was. An anomaly. A danger to all.

Alone.

Now, I had nothing.

Chapter 27

WITH 300 and the rest of my unwanted entourage in tow, I headed across campus to the line of sleek, black limousines waiting to take me and the others to the portal leading to Aethera. When I'd seen Deme one last time right before leaving my room, he'd told me the nearest dimensional doorway was in St. Augustine, a several hour car ride from our current location.

At least we're road-tripping in style.

With my luck, they'd try to stick me in a limo with Luc and my cousin. I resolved to make sure that didn't happen. The last thing I needed to do was turn into a sniveling bundle of tears in their presence.

After I'd spent a few hours crying my eyes out, I'd picked myself up and showered, and pepped-talked myself all to hell.

Yeah, I'd lost Luc, and it totally sucked. Worse, he was going to marry my cousin, and now I knew we were all expected to live together like some big freaking happy Brady Bunch family.

That sucked even worse. The thought of seeing them day in and day out, of watching as they exchanged in public displays of affection, made me want to puke my guts out.

I didn't know how I would cope with them getting married. Sharing a bed. How I would stomach knowing he had his hands on her, when I remembered how amazing they'd felt on me.

But I wouldn't let this break me.

I might not know what the future held, what sort of consequences I would face for having the misfortune of being born half dark, half light, but I would persevere.

I had to be strong. Stronger than I'd been before.

I *had* to.

As we stalked across the lawn, my gaze strayed to another group of people walking in the same direction as us. I gasped when I saw it was Aeron, accompanied by a large group of guardians.

"Aeron!" I raced toward him like he was my lifeline, trying to ignore how several of my guardians dogged my heels as if fearing I'd try to run away.

He grinned and opened his arms, catching me into a hug that swept me off my feet. "Up for some company?"

"Really?" A ribbon hope cut through the despair residing in my chest. "Luc convinced them to let you come to the palace with me?"

"Him and Professor Raymond. I don't think anyone really believes I did it anyway. The Council just doesn't have any other clues, so they needed a scapegoat." He shrugged, and even though his eyes were hidden behind his sunglasses, I sensed the sadness lurking beneath his air of nonchalance. "Beats an Earth prison cell, that's for sure."

Thank god.

I'd have someone familiar with me. Someone who didn't make my heart shatter into a million pieces every single time I saw him.

Feeling so grateful for that, I snuggled deeper into Aeron's chest. "I know you're innocent."

His hand closed over the back of my head and he gave me another quick squeeze. "Thank you. Same to you."

His comment made me laugh. I rose on my tiptoes to whisper in his ear. "Is it bad that even though we're prisoners, I'm kind of excited to take a portal into another dimension?"

He let out a chuckle. "Nah, especially when it's your home world. Think of it as a grand adventure."

Breaking away, I looked him over from head to toe. He was wearing his signature black on black.

"What's with the wardrobe anyway? If you wanted to *look* like a villain, you definitely have the clothes part down pat."

That coaxed a laugh from him. "It makes it easier to slip into the darkness. Those are practically the only color clothes back on Netheren. I guess I never dropped the habit."

"Oh." His explanation made me feel sort of guilty for teasing him. Like me, he couldn't help his heritage. "I still have a lot to learn about dark elementals."

"I'll teach you," he said simply.

His words sparked a pleasant tingle through my body. I was *so* glad to know I wouldn't be alone in an unfamiliar place. Or worse, stuck with only Luc and his fiancée, my own *cousin*, to keep me company.

I squeezed his hand. "You have to come in the same limousine as me."

Aeron grinned. "Can't stop me."

The knot of dread in my stomach eased a fraction. I turned back toward the limos and froze when I saw the group striding in our direction. My eyes immediately spotted Luc. For a brief moment I noticed he saw my hand gripping Aeron's, and satisfaction coursed through me when I realized it bothered him. Then, I took note of who he was with.

He was with my uncle. They were surrounded by several men and women who were clearly guardians, but sandwiched directly in between the two men was a tall, lushly curved woman with hair the same golden blonde hue as my uncle and eyes that looked just like mine.

My cousin, Alina.

A cacophony of emotions swelled inside me. She was family. Something I'd always wanted. Part of me was so very curious about her. Part of me wanted to her to like me. But the other part took in the sight of her, of the generous swell of her breasts under her V-neck sweater—something I could *never* hope to obtain—and the hourglass shape of her waist in the form-fitting jeans she wore, and writhed in jealousy.

She was perfect.

And Luc was hers.

A whimper of agony crept to my throat, and I swallowed convulsively until it faded away.

The world seemed to stand still as they approached, Alina's curious eyes dancing over me.

Her lips twisted in a secret smile when they stopped in front of us. "Cousin. There's no mistaking it with those eyes."

Her voice was soft and sweet, like a summer song, but something in her tone raised my hackles. There was an edge to it, a bite that made me automatically cautious.

"Nice to meet you," I said haltingly.

"We'll see," she shot back lightly.

Ah, there it was. My cousin had claws, and she wasn't scared to use them.

Luc's gaze bored into me, and I couldn't resist glancing at him. His eyes lowered to where I still absently held Aeron's hand, and when they lifted again, they were blazing with undisguised anger.

Well too effing bad. I fought the urge to drop Aeron's hand. Instead I tightened my fingers, perversely enjoying how it made Luc stiffen. If he could get married to my cousin, and I was supposed to stand back and not complain about it, then he could sure as hell deal with me holding my friend's hand.

Alina seemed to notice the interplay of emotions between us. She glanced at Luc, then Aeron, and back at me. Her eyes narrowed.

I held my breath, fearful she was going to say something. Ask us what we meant to each other, or if anything had happened between us. Instead, she only widened her grin, her eyes glinting sharply.

Something told me was going to give me trouble. I'd been around enough mean girls in my life to sense that.

Dull pain settled in my gut, and I recognized it

for what it was.

Sorrow.

I could have used another friend right now. Someone who was family. I didn't know if I would find that in Alina.

"Niece." Lord Devon gave me a formal nod. When his eyes dropped to my hand in Aeron's and he also looked displeased, I remembered.

Oh yeah. No fraternizing between the elements. He doesn't know we're just friends.

Flushing, I let my hand slide from Aeron's.

The tension eased from my uncle's shoulders. "Are you prepared for your voyage to Aethera?"

"Ready as I'll ever be," was my grim reply.

He nodded and motioned toward the line of cars.

Doing my best to ignore Luc, I turned and headed for one of the limos. I slipped inside and Aeron followed me, along with several guardians.

Luc, Devon, and Alina slipped into the limo in front of ours, and I let out the breath I hadn't realized I'd been holding.

When I turned my head, I noticed Aeron had been watching me the whole time. I stiffened, remembering how Aeron had warned Luc away from me at the bar.

"Did you know Luc was engaged?"

Aeron nodded. "He didn't really want people to know. He made me promise not to tell anyone. I'm sorry."

"It's okay." It wasn't Aeron's fault Luc had broken my heart.

Suddenly remembering how Thea had also warned me away from Luc, how she'd almost seemed concerned my heart would get broken, I murmured, "Did Thea know?"

His lips twisted and he nodded. "Yup."

Ah, now it made a little more sense. She'd known what I hadn't … that Luc would never be able to give me his heart back. She had made the mistake of falling for him anyway and had wanted to save me the same pain.

Grief twisted inside me at the thought of her. While she'd been bitchy about it, her heart had sort of been in the right place. She didn't deserve what had happened to her.

I peeked at Aeron, wondering if he knew what had occurred between me and Luc back at the cabin. If so, did he think I was the biggest fool in the world for falling for him?

If he did know anything, he didn't say. He merely looked around as the limos began to pull away, his eyes hidden by his sunglasses. Breathing in deep, he murmured, "Feels strange to be leaving this planet. It's been my home for the past ten years."

"Mine for longer."

His hand closed over mine, and he briefly squeezed it. "Ready for our next adventure?"

Was I?

Nerves rattled around in my stomach as I thought about it. In the past month, I'd learned there was a whole world of hidden magic. Six different worlds in fact, each with their own primary element. I'd learned I was royalty from one of those other worlds. I had discovered my latent magical abilities. I'd lost the man I knew as my father, and discovered by birth father was a dark elemental who wanted to rule over all six dimensions.

Now I was a political prisoner, an ex-virgin who might never be able to have sex again, and an honorary member of the broken hearts club.

Yet here I was. Still standing. Still fighting ...

Maybe I was tougher than I gave myself credit for.

I gave Aeron a slow, contemplative nod. "You know what? I think I am."

END OF BOOK 1

Read on to get your link for CHAOS AWAKENING, the free companion novella, and for an excerpt from Book 2, THE CHAOS PROPHECY.

A Note From Me and Your Free Companion Novella

Dear Reader:

The concept for this book has been in my head a long time. I plotted it all the way back in 2014, but it was in my head even longer than that. It started with a daydream of a girl who was different. So different that it would be forbidden for her to be with anyone. Of course the thing to do there would be to give her not one, but two intriguing love interests. I knew the story would be big enough that it would span over several books. As of now I contemplate this will be a 3-book series. But if you love the world and want more of it, then I'll do that. :)

So what's coming up in Book 2? THE CHAOS PROPHECY will feature even more intrigue, more action, and more of the love triangle between Jewel, Luc, and Aeron. It's about to get steamy, guys! Keep reading for an excerpt from that book. But first, if you haven't yet joined my newsletter, be sure to do so now. That's where you'll hear news from me about upcoming projects, let me know what kind of stories you want to hear from me next, and receive VIP bonuses.

If that doesn't seem spicy enough, the very first bonus you'll receive is a newsletter exclusive novella, CHAOS AWAKENING. It's not available anywhere else, and I won't be putting it up on any sales channels. It's truly an exclusive bonus for my fans, because I love you guys so much! This story spans the timeline of The SEVENTH ELEMENT and features scenes in Luc's POV. You'll even learn some things that Jewel doesn't know! So be sure to sign up for my newsletter at subscribe.rosalielario.com/elementals to get that bonus novella.

I would also really appreciate if you could take a second to review this book on Amazon, Goodreads, or any other sales channel you deem appropriate. Reviews help readers to find books, which in turn ensures I can keeping bringing you stories you like. It doesn't have to be long, just a sentence or two. ♥

Thank you for reading and reviewing, and don't forget to read on for the excerpt from THE CHAOS PROPHECY, Book 2 in the series!

Love,
Rosalie Lario

...Excerpt from THE CHAOS PROPHECY by Rosalie Lario ©2017.

There was only one person in this whole dimension who could relate to what I was going through right now, so I crawled out of bed and headed for him. Aeron was a prisoner like me. He didn't know how long he would be here, if he would ever be free again. If anyone understood how I felt right now, it was him.

The guard watching over me, a man whose name I'd forgotten, had fallen asleep standing right beside my door. I briefly considered waking him, but how fun would it be when he woke up and realized I was gone? Smirking, I bypassed him and headed down the hallway.

The castle was quiet, despite the bright light streaming in through various windows. It was nighttime, and most of the inhabitants had settled down to sleep. So it was a shock when I reached the fourth floor landing, where Aeron's room was, and bumped right into Luc. He looked just as surprised to see me, his eyes wide in his face.

I stood there quietly as he raked his gaze all over me. He looked as if he wasn't sure whether I was an apparition, but when he reached the area where my tank top gaped down to reveal the swell of my breasts, his eyes darkened.

"Hi," I murmured, unable to stand the silence.

Luc dragged his gaze back to my face. "What are you doing here?"

Suddenly self-conscious, I smoothed my damp hair and answered without thinking. "I came to see Aeron."

Luc frowned, glancing back down at my pajamas, and I realized based on my state of dress what he inferred.

"I just wanted to talk." But when I said it like that, it made it sound like sometimes we did other things besides talk. Flushing, I clamped my mouth shut.

"Dressed like that?" he asked, his voice emotionless.

"They're pajamas," I retorted. Part of me wanted to explain myself further, but I had to admit, the other part of me wanted to make him a suffer a bit. If he was sleeping with Alina, he had no reason to be mad if I was with someone else. Not that I was, but he was no longer entitled to know that.

That was when I noticed what *he* wore. Cotton drawstring pajama bottoms in a blue-and-white plaid pattern slung low on his hips, and a white cotton shirt stretched over his muscular chest.

"Where are *you* going?" I couldn't quite mask the shrillness in my voice.

His cheeks pinkened and he averted his eyes, raking a hand through his hair.

Jealousy wound through me, bitter and heart-wrenching. My fists clenched, nails biting into my palms.

"Guess you're not one to judge," I said coolly. "Excuse me."

I tried to brush past him, but suddenly his hands were on me. My back hit the wall right beside the stairs. I blinked as his palms slapped the wall on either side of me, effectively caging me in. His normally cool blue eyes darkened to the color of the ocean before a storm, and electricity practically crackled from his skin.

"Jewel," he murmured, his voice low and guttural. His tone almost pleading. "You're driving me fucking crazy."

I scoffed at him disbelievingly. I was driving *him* crazy? "You're out of your mind."

When I tried to push past him, he stepped in closer, trapping me with the heat of his body. His hips arched, and I gasped at what I felt pressing up against me.

"What are you—?"

"Please," he whispered, his eyes flashing darkly. "Don't. Not with him."

Closing my eyes at the onslaught of sensations his proximity wrought, I focused on breathing in steadily. But that only made his spicy, unique scent wash over me. Sudden tears clogged my vision and a lump grew in my throat. I kept my eyes squeezed shut until the moisture receded, then swallowed to dissipate the lump.

"I'm not," I admitted reluctantly, unable to withstand the pain in his voice. "Nothing's happened between us. He's just a friend."

Luc let out a relieved sigh, and his forehead pressed against mine.

Starved for even a scrap of his affection, I drank in the sensation of his body pressed tightly to me. But then I remembered. While my intentions were pure, he couldn't say the same.

Sliding my palms onto his chest, I pushed him back. "Isn't your fiancé waiting for you?"

He made a noise low in his throat and grabbed my wrists, pinning my arms over my head. His eyes flashed with a spark of temper. "I still want you."

My inner compass rang with truth. But it didn't matter. Because he was having *her*.

"No—"

Before I could finish my word, his firm, full lips closed over mine. When I gasped, his tongue slipped inside. Flicked against my own, coaxing it into a subtle dance. For a moment, I lost myself in the kiss, in the slow rub of his hardness right there between my thighs, where I needed it most. I moaned into his mouth and he let go of my wrist, one hand sliding down to cup my breast while the other slipped beneath my pajama bottoms. His fingers expertly found that nub right in the center of my thighs.

Whimpering, I let him devour my mouth while his fingers strummed me, coaxing my hips into grinding against his hand. Then he slid further down, stroking the moisture right between my legs. One flick and a long finger buried deep inside me. At the same time his thumb took up the rhythm along my clit that his fingers had abandoned.

I cried out at the sensations buffeting my body. My skin started to glow, a traitorous side effect of the arousal I felt.

Luc groaned, his hips bucking, and I reached out blindly, closing a hand on the thickness of his erection over the fabric of his pajama bottoms. It thumped beneath my palm and he hissed, changing the direction of his kiss. His tongue slid in and out of my mouth in a sensual imitation of what his cock had once done to me, and I cried out again. I was so close, and I needed it so bad.

I missed him so much.

But then, out of nowhere, an image hit me. Him doing these very things with Alina. Worse, him going there right after me, turned on by the fact that he was going to have two cousins all in one night.

An agonizing burst of pain squeezed my heart, robbing me of breath and practically doubling me over.

No.

"No," I gasped, letting go of him and shoving his hand away.

Luc made a sound of protest deep in his throat, his bemused gaze flashing over me. "Jewel, what—"

"No, I can't." Breathing hard, I backed away. Watched as my words penetrated his haze of lust. Hugged my arms around myself as the radiance betraying my desire for him began to wane.

His jaw clenched and his face tightened with pain as he adjusted himself through the cotton of his bottoms. I didn't look down. Didn't dare. I knew exactly what I was missing, and I didn't want anything to tempt me back into his arms.

It would only be too easy.

"Jewel," he finally murmured, forcing himself to look me in the eyes. "I'm sorry. I wish things were different. I really do."

Truth, my inner compass sang.

"Me too." I swallowed hard. "But they aren't."

Luc gave a slow nod of his head, in silent agreement with my words, and I turned away from him. Every time I thought my heart couldn't break anymore, he proved me wrong.

Other Books by Rosalie Lario

URBAN FANTASY ROMANCE

Elemental Guardians
The Seventh Element
The Chaos Prophecy

PARANORMAL ROMANCE

Demons of Infernum
Blood of the Demon
Mark of the Sylph
Touch of the Angel
Heart of the Incubus
Call of the Siren

The Fallen Warriors
For Love of an Angel
Angel's Desire
For Want of an Angel
Angel's Kiss
Heart of an Angel

Stand Alone

Spellbound in Sleepy Hollow: A Von Tassel Sisters

Anthology

CONTEMPORARY ROMANCE

The Everly Brothers
Wild Girls Rule
Good Girls Don't
Bad Girls Do

ABOUT THE AUTHOR

Rosalie Lario is the author of the urban fantasy romance series, ELEMENTAL GUARDIANS, the paranormal romance series, DEMONS OF INFERNUM and THE FALLEN WARRIORS, and the contemporary romance series, THE EVERLY BROTHERS. Rosalie double majored in Anthropology and Classics as an undergraduate student, and briefly considered becoming an archaeologist before realizing they don't actually live the life of Indiana Jones. So what was a classical geek armed with a lot of useless knowledge to do? Become a lawyer, of course!

After attending law school in Florida, she practiced real estate law for several years before finally admitting to herself that negotiating contracts wasn't nearly as fun as dreaming up stories. When not writing, you can find her on a boat somewhere along South Florida's waterways, chasing down a rainbow or pretending to be a pirate.

You can learn more about Rosalie Lario at her website, www.rosalielario.com. Sign up for her newsletter and connect with her on Twitter or Facebook.